Return... François Stood at the Door to Nicolette's Chamber...

"My lady," he greeted her.

"My lord and husband," she replied, softly. Nicolette stared at him. Suddenly her head went light, for as she stared she saw her beloved Davide before her.

"I fear my return has unsettled you, my lady," he said as he moved towards her. "I have missed you." His voice was François' but something nagged from her memory. As he brushed back a lock of hair from his forehead, it came to her. She prayed she could restrain herself for but a moment, for she had to be sure!

"I have missed you too, François," she said, lowering her eyes in pretended shyness.

Davide's heart shattered. She believed him François and she spoke with a shy, but loving intimacy. Did she do so for show or—

His despairing look removed her last doubt. "Would you come to my side and kiss me, my husband?" she asked. "For I have missed you so desperately, my Davide . . ."

Dear Reader,

We, the editors of Tapestry Romances, are committed to bringing you two outstanding original romantic historical novels each and every month.

From Kentucky in the 1850s to the court of Louis XIII, from the deck of a pirate ship within sight of Gibraltar to a mining camp high in the Sierra Nevadas, our heroines experience life and love, romance and adventure.

Our aim is to give you the kind of historical romances that you want to read. We would enjoy hearing your thoughts about this book and all future Tapestry Romances. Please write to us at the address below.

> The Editors
> Tapestry Romances
> POCKET BOOKS
> 1230 Avenue of the Americas
> Box TAP
> New York, N.Y. 10020

Most Tapestry Books are available at special quantity discounts for bulk purchases for sales promotions, premiums or fund raising. Special books or book excerpts can also be created to fit specific needs.

For details write the office of the Vice President of Special Markets, Pocket Books, 1230 Avenue of the Americas, New York, New York 10020.

Song of The Rose

Johanna Hill

A TAPESTRY BOOK
PUBLISHED BY POCKET BOOKS NEW YORK

Books by Johanna Hill

Daughter of Liberty
Gilded Hearts
Song of the Rose

Published by TAPESTRY BOOKS

This novel is a work of historical fiction. Names, characters, places and incidents relating to non-historical figures are either the product of the author's imagination or are used fictitiously. Any resemblance of such non-historical incidents, places or figures to actual events or locales or persons, living or dead, is entirely coincidental.

An *Original* publication of TAPESTRY BOOKS

A Tapestry Book published by
POCKET BOOKS, a division of Simon & Schuster, Inc.
1230 Avenue of the Americas, New York, N.Y. 10020

Copyright © 1986 by Johanna Hill
Cover artwork copyright © 1986 Pino Daeni

All rights reserved, including the right to reproduce
this book or portions thereof in any form whatsoever.
For information address Tapestry Books, 1230
Avenue of the Americas, New York, N.Y. 10020

ISBN: 0-671-62903-4

First Tapestry Books printing August, 1986

10 9 8 7 6 5 4 3 2 1

POCKET and colophon are registered trademarks
of Simon & Schuster, Inc.

TAPESTRY is a registered trademark of Simon & Schuster, Inc.

Printed in the U.S.A.

In memory of the late Diane Thomas, screenwriter of Romancing the Stone. The Cinderella who created her glass slipper with talent, hard work, and lots of class!

Song of The Rose

Chapter One

Northern France
1191

'TWAS A GLORIOUS MAY MORN, YET NICOLETTE Duprey's heart was as heavy as her footsteps were quick, as she hurried down the rutted road from the castle of St. Aliquis toward the forest. Although she had prayed with the deepest reverence to the Virgin Mother at this morning's Mass in Baron Perdant's chapel, she knew that not even Mother Mary could save her from her fate.

The morrow would bring sweet, dear Bruge's thirteenth birthday and the thirteenth anniversary of their mother's departure to Heaven. Nicolette had been barely three, yet she remembered her mother clearly in her dreams, smiling down upon her with a smile as sweet as that of the picture of the Lord Jesus's own mother in Nicolette's Bible. Nicolette fought back her tears as she remembered her own thirteenth birthday. On that day they had learned from their stepbrother, Henri, Father's son from his first wife, that Father had been killed in battle for Baron Perdant. Henri, knighted by the baron shortly after Father's death, had been richly rewarded for their valiant father's death.

But for Nicolette, the nightmare had begun. She could not save herself, she had soon, bitterly learned. If only Henri had died in battle rather than Father, God forgive her. This morning she thanked the Virgin Mother for at least sparing Bruge, far more delicate and trusting than herself. For in a pique of anger at her attempted defiance, Henri had declared that if Nicolette would not agree to marry François Perdant, the good baron's youngest, prodigal son, then Henri would cajole François into taking her young sister Bruge instead.

Henri had won. Only in her prayers to the Father, the Son, and the Blessed Mother had Nicolette ever asked for mercy again. Last month, upon François' dubbing—his confirmation as a knight on his eighteenth birthday—Father Gregoire, the chaplain, had come to the castle chamber to hear Nicolette's consent to her betrothal. For the church demanded even a woman's consent. A consent that only a maiden as noble as Mademoiselle Alienor, François' sister, who she and Bruge served, might dare deny.

"Good day, my lady," a peasant, carrying heavy sacks of grain on his hunched shoulders, respectfully bid.

SONG OF THE ROSE

"Good day," she replied, forcing a smile. The peasant headed toward the castle, where his wife was most probably baking bread at the great oven.

Dressed as she was, in but a modest gown, mantle, and her delicate white slippers that she had impetuously decided to wear, despite the sometimes rough underbrush she would encounter in the forest, she knew she appeared to the "villein" as a noble maiden. But despite Henri's pretensions, the Dupreys were but "petty nobles." The proud death of their father made Henri knight and vassal to Baron Perdant and allowed Henri to move them from the thatched roof country house where Nicolette had happily lived to the dank chambers of the palais itself. Nicolette and Bruge were ladies-in-waiting to Alienor, the baron's only daughter. Service to Alienor, as kind and sensitive as she was beautiful, was as much a pleasure as honor. Nicolette and Alienor were but weeks apart in age, and soon, despite their difference in class, became as much friends as mistress and maid. It was Alienor who sent her off, after Mass at five, on a supposed errand with a love note to Sire Guy, the handsome knight to whom she was most happily betrothed.

Nicolette laughed aloud as she recalled Bruge's disappointment in not being permitted to accompany her. How Bruge *loved* romance! . . . Nicolette's laughter disappeared as she remembered her own dreams of falling in love with a tenderly handsome, gallant, romantic, brave knight in his mailed suit of armor, sitting high upon his destrier, his white fighting horse. This knight, to whom she would have given her silk sleeve and stocking to hang upon his lance, would ride off to battle with a lock of her hair set around a gold ring and a larger blonde lock which he would twine about his helmet. Until her cavalier returned, she would hold the gold ring he had presented to her with a passionate kiss close to her heart. How clearly she had pictured the ring, one just like Sire Guy had presented to Alienor with both his name and hers engraved thereon. Her beloved would return from battle and carry her off to his castle where they would marry and live most happily forever—

"Watch where ye go, girl!" Michel, one of the baron's squires, shouted as he rode quickly past her, causing Nicolette to scurry out of his way. But it was too late. For his horse's galloping hoofs had splashed the muddy water from a puddle all over her mantle and slippers. Arrogant Michel had not even turned back to notice the damage! How she disliked him, ever since he had attempted to steal kisses from her the night they had arrived at the castle. She had fought him off and he had tripped and fallen into a mound of horse manure. Instead of running away, Nicolette had stood and laughed so loudly that a passing group of nobles visiting the baron had walked upon the scene. Michel had been properly cuffed and word quickly spread that Nicolette was a maid who took "unkindly" to amorous advances.

He probably had splashed her on purpose, Nicolette realized, as she turned off the road and onto the footpath that would lead her into the dense forest. How happy she would be if Michel's punishment was to be the worst to befall her. For compared to Sire François, Michel was almost a saint! She had fended off François for almost two years, but now with Henri deaf to her entreaties, when François arrived at the castle tonight she would be as helpless to save herself from him as if she were bound to the torture rack. Well, he could take her body, force her to become his wife with Henri's greedy complicity, but he would never have her heart or her soul!

Nicolette trod gracefully through the forest's thick underbrush. How she loved the peaceful beauty of the forest. She headed purposefully toward the mossy stream. There she would find the wildflowers that she would pick and weave into a beautiful chaplet, her secret birthday present for Bruge. On the morrow, no lady of the noblest rank would wear a garland more glorious than Bruge! Bruge, now of age, would win the heart of the finest, most gentle young squire. She would win a match that would have made their father happy. Bruge would live and love for both of them. This vow Nicolette had made upon her forced agreement to marry François. A silent vow to her dear departed mother, father, and the Holy Virgin!

Yes, it truly was a glorious day as the first of the sun's rays streamed through the redolent branches of the newly reborn trees. The dew still clung to the underbrush and seeped through Nicolette's already muddied slippers, yet she did not mind. She would wash them and her mantle at the stream and lay her slippers and cloak upon her favorite rock where they would dry beneath the bright morning sun. The sweet scent of the honeysuckle further filled her senses with joy. It would be this woodbine, her favorite, the flowers tiny yellow and as lovely as they were sweetly redolent, and hawthorn, the delicate pinkish flowers that blossomed on the thorny bushes already in purview, that she would use to make the chaplet. With the colored ribbons that Alienor had generously given her, they would form the crowning beauty that Bruge would find on her chest before the morrow's matin Mass. Nicolette began to sing a song she had learned from a *trouvère* who had entertained at the barony a week before. She retrieved her small, sharp knife, tied at her girdle, and deftly cut her first branch of hawthorn.

"Can par la flor justal vert fuelh," she sang. How she loved to sing, though it embarrassed her when Alienor had her perform for visiting knights and nobles. Yet the joy of the melody and words of this May song lifted her heart as she sang out into the serenity of the forest.

"Oh!" she cried out, as a thorn pricked her finger, then laughed and began her song again. "When the flowers appear beside the green leaf, when I see the weather bright and serene . . . and hear in the wood the song of the birds which brings sweetness to my heart and pleases me . . ." Lost in song, she carried the flowers carefully toward the brook. "The more the birds sing to merit praise, the more joy I have in my heart and I must sing, yea I must sing . . ."

The young knight knew not how long he had stood transfixed, gazing at the vision of the maiden as she wove a garland, singing ever so sweetly. On his way to join the Count of Champagne on the Crusade, he had detoured from the main road although he had ridden his proud destrier for two days since he had left his father's castle and still had two days of journey before him. But something had caused him to return to the barony of St. Aliquis, where he had spent the earliest years in his life. Years so long ago that they seemed more like fragments of a dream than a reality. Fragments of an unhappy dream at that, except for his flash of memory of playing in this forest.

He had watered his horse and walked him up the steep cliff above the stream when he had heard the first enchanting sweetness of a maiden's voice. Quickly he tied his horse to a tree limb out of sight and sat in wait for a glance at the maiden who sang the May song. From the moment she filled his vision he knew that it had been providence that had brought him to these woods this morn. This gentle damsel was the promise of all the songs and stories of romance he had learned when he had been "nourished," trained, to be worthy of knighthood. Since he had been "dubbed" into knighthood almost two years before, he had traveled throughout the French kingdom and across most of the Christian world. He had been introduced to maidens and fair ladies from the rank of queen to servitor, yet he had never met one woman who had made his heart pound and his palms dampen as this unknown maiden now did.

Again he tried to make himself either slip away or find the courage to bring himself down the cliff and on his knee before her. But he feared he might frighten her away or that she was merely an apparition that would disappear should he move a muscle. Only twenty-three and he had already fought valiantly for his count. Now he was off with the Count of Champagne to join King Philip Augustus. They would drive the infidels out of the Holy City of Jerusalem. He feared not fighting mighty Saracens, their leader the fierce Saladin, Sultan of Egypt, just as he had never feared following his liege lord into previous battles against rebelling counts who had sought to seize his lord's power. Yet here he stood in mortal fear of a lovely damsel whom he could carry away with one arm. Oh yes, the monks were right. Woman was the undoing of man as Eve had been to Adam, he thought with a sudden, deep knowing laced with wry humor. He must summon his deepest courage and seize the moment. He had to know this bewitching creature, who sat upon a smooth rock at the edge of the stream, her blonde hair unbraided and falling down her shoulders to her arms as she nimbly and industriously wove a brilliant garland. Yet the flowered chaplet paled in comparison to the damsel's beauty.

Soundlessly he edged closer. A twig snapped beneath his boot and he feared discovery, but the maiden's sweet trilling kept her innocent of his presence. When he viewed her more closely, his heart pounded beneath his mailed hauberk. She was more beautiful than he'd thought possible. As she raised her head and smiled at a bird on a beech tree limb who sang with her, he had a full view of her face.

Beneath her golden hair, affixed with little lovelocks, shone her forehead whiter than lilies. Her eyes were blue saucers and laughing; her face most dainty

SONG OF THE ROSE

with lips more vermeil than ever was rose or cherry in the time of summer heat. Her face outvied the white and pink of the flowers she wove. She had a witching mouth, a delicate nose, and an open brow.

Suddenly she rose, taking him by surprise. She reached into a purse tied to her white girdle that emphasized her slender waist and bodice. "Here, my friend," she called in a voice as melodious as her singing. She tossed crumbs of bread upon the ground beneath the tree. "I have brought you dinner, as I always do. You shall eat this morn as well as the baron supped last eve."

She stretched, raising her face and slender arms to the sun, unknowingly showing off her white bodice beneath which her breasts pressed so firm, like two rounded sweet nuts. Her throat was whiter than snow on winter branch, and as she suddenly raised the hem of her pale blue tunic and massaged her finely formed calves, most probably stiff from having sat cross-legged as she wove, he saw the delicacy of her instep, as white as the rest of her flesh. How he suddenly ached to see all of her.

Nicolette turned to stretch her neck that had stiffened. "Oh!" she gasped as she saw the blond, curly-haired knight staring at her. She dropped her gathered hem and stood rigidly uncertain. It could not be but it was! Somehow Sire François had discovered her secret place. She covered her mouth to suppress a frightened, despairing cry. She must *never* let him know the depth of her fear of him. Why had the Lord made a man so beautiful to the eye and so brutish and evil in the heart?

SONG OF THE ROSE

He did not know what to do, but the look of horror upon the maiden's face made him flee from her view. How could he have evoked such fear on the face that had burned a spark into his heart? He had caught her by surprise but she had reacted with more than fear. Her blue eyes had darkened with visible terror and hate. Why had she looked upon him, a stranger, with such abhorrence, as if she had despised him forever— That was it. The maiden had thought he was another! A knight who had given her cause to stiffen and be reviled at his sight. He must rush back to her, if she had not already run away, and apologize and allay her fear, plead her forgiveness for the fright he had caused her.

The knight had disappeared and Nicolette found her breath once again. Should she gather her things and hasten back to St. Aliquis? She had been so certain that the figure on the cliff above the stream had been François. But it could not have been. For François would have laughed viciously in triumph at her fear and come after her. In her immediate fright she had not been able to absorb the expression of panic on the handsome face of the knight who watched her before he fled, she suddenly realized.

Nicolette sighed deeply. She was safe. It had been her imagination at work! For as much as she drank in the serenity of the forest and enjoyed the work of weaving Bruge's chaplet and the image of Bruge's joyful face on the morrow, she had not been able to erase her fearful hopelessness. With the tacit approval of her greedy stepbrother, she would be forced into François' bed tonight. She had overheard François and Henri in collusion the other day, right before François had ridden off to the Duke of Quelqueparte for a few days' visit.

"I shall return in two nights and I want your sister to finally be mine. For surely I must test that her beauty satisfies me as fully as I imagine, if I am to wed the wench and make you the lord of a large fief of land, Henri! The church be damned with their injunctions. We speak man to man, do we not, Henri?"

Henri had laughed. "Certainly, my liege lord. And I am certain that you will break her in, to your liking, as easily as you did this fine fighting horse you sit upon. And a fine ripe virgin she is. Were I not her kin by our mutual father I might have wanted her for my own. But I am but your vassal and she is destined to serve and pleasure a cavalier of noble blood," he answered and sighed with feigned obsequiousness.

"Yea, you are as wise as you are ambitious, my friend Henri. Soon I shall say my brother, Henri? Have her as pliant as she is tasty and you will be rewarded with a fine wench for your own as well as the Castle Petitmur. For I hear tell that a certain neighboring baron has died, leaving his castle and daughter, his only heir, unprotected. The Count of Champagne must find her a fine husband. And although she doesn't exhibit the exceptional beauty of your sister, I believe that her father's castle and fief may act upon you as deeply as the strongest aphrodisiac? Do you gainsay, Henri?"

"No, Sire. I most heartily agree! I have heard of this lovely maiden and am most desirous to experience the sweetness of her great charms. Thank you,

François. Nicolette will be waiting *eagerly* for you upon your arrival home night after next. You have my word."

The men's raucously shared laughter had caused Nicolette, hiding behind a stable post, to shudder even more deeply.

She shuddered again as she wove and cried out as she pricked her finger on an unseen sharp thorn. Suddenly the sky darkened. Too late she realized that a cloud had not passed before the sun but that a figure stood before her, the gold tassels of his mantle glinting. She cried out despite herself. She gazed up at the towering figure of François and cursed herself for her dangerous misjudgment. It had been François watching her! But no! She tried to think through her confusion as the garland fell into her lap. She had to have full control of her senses. The knight had *not* been François. For here stood François in an aggressive open-legged, crossed-arm stance before her dressed *not* in knightly raiments but in a brilliant blue bliaut and linen, white leggings, and fine, jeweled slippers.

Unbeknownst to her the knight watched from his hiding spot and quickly withdrew his sword from his scabbard, his eyes steeled upon the lord standing before the damsel. He was ready to come to her protection, but the question was, did she require it? Or had she been so badly shaken moments before that she now was frightened by the surprise of the young sire who smiled benignly and familiarly at her?

"Good day, my sweet Nicolette! I am sorry if my sudden appearance caused you a moment of fright," the lord, wearing the blue of St. Aliquis, said so kindly that the knight was further uncertain.

"Good day, Sire," she responded evenly. She would not show him another taste of fear. For like a wild boar, it would only make him bolder. "Fright no, my lord. You startled me, for I was lost in my weaving and my thoughts." She forced herself to meet his eyes with head held high, jaw firm.

"And such a lovely, delicate garland you weave, my dear." He looked down at her lap, then his eyes rose to her waist, then bodice, openly and slowly appraising her. Indelicately he stared at one breast and then the other, making her want to cover herself, but she dared not acknowledge his lust. "But of course not even nature's finest flowers can match your succulent, ripe beauty, Nicolette. May I hope that your dreamy thoughts were of me, your husband-to-be?"

The knight's heart was crushed at the utterance of the lord's last words. Suddenly weary, he placed his sword back into its scabbard and turned away. Most unmanly tears filled his eyes and his knees became so weak that he had to rest beneath the tree for a moment until he could compose himself.

"They were not, my lord," Nicolette answered evenly and wanted to laugh at the expression of shock at her honest defiance upon his face. However, as he boldly sat himself beside her, fear clenched her heart again.

"I adore not only your beauty but also your feisty manner. For that is a quality I seek in a wife as well as in my finest destriers." He grabbed her by the shoulder and pulled her into an embrace as his mouth tried to devour her lips.

SONG OF THE ROSE

For a moment the cry she tried to utter was trapped in her throat as his hands grasped beneath her chemise and pulled at her breast. All thought fled and Nicolette bit so hard at his lip that she could taste his blood.

"Bitch!" he screamed in pain as his hand went to his bleeding mouth. "I will not wait until tonight. I shall have you now and teach you how to treat your lord and master!"

The knight jumped to action. Withdrawing his sword he quickly grabbed hold of a strong vine which would enable him to fly across the stream and come to the maiden's rescue.

Nicolette rose, but François grabbed her ankle cruelly, causing her to lose her balance and tumble toward the stream. Had he not held her fast she would have fallen in. But he was upon her, as if he had a dozen hands, ripping at her chemise, pulling at her tangled bliaut as she heard the rip of the girdle that held her chemise tied at her waist. Suddenly she realized that she had the sharp knife still clenched in her right hand. But if she used it, what fate would befall her sweet sister?

François caught the glint of the knife, and having the wench securely immobile beneath his strong thighs, he stopped for a moment. She would either hand over the knife or woe the day she was born! Tears filled her large blue eyes as she wordlessly dropped the knife that fell into the stream. Her tears of submission made him laugh lustfully as he felt his manhood throbbing in demand for release. He ripped off the sleeve of her pale blue bliaut and then the

SONG OF THE ROSE

chemise beneath it. He grabbed her breast and tasted her shoulder as his hands roamed her body, her skirts having risen so he could reach the seat of her maidenly womanhood. Suddenly, she twisted in such a manner as sent him off balance.

"Damn you, whore!" he screamed as he tumbled into the stream, suddenly enjoying the hunt as much as he would enjoy his inevitable victory. For he righted himself as Nicolette unsteadily tried to flee. "Run," he called out, laughing heartily. "For like the hunt of the wild boar, that will only make the chase more exhilarating, wench. And I shall show you no mercy, this I promise you. You are mine!" he yelled as Nicolette tripped upon some underbrush a few yards away. He would take no chances with this wild one, he decided and started to reach for his sword, but something clenched his neck. An arm in a mailed hauberk. A knight.

"The chase is over, my lord," the voice shouted. "The sweet doe has escaped, hasn't she?" François felt the edge of the cold steel against his throat.

"You misunderstand, my fellow knight. We are but lustfully gaming. The maiden is my betrothed. I am Sire François Perdant, son of Baron of St. Aliquis. Ask the lady. Her name is Nicolette. Ask her if she is not my duly intended wife and lady-in-waiting to my sister, the gentle Mademoiselle Alienor!"

Nicolette stood in shock, unaware that her ravaged clothing gave view to her small, pink-nippled breasts. The knight could save her. Perhaps he would take her from St. Aliquis forever, but if she saved herself what would become of Bruge? "Yea, what he speaks is true," she said weakly as her bitter tears fell, though she tried to fight them back.

The sight of Nicolette's surrender for reasons he didn't understand, the tears that streamed down her delicate face that she tried to wipe away as she pushed back her tangled hair, made the knight want to slash the Sire of St. Aliquis' throat all the more! For the rich, cowardly knight's unchivalrous deeds were widely known throughout the kingdom. He had despised François' very *name* for years now, but had never expected to come upon him in this way! But the knight could not slash the throat of a fellow knight who was unarmed. Moreover, what *François* did *not* know was that they would be riding together on the morrow's eve with the Count of Champagne for King Philip Augustus. The knight was now glad he'd placed his helmet upon his head before swinging across the stream, for François would not easily identify him in his mailed suit of armor. But what to do about the maiden? He could not leave her to François.

"Sire Perdant. I am much surprised to come upon you behaving such when the lady is not in the mood for amorous adventure. For I have heard of your gallantry and august reputation as a gentleman and a chevalier of honor." The knight released his hold.

François turned and glanced through blurred eyes at the helmeted knight who matched him in height and build. The sun prevented him from distinguishing much else about the knight who was not carrying an identifying shield. François did not want to challenge him to a duel, for bully though he was, François had no taste for dueling and fighting, much preferring whoring and drinking through the night. He cleared his throat and glanced at Nicolette who now sat, trying to cover herself with maidenly modesty.

"You are right, Sire, eh, what is it?" he asked, feigning camaraderie in an attempt to learn his attacker's name. But the knight did not offer his name nor any word. Nervously, François continued. "I am so enchanted with my Nicolette that my *love* overwhelmed me, as I'm certain you must understand. Yea?" The knight remained silent, his sword lowered but ready. "Being a man of the world I had almost forgotten the, uh," he whispered, "the modesty of a virgin. My dear Nicolette had asked me to meet her in this secret place, but I can now see that the damsel, so reverent a lady, hears the incantations of the church louder than her own passion. I so adore her that I think it best if I wait for our wedding eve. It was upon *her* insistence that we met today, for I am riding with the Count of Champagne and the great suzerain lord himself, King Philip Augustus, in the Crusade on the morrow. Are you riding with us, perchance?" François asked in bold, casual voice again, hoping once more to trick the knight into revealing his identity.

"Then perhaps you should ride off," the knight said, glancing at François' horse, peacefully watering at the stream bank, "and leave the maiden to regain her composure and suffer her embarrassment at her understandably passionate invitation to you, my lord?" the knight asked amiably, pretending to believe the despicable coward's story. If François were half a man, he would have challenged him to a duel. But this was François Perdant, a knight who believed that his father's wealth and power could buy him anything.

The knight knew something François did not. François had no more intended to ride off on the Crusade on the morrow than the lovely maiden Nicolette had offered herself to him. François intended to pay scutage—a fee—to a poor knight who would take his place in the Crusade. For the knight expected to replace François had told him so at the inn, shortly before the fool had died in a drunken brawl last night. So, unknown to François, his plan had been foiled.

"I think you speak wisely, man to man, Sire," François said. "I am hungry and from the look of the sun it must be nearly nine and time to dine. Would you care to honor us with your presence at dinner?"

"Thank you, but no. Perhaps another time. For I am certain that we shall meet again, Sire."

"Then I shall take my leave. I must pay my thanks to you for the chivalry you showed my lady, though misconstrued."

"The pleasure was mine," the knight replied evenly.

François smiled charmingly and then turned and walked downstream to his waiting destrier. The knight watched as François turned his head to the maiden but apparently decided to leave without a word. Then he turned back to the maiden on the bank and called, "I shall see you tonight, my sweet Nicolette. I bid you a good day, my lovely betrothed." The knight watched Nicolette fight back a shudder in response.

SONG OF THE ROSE

If only God would strike you dead and save us all, Nicolette thought. But she had to appease him or only the Devil could know what he might do if he left the forest in abject humiliation. "I am sorry for my silly behavior, my lord. I *beg* your understanding and forgiveness. I will try to make it up to you, François"—she forced the words out—"my dearest, kind husband-to-be." The delight on François' face made the bile rise in her stomach. For only a man as vain and arrogant as François was so easily appeased. Bruge should be safe. Nicolette doubted that François would report this morning's events to Henri now.

"You have my forgiveness, my lovely songbird. Tonight I shall prove it to you," he replied, laughing.

François jumped on his horse and galloped off as the knight stood in the stream and watched. Nicolette rested her head in her lap and cried bitter tears of relief. She cried so hard she couldn't raise her head when the knight who had saved her called her name.

"Sweet lady, you are safe," the knight said tenderly. She looked through swollen, blurred eyes at his face as he crouched before her. She gasped in shock for a moment, for he was again unhelmeted and he looked *so* like the monstrous François. But she saw the gentleness in his eyes and the softness in his smile and she realized he was as far different from François as the Lord was from the Devil. Tentatively, so as to not frighten her, she realized, the knight reached for her hand.

"Cry the terror away, fair maiden. Then we shall talk," he said.

She gazed into his eyes, bluer than her own, as he brushed a blond curl from his forehead. Suddenly she felt a sense of safety that had died with her father. Nicolette fell into the knight's arms and sobbed with despair. And unexplainable hope.

Chapter Two

"'Tis finished." Nicolette, her dried mantle wrapped around her shoulders, shyly held up the garland she had completed as she had poured out her story to the knight.

"An object of beauty that Bruge will adore, I am certain," the knight answered. His sparkling blue eyes held her own as he smiled for the first time since she'd begun to unfold her tale of woe. Such a fine mouth he had, thought Nicolette.

As he admired the chaplet, Nicolette studied the man beside her for the first time. He sat cross-legged in his doublet, a short quilted jacket, and dark green chausses, his tight-fitting stocking that covered his body from his waist to his boots. His hauberk, the garment of chain mail which had covered his body from neck to knee, he had removed after he'd brought his horse, saddled with his leather bags, shield, and mace club, to a spot beneath a shade tree just yards away. He had quickly laid a blanket upon which they now sat and had offered Nicolette a dinner and wine. She could not touch the food but did sip from his flask of wine to wet her dried throat as she spoke.

Nicolette handed the knight the garland, which he examined carefully. "To be able to create beauty, as women do, has always left me in wonderment," he said shyly and studied the garland with the serious expression he had worn as he had listened to her story. "I am not only studying the magic of your weaving"—he looked into her eyes and his face broke into a shy smile that displayed his deep dimples—"but I am thinking about your dilemma and cannot think logically when I gaze upon your face, for your beauty —outer and inner I now know—tosses me into a maelstrom of emotions." The blush rose to his cheeks and Nicolette felt herself blushing. She laughed shyly, and wondered what his name was.

Nicolette was grateful for the knight's intentional distraction for she was experiencing feelings unknown to her. With his eyes cast down, she found the courage to gaze forthrightly at him. It was quite remarkable that at first glance he could pass for François' twin— the same stature and handsomely molded visage. But in the hour or so they had passed, with the help of the kindness of his heart that sang through his brilliant blue eyes and finely shaped mouth, the image of the boorish, cruel, heartless François had faded.

A curly blond lock of his hair had again fallen on his

SONG OF THE ROSE

high white forehead, just above his black arched brow. Nicolette found herself wanting to brush it away but dared not. She continued instead to study his face. She drank in his laughing blue eyes, serious as he sat deep in thought, his nose as straight as an arrow shaft, ears finely shaped. Her eyes again fell to his mouth. "A fine and amorous mouth she loved to kiss . . ." the troubador's song had gone. The lyric suddenly popped into her head and for the first time she *understood* the love songs of the *trouvères* and *jongleurs*. The knowledge made her heart beat in fear. Fear of her own sudden desire to press her lips against his own. To touch his slightly cleft chin and caress his straight neck and the white skin of his broad-shouldered chest that revealed itself beneath his top unbuttoned doublet. Nicolette reached for the flask of wine with shaking hands just as the knight looked up. Their eyes met and held this time.

He took the flask from her soft, white hands and the touch sent shocks of desire through him. The blush that rose from Nicolette's throat to her cheeks and the expression in her eyes told him that she too was feeling the stirrings of passion which frightened her so that she had brought her hands to her face, as if to hide.

He rested the flask beside his scabbard and moved closer, taking her hands that were now icy cold into his own that burned with the heat of passion. But he did not merely desire to possess her body and thrill in the delight of her flesh. He wanted Nicolette to be his wife and share his heart and soul forever. That was why it was imperative that he think now of a plan that could save her from Perdant. Oh, he could simply ride her away and ensure her safety in his father's protection until he returned from the Crusade. But that would leave her younger sister Bruge to the mercy of both Perdant and Henri, damn them both to hell! There had to be a solution! As she gazed with sky-blue, trusting eyes at him, the knight had to kiss her.

Nicolette sat with quiet anticipation, though her heart beat wildly, as the knight gently placed the chaplet upon her head. His hands caressed her hair and then her chin and she unknowingly tilted her head back. His sweet lips touched hers and her hands cupped his large, strong hands that so delicately caressed her face. His kisses were chaste and gentle but then her body, possessing a will of its own, urgently demanded more as her mouth opened and she pressed herself into his arms. The deepness of his kiss caught her breath in her throat and her yearning grew stronger still. Abruptly, he pulled away, causing her to sigh.

He commanded his heart to still and was determined to ignore the heat and hardness of his groin. They had to talk. He swallowed heavily the wine from the flask, for his throat was hot and parched. Nicolette's mantle had slipped off her shoulder in their impassioned embrace, though she knew it not, revealing her ivory shoulder and small, pert breast with her nipple now taut and pinker than the flowers in the garland. "We must devise a plan, Nicolette," he said as he forced himself to cover her glory with her mantle or all would be lost.

His words brought her back to her real world and

she shook her head bitterly. "There is no way to save myself. I have thought it over and over. I had even contemplated speaking candidly to dear Alienor. But she would be unable to help. She does not speak of it, but she holds her brother in quiet contempt. I have seen it often in her eyes when his back is turned. Yet their father, the baron, is old and ailing. There is talk that he is not to live through the month. Alienor will not be married until Sire Guy returns from the Crusade, so she too will be under her brother's mercy. I have seen her venture to speak to me but sadly decide otherwise . . . I am betrothed to François. Tonight he will"—tears strangled her throat and again filled her eyes, but she forced herself to continue—"take me and I shall be forced to marry him next month." She fought back the sobs.

He took her hand but allowed her to continue as each word cut through his heart like the sharpest sword of steel.

"You see, I learned that François has paid for a gallant but poor knight to fight in his place. He will *not* leave on the Crusade on the morrow. He is as much a coward as a brute. He will use his father's illness as an excuse. So, there is no hope . . ."

Her sobs drove him to a violent inner frenzy he had to hide from her. He had to tell her now what he knew, although he could not reveal even his name to this maiden he would love for eternity. He could not tell her his story for her own safety, in the event that the plan he must formulate failed. "Nicolette, hold your tears and listen carefully . . . I loved you from the moment I gazed upon you singing and weaving from across the stream." He waved his hand toward the spot where he'd first seen her what felt like another lifetime ago. How her lack of coyness thrilled him, for she did not attempt to hide her delight at his words. Her smile of unspoken returned love was more glorious than anything he had ever witnessed.

"I—"

"Hush," he gently interrupted. "Hear me out, for it is imperative for both our lives and your sister's as well. I cannot tell you my name or from whence I come. But I *long* to hear my name uttered from your sweet lips. So pick one for me and it shall be mine between us forever."

She gazed into his eyes for just a moment and then she knew. "Davide," she said. "For he slew Goliath," she answered simply.

His smile made her heart soar. "Davide . . ." he repeated. "I like that. Do you know what it means?"

She brought his hand to her lips and gently kissed it. "Yes . . . beloved . . . you are Davide, my beloved . . . All my life I have dreamed of you—but now it is too late!"

"It is not too late!" he implored. "François will be *forced* to ride with our king on the morrow. Despite his wealth and cowardliness. The knight to whom he offered scutage is dead. François will not learn this until it is too late. Do you take me at my word?"

"Yes, oh, yes, my Davide, I do! But how do you know—I am sorry. I will not question what you cannot divulge."

The knight's heart filled as he saw the first true glimmer of hope sparkle in his beloved's eyes. How he wished he didn't have to speak the next words. "However, I too shall have to ride. I cannot tell you specifically with whom. Therefore, I could easily steal you and Bruge away from St. Aliquis tonight, but I would not be able to ensure your protection— If only there were but a few more days!"

His rage at his impotence forced him to rise, grab his mace, and swing the short, spiked war club against the ground. Again and again. When he turned back to her, Nicolette looked pale. The hope that had shone in her eyes was but a memory. He sank wearily to the ground. "If only I could save you from tonight, then I know I should be able to protect you and love you forever." He did not try to hide the unmanly tears of frustration that filled his eyes. He held his head in his hands, for although there had to be some way, he who was supposedly as quick in mind as he was agile with his sword, could not find it.

"Davide," she called softly. He raised his head and saw that Nicolette kneeled before him. She had removed her mantle and her ravaged chemise hung in tatters, leaving both shoulders bare and her breasts exposed as she leaned toward him, took his hands in her own, and bent to kiss first the right then the left.

"Nicolette . . ." He could not speak as she raised her head and brought her mouth to his.

"Davide . . . there is *only* one way you can save me in this life. For I am sure we will meet in eternity."

"No. I shan't accept—"

"Shush." She placed her fingers to his lips. "You can love me *now*. So that I will know what love is *meant* to be. Then, no matter what, I will *always* know what love is and I will hold each moment in my heart and memory. You, Davide, will be my first and only love. Please."

He gazed at her jutting breasts and then fell into the pools of deep blue that were her eyes and the door to her soul. His desire threatened to engulf them if he did not rein it hard, for he felt the heat rise from his groin as she placed his hands on her alabaster breasts and he felt the tautness of her nipples against his palms.

"Davide . . . please. Take me now and possess me forever—"

He caught the last of her words in his mouth as he pulled her down upon the blanket and explored her mouth with his unleashed, smoldering passion. His hands deftly removed her ravaged raiments from her quivering body.

With the last of her garments removed, he sighed in awe at her beauty. His eyes traveled from her breasts, tracing the gentle contour of her waist and belly until they feasted upon the soft blonde triangle and seat of her womanhood, which he would be the first to know. He dared not think of François Perdant now!

Nicolette did not feel embarrassed by Davide's loving gaze, for in her soul she knew that had not the Lord intended for her to feel the joy of the passion that fevered her body he would not have given her the senses with which to feel it. She looked upon Davide with wonder as he slowly removed the last of his clothes. How very beautiful he was. The rippling muscles of his broad shoulders tapered to narrow waist and hips and heavily muscled thigh and buttock. He turned as he stood above her and she gasped at the sight of his large, erect manhood.

This morning she had thought she would never know tender lovemaking and the ecstasy spoken of in

Alienor's tales of romance. Now, as Davide lowered himself onto her, his musky scent, his tautness pressing against her, the silkiness of his skin, the hardness of his muscles made her senses reel as he caressed her with his mouth and hands until she cried out in pitched desire. She knew she would never forget, no matter what befell her. She opened her thighs to the tip of his manhood. Soon his penetrating hardness filled her to her core. She would never forget . . . She held him tight as she gave herself to him and melded into him until they were one and only feelings and colors filled her mind and took her to a place she had never been.

"You are a lusty wench, Nicolette," Davide teased. He gave her a mockbite upon her shoulder as she hungrily chewed off a piece of dried beef he'd unwrapped along with a loaf of fresh, crusty bread. "First you devour me, then my food and red wine. I shall not be surprised should you turn into a stout madame in a few years."

"And will you still love me when I am old and fat, or will you have taken a pretty young maiden or two as your lovers?" she easily teased back.

"You will leave me too weak with constant hunger for food and too weary with your insatiable demands in our bed to even *look* at another damsel!"

Nicolette fluttered her eyelids coquettishly, grinned, and then took a huge, most undainty bite of his beef again, causing Davide to break out in a hearty burst of laughter. Oh, how he adored everything about her! In truth she had exhausted him during their long, tender passionate, lusty interlude of lovemaking. She was a quick learner and an innately passionate and loving creature, surprisingly unabashed in her questions about his body and her own. She was as playful and chattery as a child and he regretted having to remind her of her plight, but he had found the answer, he thought. He prayed!

He caressed her hair that was still drying from the bath they had shared in the stream, and Nicolette snuggled closer to him. He offered her another bite of meat, but she declined, her playfulness lost. So, she too had returned to her troubles, he thought.

"Nicolette?" She did not answer but instead clung to him. He pushed the food aside and turned her face to his. As he thought, she was fighting back tears.

She kissed him tenderly upon the mouth. "Davide, I do so love you. You have given me the happiest hours of my life and I shall never forget them although I shall never see you—"

"Don't even speak such words," he sharply interrupted. "For I have found our solution. I see in your eyes the despair of doubt. Do you trust me, Nicolette?"

"I trust you with my heart and soul. With my life."

"Prove it to me. Look into my eyes until your fear transforms itself into a smile of renewed hope." He watched as her blue eyes darkened further until the few tears fell. After she brushed them away, the glimmer of hope slowly lighted her eyes to sapphires smiling at him from the depth of her soul. We have just truly wed, he thought, and thought to tell her. But as they gazed deep into one another he realized it was unnecessary. She already knew.

SONG OF THE ROSE

"Tell me your plan now, Davide," she asked as she took his hand into her own. "Tell me . . . my husband, lord, and master . . ." Her solemn countenance broke into a wide, bright grin punctuated with a bold laugh. "Although I think I will prefer to think just husband and lord for I am *sick* of masters!"

"Is that so? I shall have to show you otherwise, wench!" Laughingly, he grabbed her but her quick knee at his groin caused him to groan in pain. The look of shock so quickly filled her face that he burst into laughter and raised his arms in mock surrender. "Show mercy, my fair lady. I will be *your* vassal if you so desire!"

"Does it really hurt?" she asked anxiously.

"A bit," he responded, unwilling to allow her the knowledge of the pain that had ensued from her playful blow.

"I will make it better, my lord," Nicolette whispered. A smile played on her face. "I will make it better with a kiss," she said and she lowered her head to his thighs.

The shadow cast by the lowering sun told them it was nearly three o'clock as they lay entwined beneath Nicolette's mantle.

"You shall make me an old man before my time if I am not careful, my sweet Nicolette," Davide teased with only half-pretended exhaustion as he stroked her neck.

"Ummm . . ." she whispered back. She lay contentedly in Davide's arms, her eyes heavy. She yawned.

As greatly as he too desired to sleep, they dared

not. Time was too short and he had to instruct her as to the plan. He tickled her unmercifully and she fought back until he ceased and they sat, once again alert.

"The plan," she said. "Tell me." She glanced at the sun and became somber. "There is little time left."

"Nicolette," he began. "You truly believe that Alienor would come to your aid as long as she did not have to give herself away?"

Nicolette thought deeply. Alienor loved her like a sister. "I do."

"Good. Then I believe I have thought of a ploy that with Alienor's help and God's blessing just might work."

"I believe the Blessed Mother looks kindly upon us, my love. I will do whatever is necessary."

"I would lay down my life happily to spare you this night but there is no other way out, I think. I will explain my idea but it requires your aid in the finer details."

"Tell me quickly then, my dearest lord. For I know now I am no longer alone, my angel."

"Nor will you ever be again," Davide responded. "Above all, no matter what happens or *seems* to happen, you must hold that certainty in your heart."

Nicolette kissed him gently on his mouth in reply.

Davide began, "I can spirit you back to the castle. Your mantle will prevent any notice of your ruined upper garments. You must go immediately to Mademoiselle Alienor's chamber and speak with her in secrecy. Can that be managed?"

"I believe so."

SONG OF THE ROSE

"You must tell Alienor of everything that passed this day, woman to woman—but for your sake and hers you must make *no* mention of what has passed between us, no matter how sympathetic a heart she offers. This is essential for her protection as well as Bruge's and your own. Nor may you confide in Bruge."

Davide spoke with quiet authority, and she nodded in assent, anxious for him to continue.

The sun hid behind the trees. Nicolette and Davide sat closely, each lost in private thought.

"Davide." Nicolette broke the silence. "Your plan will work. I feel it in the depth of my soul."

"Our plan, Nicolette. For truly we have become partners," he answered with newfound respect for the woman who would share his life once he returned from the Crusade. For in the course of the day not only had she gone from maiden to woman in the knowing ways of love, but during their discussion she had demonstrated quick wit and courage beyond her years. He had no doubt that if Alienor could be counted upon, their shared scheme could not fail.

"Yea, this is true. We have become partners," she agreed so honestly that Davide laughed.

This lady would never allow his male arrogance to overtake him! God had truly presented him with a gift more precious than all the jewels and kingdoms in the world. He took her in his arms and kissed her passionately, then pulled away, for they had to dress and prepare to ride her back to the castle. But her witching mouth and insistently wanton fingertips

SONG OF THE ROSE

would not let him be. "Nicolette," he whispered halfheartedly between deep kisses.

"No, my beloved. Once more. I want you once more today. For you say yourself you cannot promise when you will return for me, only that you will . . ." She kissed his eyes as her fingertips caressed his chest, playing at his nipples. "And return you will. That I shall never doubt," she whispered in his ear, and then her tongue and lips sent quivers up his spine. He lay back and lifted her on top of him and brought her breast to his mouth, teasing and taunting her nipple until it was rosy and hard while his hand ran down her waist, caressing her firm buttock and lifting her higher until she came to rest upon his hot, hard manhood.

Nicolette laughed with abandoned pleasure as he flipped her onto her back and crouched above her so that the glory of his manhood almost touched her lips. Her laughter turned to a tortured sigh of pleasure as his head lowered between her thighs and his tongue danced upon her vulnerable spot, causing her to cry out in ecstasy as undulating waves of pleasure coursed through her. Her cry was answered with his hardness and she sucked him as naturally as a babe suckles its mother's breast.

There was no greater pleasure to feel, she thought, until he turned her for the first time onto her belly and side and kissed her neck and caressed her breasts. She felt his hard, driving thrust as he entered her more deeply than before and she danced to his rhythm, as old as time, as he thrust into her again and again until she could neither see nor hear nor think.

He turned her onto her back. She rode the waves of

ecstasy with him as Davide arched his back and plunged into her again and cried out as his heart beat wildly against her breast. Then the wave overtook her again and she shook to her core as she wedged her mouth to his and their breath became one as her legs clung tightly round his back.

"Oh, how I love you, Nicolette," he whispered, as they came slowly to their senses.

"And I you, my Davide . . ." She allowed her tears of joy and sorrow of parting to flow freely. She saw his own eyes fill with tears as they clung fiercely to one another.

Gently he withdrew from her and turned onto his back as Nicolette cuddled against him. "I cannot give you my gold ring today but I will give you a present otherwise."

"Another?" she teased with a seductive voice and then grinned impishly.

"So witty my lady is." He laughed. "One of the least important of the *many* things you know not about me is that I am something of a *trouvère* myself. Though I do not sing with the gift of voice that you have been given."

"You compose your own songs?" she asked excitedly. "How wonderful! I have no talent thereof, for I can merely learn and sing another's." She scrambled upright. "You will sing for me now, then? Oh please do, Davide! Please!" She pulled at his shoulders, anxious for him to rise.

"I will sing to you. It is a song I composed only a fortnight ago. No one has heard it. It came to me one night in a dream and I knew that I should not sing it

SONG OF THE ROSE

until I'd found the damsel of whom I dreamed. To you, Nicolette, that dream's damsel, I will sing," he shyly declared. "I call it, 'La Chanson de la Rose.'"

"'Song of the Rose,'" Nicolette repeated, awed and humbled by his words.

"She is the rose," he sang in such a lilting baritone that it broke her heart. "The lily too. The sweetest violet . . . and through her noble beauty, stately mien, I think her now the finest queen which mortal eyes have seen . . ." He took her hand as he continued. "Simple, yet coy, her eyes flash joy . . . God give her life without annoy and every bliss whereof I ween . . ."

Nicolette could barely speak. "How beautiful," was all she could say, unable to find words that would convey how deeply his song had touched her. Davide's eyes held that serious expression she had already come to understand.

"It pales now that you are a reality rather than a dream, but it is the best I can do . . . More importantly, you must know that I will *never* sing your song again until I hold you in my arms once more. Should something go amiss you *must* remember my song to you," he explained, his eyes taking a mysterious cast she knew not to question.

"I shall no more forget it than the taste of your sweet lips," she said softly and ran her fingertips across his mouth, "or the scent of your skin . . ." He drew her into his arms. "Or the touch of your cheek against mine." They kissed deeply and held on to one another tightly. "I have something for you, too, my love."

"What? Are you going to give me Bruge's chaplet to wear upon my helmet as I ride into battle?"

Nicolette cuffed him lightly on the shoulder. Then she reached behind her, beneath the garland. She withdrew the pale blue linen, flowing sleeve of her bliaut that she had salvaged from her tattered raiments. "Will you carry this upon your lance as other knights do?" she asked shyly.

"Oh, but I wish I could, for to me it is the most precious object I now possess. But I cannot tie it to my lance for it could endanger you—"

"You are afraid that François will recognize it! So he will be riding with you!"

"Nicolette! Do not speak another word of it if you love me half as deeply as I you!"

"I'm sorry . . . I forgot." She hung her head in shame, for she knew it tortured Davide to hold back all he wanted to share as much as it tortured her not to know. "I should not have—"

He cupped her chin and brought her eyes to his. "You understand, do you not?" Desperation tinged his voice.

"I understand, Davide."

"This sleeve I will carry with me into battle but it shall be wrapped around my heart until my return." Her understanding smile soothed his frustration at the necessary evasion. "And return you to the castle now we must, my darling."

They walked arm in arm to his destrier. Davide mounted and pulled her up behind him. Nicolette wrapped herself tightly around his body. "Davide," she inquired urgently as he walked his war-horse through the underbrush. "How will you *know* that all went as planned tonight? And how will *I* know that *you* know?"

"I will know. And you must remember that. No matter what *seems* to be. For I regret that things may appear quite different than they are. No matter how dark a day may seem, know that I am always with you and that you and Bruge shall always be protected."

"I will hold fast to your words. I shall forget nothing, my lord. Not a single moment, touch, word, caress, or note of 'The Song of the Rose.' Do *you* trust me to *my* pledge, Davide?"

"I trust your pledge as deeply as I trust there is a God in Heaven and that the sun shall rise on the morrow. If we do not leave this moment I fear that I shall lose all reason and steal you away this moment, forever. But that is not the way, is it, my lady?" He sighed deeply.

Nicolette thought of the smiling face of her pretty younger sister. "No, that is not the way, my beloved," she whispered and wiped her tears away. "The plan *will* work and I will wait patiently, filled with loving devotion until you return to me." As they galloped away from the forest, Nicolette gazed behind her, knowing that somehow, someday, they would return.

Chapter Three

NICOLETTE CROUCHED, HIDING BEHIND THE HEAVY BLUE taffeta curtain of Alienor's bed. She heard Alienor, Bruge, and Denise, the daughter of another petty noble who was Alienor's third lady-in-waiting, enter Alienor's chamber.

"Nicolette?" Bruge called out as Nicolette held her breath. "It is nearing five. I was certain she should have returned by now," Bruge said in a worried voice.

"Check her pallet, for perhaps she has returned and is somewhere about the castle," Denise offered.

Nicolette heard her sister's footsteps as she crossed to Nicolette's narrow, straw-filled bed. She listened as Bruge opened her chest that sat before the pallet.

"There is no such sign. Her pallet is undisturbed as

you can see. Her mantle is not hung on the hook and her white slippers are absent from the chest."

Nicolette heard more footsteps in the direction of her pallet, which most fortunately lay on the other side of the chamber.

"Bruge, do not frown," Alienor instructed. "It is most unbecoming. Besides, I am most certain that she has returned and is perhaps somewhere within the castle's bailey. For you know how your sister prefers the fresh air of the out-of-doors, and it is still relatively warm outside."

Nicolette knew that Alienor was trying to disguise her own worry for Bruge's sake.

"Methinks that you and Denise should look for her. Perhaps she is visiting 'Crooked' Herman in the garden. Why do you not check there, Denise? Or perhaps she has gone to the chapel and is with Father Gregoire. Go seek her there, Bruge."

"Perchance you are correct . . ." Bruge's voice trembled less than before. "For Nicolette spends much time in prayer these days."

"Take your mantles so that you do not take a chill," Alienor spoke in a motherly way to the younger maidens.

Nicolette listened as they obeyed and Alienor saw them to the door. "Do not tarry, for I must be dressed for supper at five." The chamber door closed and Alienor's footsteps continued within the room. How could she now get Alienor's attention without frightening her? But she had no time to waste! She would just have to call out Alienor's name and come out from her hiding place.

"Where are you, Nicolette?" Alienor suddenly

spoke aloud to herself. "I should never have participated in your scheme, for if anything befell you in the forest I shall never forgive myself. I thought for sure that François would have ridden you home, but he said he never found you on his morning ride. At first I rejoiced for his not finding you. I know how unhappy you are, betrothed to my brother, though I can't say so! I would do anything in my power to spare you your fate! You are not merely my lady-in-waiting, Nicolette. You are my dearest friend . . . But alas, I dare not defy my brother with Father so ill . . . Where are you, Nicolette?"

Nicolette knew that Alienor worried that she had been abducted by some highway robbers or worse. She had to make herself known. "I am here, Alienor."

"Oh!" Alienor responded, startled.

Nicolette quickly walked before Alienor, who stood at the fireplace. "I am sorry for giving you a fright but I must speak with you alone!" Nicolette pulled off her mantle and stood before her in her tattered clothes. Alienor's face paled in horror as she pulled Nicolette into her arms.

"Oh, dear Lord!" Alienor exclaimed. "What has happened to you? Did some barbarian come upon you in the forest and—" Alienor lapsed into tears, obviously unable to utter the words.

"I was almost ravaged by a brute but was saved by a passing knight, thanks be given to Mother Mary."

"Did you know the man's face, for we will send the provost to bring him to the *donjon*—"

Nicolette took a deep breath. How she hated to hurt her kind friend, but as Davide had shown her, there was no other way. Nicolette led Alienor to her canopied feather bed, seating them both. "I do, but you shall not be able to call the provost upon him. The man was your brother."

The disgust on Alienor's face caused Nicolette to despise François even more deeply. To think that these two were brother and sister. "I need your aid, Alienor. I think I know of a means whereby your brother will never know your participation. Will you help me?"

"Anything! I will go to Father if you wish—"

"Oh, no one could have a better friend than you." Nicolette forced away her tears of gratitude for there was little time. "But I think that will not be necessary. Can you calm yourself enough to listen carefully?" she asked as she took Alienor's icy hands into her own.

Alienor brushed her tears away. "Yes. Tell me that which you wish me to do."

Nicolette closed her eyes for a moment. She saw Davide's face, his eyes smiling at her. She heard his last words: "No goodbyes. We shall never say goodbye until the Lord calls us to Heaven. We are bound forever and unto eternity. So off with you, my lusty wench!" Now she could begin. "The knight who saved me from François—and I shall tell you the wretched details of the morning—only *delayed* the inevitable. For tonight, I will be forced by my own brother"—she spat out the word—"to allow François to bed me. And François let me know *most* clearly that he would take his revenge for my years of rebuffs and his humiliation today . . . You see, I was sitting by the stream at my favorite spot, weaving Bruge's garland," she began.

Alienor sat upon her bed chest as Nicolette quickly tore off her ruined clothing and slipped into first a fresh chemise, a shirt of white linen, over which she placed her pelisson, like the one of pale blue that she had worn today, the sleeve of which Davide now carried next to his heart. As she slipped her arms into the wide sleeves of the pale yellow pelisson, it fell gracefully to her feet. Alienor handed her her bliaut. She put on the darker yellow tunic, which she tied closely around her waist with her best girdle, woven with silver and gold threads. This belt had been her last birthday gift from her father.

Alienor handed her a small, embroidered purse which she tied to her girdle. Then Alienor gave her the tiny brown vial that Alienor had sent a servant to procure with a note to Alienor's private physician. The servant, who could not read, had quickly returned with the vial wrapped in cloth. Nicolette trusted Alienor's assurances that her physician would never utter a word to anyone concerning Alienor's request for the sleeping potion. She was ready, the vial secure in her purse.

A quick knock upon the door and a distraught Bruge appeared, Denise on her heels.

"There you are, Nicolette!" Her sister ran to hug her. "Where were you? Such a fright you gave me!"

Nicolette forced her brightest smile. "Oh, Bruge. Sometimes you are still such a foolish child! I am fine. In fact I had a most wonderful day," she pretended.

She patted Bruge's dark brown braids. "Sire Guy's sister's lady-in-waiting took me to their garden. And then I was invited to go on a hunt with Marguerite and her ladies and some noble guests in Sire Guy's forest!"

"A hunt?" Bruge asked, bewildered. "You dislike hunts."

"Yes, as I well should." Nicolette grimaced and rubbed her hip. She looked from Bruge to Denise. "I shall tell you the reason for my delay home, but if either of you breathes a word of my humiliation, I shall never speak to you again!"

"I won't, I swear," Denise promised, as she crossed her heart, anxious to hear the story. Bruge did likewise, though her tiny face was still pinched with worry.

Nicolette sighed. "I have told Alienor in detail and since we have yet to dress her for supper—"

"And proud Nicolette *hates* to tell of making a *fool* of herself—" Alienor cleverly added in a playful tone.

"My lady, how can you accuse me of false pride?" Nicolette responded with such apparent injury that the maidens fell into gales of laughter. How it eased Nicolette's heart to see Bruge laughing again.

"I can guess what happened," quick, pretty redheaded Denise interrupted, playing right into their hands. "She fell off her horse. Didn't you, Nicolette! That is why you keep rubbing your side!"

"I did not *fall* off my horse because of lack of riding skill," Nicolette declared hotly. "The Devil himself took hold of the stallion and sent him galloping until *he* lost step and tumbled into a stream! Leaving *me* sore, but unharmed, and my favorite bliaut in tatters!

So I was taken back to the castle to be examined by their physician, despite my protests that it was unnecessary. Marguerite offered me fresh clothing, but she is a bit stouter—"

"She is as fat as she is tall!" Denise said without thinking and then looked to Alienor in contrition, quickly relieved when she saw Alienor giggling as well. "I spoke out of turn, I am afraid."

"Marguerite is sweet and kind, but she *is* fat, though we should not fun about it," Alienor said but broke into a giggle which set the two maidens off again. Nicolette pretended disapproval.

"Marguerite was very sweet and remembered that Alienor had left some clothing upon her last visit to the castle. So I wore, rather than carried, Alienor's raiments home after I had dined and rested. I fell into a deep sleep and no one awakened me, thinking I needed the recuperation. That is the entire story and I want not another word of it ever mentioned! Now, are we to dress our lady or are we not?" Nicolette said so sternly that the two maidens scurried to their tasks, leaving Alienor and Nicolette a precious moment to smile gratefully at one another. If only the rest would go so easily, Nicolette prayed. But she would think now only moment by moment if she were to get through the night! She quickly turned away to lay out Alienor's raiments upon her bed.

Chapter Four

FRANÇOIS RUBBED HIS HAND DOWN NICOLETTE'S THIGH as she sat beside him at the heavy oak-planked dinner table, long and narrow, that stood upon the dais in the great hall. She gritted her teeth and forced herself to endure his repulsive advances as she had throughout supper. Baron Perdant's canopied chair at the center of the dais remained empty again tonight. Although François had toasted his father after Father Gregoire's prayer before the squires served the first course, word was whispered that the baron's condition had worsened, despite his physician having bled him just yesterday. His father's imminent death had not seemed to sober François. Nicolette had caught him stealthily glancing at the canopied empty chair, the symbol of high seigneurial privilege that would be his upon his father's passing.

"A bite of a pear, my lady," François insisted, pushing the baked pear at her mouth as he had done with the rabbit and leg of mutton of the earlier courses. Nicolette implored herself to take a bite and chew, for she must do nothing to arouse François' suspicions. He brought the silver chalice of spiced wine to her mouth and smiled as she readily drank the heated wine. She forced herself to resist the temptation of drinking enough to soothe her nerves for she dared not lose her wits. François drank the wine and then lifted his flagon of beer, which he guzzled with zest. A man less a drunkard than he would have passed out by now, Nicolette thought with contempt. Then she realized that if the plan were to work, François was not to pass out. Not until she was alone with him in his chamber.

He kissed her sloppily upon her cheek and raised his flagon at someone across the room. Nicolette knew without having to look again that he toasted Henri, for she had caught their conspiratorial grins throughout supper. Someday she would have her revenge upon her venal stepbrother but for now—

François abruptly staggered up from his chair and pounded his flagon on the table. "I wish to make an announcement," he roared drunkenly. The chatter in the room filled with family and guests ceased. "Two announcements!" he continued. "The first of regret." Whispers echoed until he pounded his flagon again. "As you all know, my dear father, Baron Simon Perdant, is ailing. Though I am assured that he will make a most speedy recovery, thank the Lord in

Heaven, my duties as his only son have forced me to send a message to the Count of Champagne. On the morrow I was to ride with my mounted party of knights from St. Aliquis and partake in the glorious third and final Crusade. But I *must* forsake my own honor and glory to safekeep that of our barony until our baron can take his rightful place in his honored chair once again!"

This can not be! Nicolette's hands trembled. She felt herself pale. For Davide had assured her that François would have learned, *before* supper, that the knight he had hired was dead. It mattered not now that she had secured the vial of sleeping drops, for there would be the night on the morrow and the one after that. Endless nights!

". . . and of course I have entreated a most noble knight, a reknowned knight from Troyes, to ride in my place, holding the banner of St. Aliquis high! He shall arrive before tonight's entertainment ends. Oh, that Jesus himself would intercede and make my father well before morning so that I might mount my magnificent destrier and lead my fellow knights in glory!"

Nicolette sat frozen as cheers and applause filled the great hall.

"There is but one joy this bitter cup of life brings me tonight."

Nicolette stared at François. Mother Mary, she thought, what new surprise would he spring?

"On the morrow, we will sanctify it, but I wish to announce my betrothal to the fair maiden Nicolette Duprey. We had planned to make our bliss known at a later date. But with Father so ill, dearest Nicolette, the next Baroness of St. Aliquis, may my saintly

SONG OF THE ROSE

mother rest in peace, has consented to fulfill Father's deepest wish to see us joined as man and wife. Therefore we will forgo a gala wedding celebration and take our vows in Father's chamber on this Friday."

Two days from now, Nicolette thought, as a fog engulfed her. She felt herself being pulled to her feet and heard a toast and the ensuing cheers as if she were off at a great distance. The wine poured down her throat jolted her awake again, as her knees began to buckle. There was no hope and she began to let herself drift, though she remained standing for François' arm held tightly around her waist. Numbly she felt his vile lips upon her own. Suddenly Davide's smiling face filled her mind and she heard his words echo through her head. "You are safe, Nicolette. We are already husband and wife. *Nothing* shall ever separate us. You must hold on, my beloved!" I will, she silently declared. The room came back into focus and fortuitously François again brought the chalice of wine to her mouth. She drank greedily and felt the lightness in her head evaporate. Then she found herself seated once again and lowered her head in feigned modesty.

"Sire." Gervais, Baron Perdant's second squire, stood before François. He had an envelope with an embossed seal in his hand. "A messenger just delivered this. He said 'tis urgent that you read it immediately."

François drunkenly opened the letter. He read it once and then again, visibly paling. "This cannot be!" he muttered to himself. "It cannot be."

"Is everything all right, my dear brother?" Alienor,

seated at his side, asked innocently. Nicolette dared not look at her. Oh, thank you, Mother Mary, she silently offered. She was certain that nothing other than the news of the death of the knight to whom he had offered scutage could have paled and sobered François so rapidly.

François rose. "Henri," he called across the room and beckoned. Then he turned to Alienor. "Everything is fine but I must speak with you in private for a moment after I have a word with Henri."

"Of course, brother," Alienor replied evenly. "Where do you wish me to be?"

"In my chamber in five minutes." François marched off the dais and walked toward the entrance to the family chambers where Henri met him.

Nicolette watched as François spoke a few words to Henri. She observed her brother's face as he strove to maintain composure. Henri glanced at her once but she met his eye with equanimity. He returned his attention to François, nodded, and strode in her direction. As she breathed deeply in preparation, Henri quickly approached.

"My sweet sister," he said loudly with a forced smile on his long, pallid face. His Adam's apple pulsated as it always did when he was upset, and the tightness of his mouth emphasized his hawklike nose.

"Brother," Nicolette said evenly, giving him a bright smile that further enraged him.

"I suspect that you are about some scheme. If you are not in François' chamber," he whispered in her ear, "before the music ends, then I shall send Bruge in your place. Is that clear?"

"I shall not gainsay you, brother," she answered

obediently. She lowered her eyes in a submissive gesture that seemed to appease him. And you too shall burn in hell for eternity, she thought.

"Are you not going to bed too?" Bruge asked, her voice heavy with sleep, as Nicolette sat beside her on her straw bed.

Nicolette stroked her sister's silky dark hair. She smiled into Bruge's sleepy brown eyes and bent to kiss her rosy cheek that glowed in the candlelight. "Soon. For I too am very weary. And sore." Her allusion to her "fall" today brought a giggle from Bruge, causing sleeping Denise to stir. "Shush," Nicolette gently admonished. Oh what joy her sweet sister brought to her heart!

"Nicolette," Bruge whispered insistently as Nicolette started to rise. "I must ask you an important question or I shall not sleep a wink."

"Pray tell?" Nicolette whispered back.

"Are you happy that you will be marrying François? I had always thought you disliked him."

"Oh no, my sweet. I am very happy." She forced a believable smile for it was difficult to fool Bruge who was so sensitive. "I will be a baroness and we shall all live happily ever after. For a handsome, gallant knight will one day *beg* for *your* hand and we shall all live here at St. Aliquis. You are happy here, are you not, Bruge?"

"Oh, yes. Very. But no handsome knight will ever choose me . . . I am not beautiful and talented as you are, Nicolette." Bruge sighed.

"How dare you gainsay me, my foolish sister. For not only are you most talented and quick, but your beauty lights any room you enter! But more importantly, the beauty of your soul shines even more brightly, if that is possible. I love you deeply, my sweet, foolish, pretty little sister." Nicolette kissed her tenderly upon her forehead. "But I must attend to Alienor and you must go to sleep. Remember what father made you recite each night before your prayers?"

Bruge smiled in memory. "Rise at five," she began the child's rhyme, "dine at nine, sup at five, to bed at nine"—Bruge yawned—"is the way to live to be ninety and nine."

"I will see you in the morn," Nicolette said. Bruge's eyes closed; in a moment she fell into deep slumber.

Nicolette hurried from the room.

Henri stood posted outside François' chamber as Nicolette approached with the two gold goblets and a decanter of wine. He smiled with satisfaction and knocked upon the door for her. "Enter!" François' voice commanded. Henri opened the door. He sends me in like a whore, Nicolette thought bitterly as she heard the door close behind her, but she forced a shy expression upon her face.

François sat upon his canopied bed, wearing only his chemise. He leered at her, his full mouth curled lustfully, but said nothing.

"My lord." She curtsied and carried the wine to a chest across from his bed. "I have brought wine for a toast to our marriage."

"You sing a different tune than this morning, my lovely songbird," he mocked.

"I am sorry for my actions this morning, François,"

she replied softly, meeting his eye. "I have been a foolish maiden."

"That you have. But you shall be a maiden no more, for I will make you a woman tonight."

"Will you be gentle with me, my master?" she asked with an intentional tremor in her voice that seemed to convince him of her sincerity, for his expression softened.

"That shall depend on you, my lady. Come here," he commanded.

She forced herself to walk slowly and gracefully to him and stood before him, meeting his eye.

"Tonight I will finally have you. And have you I will, for on the morrow I must ride, after all, to the Crusade," he stated dourly.

"Oh no, my lord! But then how are we to marry Friday?" She pretended confusion. "It can not be possible."

"But it is. I must say I am pleasantly surprised to see that you are truly distressed. When I return I will marry you. But tonight we shall become man and wife in all but ceremony, shan't we?"

"Yes, my lord." She lowered her eyes and blushed with maidenly modesty.

"The knight that came to your protection today?"

"Yea, François?" she asked, feigning innocence.

"Did he tarry long after my leave?"

"No. Just a few moments."

"Did he speak his name to you?"

Just as Davide had said François would ask, he did! "Yea, my lord."

"Do you recall it?"

"I do. He said his name was Guilbert Mathieu. And

that he was a vassal for the Duke of Burgundy," she offered as planned. "Why do you inquire, my lord?"

"I was merely curious . . ." He ran his hand across her cheek and down her neck, staring into her eyes. Nicolette was careful not to give herself away. He grinned lustfully but erased his smile abruptly. "Bring me some wine, Nicolette."

"Yes, my lord." Slowly she turned toward the chest and as she walked with her back to him she removed the vial from her purse. She filled one goblet in his vision, then turned most naturally and poured the other as she quickly dropped the sleeping droplets in the second cup. Please, Mother Mary, she prayed, as she turned and shyly carried the goblet with the potion in it in her right hand and the untouched goblet in her left. "A toast to my husband-to-be," she whispered, holding her breath as he hesitated, then reached for the goblet with the potion.

"A toast to my most lovely wife-to-be," he responded, clinking their goblets. He downed the wine in one gulp and tossed his goblet into the fireplace across the room.

"Nicolette," he said sternly, no longer feigning a smile. "You humiliated me today in front of a fellow knight. You must be punished for your travesty so that you will learn your lesson."

Her heart pounded in fear and rage. She lowered her eyes. "I am sorry, my lord. I beg for your mercy."

"Just a taste of humiliation, so that you will forever know your place, my beauty. You are a virgin, are you not—Look me in the eye, Nicolette."

"Oh!" she exclaimed at his violent jerk of her head. He laughed in response and continued to cup her face harshly. Oh God, let me find the courage to continue, she thought. "I am, my lord."

"Have you ever stood naked before any man other than the physician?"

"I have not."

"Answer with 'my lord,' maiden. For it pleases me to hear the words from your cherry lips."

"Yes, my lord."

"Good. Now I want you to do as I say." He drew the candle closer so that it shone brightly upon her. Only his yawn gave her the courage to suppress her tears. "Take off your girdle. Quickly."

Nicolette undid her belt. She understood now what was to come next. She knew he intended to humiliate her by making her undress, standing before him. She had to do so. But ever so slowly.

"Now the bliaut," he said, the churlish smile playing on his lips. He yawned again.

Very slowly she removed her tunic. He took it from her and tossed it across the room.

"Now your pelisson," he commanded, his eyes fixed upon her. Again he took the garment and tossed it across the room. Nicolette stood in linen chemise that fell only to her knees. Her blush now was no artifice. "Come closer." She stood just an arm's distance from him as he yawned deeply. "Forgive me. It must be the wine, for certainly your charms do not bore me. Take off your chemise. Very slowly."

"My lord," she pleaded. "I can not."

"Do you still defy me!"

"No, my lord." Her tears fell, causing François to smile with satisfaction. She could not bear the look on his face and lowered her eyes. Again he jerked at her chin but this time she did not cry out, though she shook in fright. I will see only you, Davide, she thought. Touch only you. Feel your love engulf me and protect me. Slowly she finished disrobing. She stood before him naked as a babe.

"As lovely as I imagined"—he yawned again—"more lovely . . . Turn in a slow circle, for your blush becomes you and I want to see if you blush all over."

Before she had completed her turn he pulled her roughly to him and his hands plundered her body and pulled her onto his bed.

"Kiss me, wench. And beg me to take you." His speech had grown heavy and slow, she realized, through her panic. She must prolong her kiss. Make it impassioned. Make it the last thing he remembered once he awoke. She brought her lips to his and he rolled her onto her back, beneath him. Abruptly he pulled away. "Say it."

"Take me, my lord, but kiss me again first. Please."

"See, I always knew in your soul you were a lusty wench like them all . . . So you like my kiss after all, do you?" he said in a sleepy, sing-song voice.

Nicolette smiled and brought her mouth to his in response. She endured his tongue's assault as she remembered the wonder of her passionate kisses with Davide. After what felt like an eternity but was just minutes, he rested half upon her, snoring and breathing deeply.

It had worked. He had humiliated her and raped her with his eyes and words. Only. But he was asleep. She rolled from beneath him and he fell heavily onto the mattress but did not stir. It had worked!

Quickly she gathered her clothing and dressed. She

would lie awake on the pallet near his bed until dawn. He would awaken to find her dressed and assume she had merely risen before him. She would go to him shyly and thank him for making her a woman and his wife. Never would he know otherwise. By noon he would be *gone* and Davide would come for her and Bruge before François' return. Nicolette climbed onto the pallet and quietly sobbed in exhaustion. Behind her closed lids she saw Davide. He held her and she fell asleep, comforted by his loving, handsome face as he sang "The Song of the Rose."

She awoke before dawn, smiling, for she had dreamed of her Davide. Her smile turned to alarm as she remembered where she lay and what had passed. The worst is over, she soothed herself, forcing her frightened heart to still.

A sharp rap came upon the door. "Sire," Henri's voice called. François did not stir. For *once* her brother had come to her aid, however unknowingly.

"One moment, my brother," she said as she opened the door and smiled. Had she actually caught a fleeting expression of guilt in his eye? She closed the door again and walked to the sleeping François. "My lord," she said. She shook him until he stirred. She kissed him on his lips quickly when his eyes opened. "My brother is at the door. How I hated to wake you, my husband," she said shyly and kissed him again.

"Was it not wonderful last night?" François asked as he shook himself awake. She thought he could do no more to shock her but his eyes asked for genuine approval for what he *imagined* had taken place.

"It was wonderful, François," she whispered. Henri knocked again, most insistently.

SONG OF THE ROSE

"Let your damned brother in, Nicolette," he ordered as he stretched himself to consciousness. "It was absolutely wonderful," he repeated, as he rose. "Such perfection that I have *just* decided Father Gregoire must marry us this morning. Before I ride, you shall become my wife, my love!"

Chapter Five

NICOLETTE HAD BEEN DISMISSED FROM FRANÇOIS' CHAMber with orders to have herself dressed to be wed at noon. Sire Eustace, the baron's seneschal, who supervised both the baron's estates and his household, passed her as she fled down the long hall of the palais. Nicolette turned and watched as the seneschal approached François' room. The hasty arrangements that would condemn her to become François' consort would no doubt be carried out with great efficiency, Nicolette knew. There must be *something* she could do to save herself.

She halted at the steps that led down to the great hall of the palais, for although she had started for the chapel where she would pray for reprieve, she realized that action, not prayer, was her only chance for salvation. She must speak in private to Henri. For surely, in his heart of hearts, she could find a drop of compassion for his blood sister. She would fall to her knees at his feet and plead for a boon. An appeal for one favor in the name of their mutual father might soften the steel of Henri's greed and ambition. Nicolette slipped behind the heavy drape before Henri and Sire Eustace, who stood in the corridor outside of François' chamber, saw her.

"I shall at once inform Father Gregoire that the marriage vows are to be made at the baron's bedside. The prior, Brother Matthew, arrived from the abbey before dawn. He and the father are administering last rites to the baron presently," said the imposing Sire Eustace.

"Last rites!" Henri whispered, feigning alarm. "Do you say that our seigneur is that near the gates of Heaven?"

"With deep despair, I do. For Messire has been more than my lord these long years since we fought in the last Crusade. We were but damoiseaux, young knights with our first beards fighting for our suzerain, the present Count of Champagne's father. The baron is quickly slipping from this world. He is as pale as death itself and so weak he cannot lift his head. His physician believes he will not last the night."

"Then it will please Messire to see Sire François properly wed this noon, will it not?"

"Aye. For he cherishes his only surviving boy child more than life itself. Two wives before the late baroness died in childbirth taking his sons with them to heaven. Then, when Lady Adela, the baroness, may she rest in peace, still carried François in her belly, she was kidnapped on the road to the cathedral and held for ransom by the Count of Reims. The king intervened, threatening to invade the count's castle if he did not return Lady Adela and the boy child, François, who had been birthed during her captivity."

"I have heard tell of the horrific kidnapping those long years ago," François answered with practiced sympathy.

Nicolette had also heard the well-woven tale of the *supposed* kidnapping of Lady Adela. But she remembered the night before Henri was sent off to St. Aliquis to be "nourished" by the baron. Father had thought her asleep, for she was but a young girl and Bruge just a small child, when he sat Henri by the hearth to tell him the true story. Father had been one of the knights who had returned Lady Adela and the baby François to St. Aliquis. Lady Adela had wept in Father's arms and sworn him to a confidence he had not broken until that eve. For in truth he held the baron in contempt and sent young Henri to learn to become a knight under the "nourishment" of Baron Perdant with the greatest reluctance. Only his desire to caution Henri as to the true character of the baron had made him break his vow to Lady Adela.

Father did not live, thank the Lord, to know that he had done so in vain, for Henri had become as vile as the baron and François. Worse, for he trampled upon the values of chivalry and the teachings of Christ which Father had striven to instill into his only son. Nicolette had never forgotten a detail of the story meant not for her ears that night. Yet Henri now stood with the seneschal, clucking in sympathy for the dying baron, offering praises to his honor and gallantry. How she despised her stepbrother. Still she would supplicate herself before him as soon as she could steal a moment of privacy.

Sire Eustace completed his lauding of the dying baron, suggesting that it was the baron's charity that allowed him to be joyful of François' betrothal to her, though by wedding a maiden of a lower rank François "disparaged" their name. Nicolette's blood boiled as Henri carried the sham further, speaking his "gratitude" that the angels had deemed it fit to bless his "fair, loving sister with the prize of Sire François' noble adoration." Sire Eustace knew, perhaps better than most, that Baron Perdant had not been able to negotiate a marriage for the boorish, profligate François with any higher-ranking count or duke in the kingdom, so widely spread was François' ill reputation. Nor had he been able to finalize an agreement for betrothal with a plain and simple twenty-two-year-old maid of a neighboring, poorer baron. For it had been whispered through the barony that even for the promise of a large fief and larger castle, that loving baron could not bring himself to deny his daughter's entreaty to send her instead to a nunnery.

"Yea, we Dupreys have been blessed by our deepening ties with the noble Perdants . . . Nicolette is most probably in the chapel right now giving thanks to Mother Mary. So overcome with happiness was she to learn this morn that François would forgo the pageantry of a noble wedding ceremony in order that the baron bless their marriage before he forsakes us for the glories of Heaven."

"Nicolette—I should properly say Lady Nicolette—methinks will make François a fine wife. They will bring happiness to the baron in his last hours. Should I not offer my congratulations to you, Henri, as well? I believe that Sire François was wise in appointing you his commander of his men-at-arms. He will be able to ride out with his knights to the Crusade assured that St. Aliquis will remain well protected during his absence, even in the event of the baron's passing."

"No words of congratulations, for it is my humble honor to assume the position. I do look for your wise guidance during his absence, Sire Eustace," Henri replied with a clever show of humility.

"Of that you may be certain. But I must see to the arrangements for the wedding now. Time is of the essence."

"I cannot gainsay you, Sire Eustace. I, too, must attend to my duties at the barracks."

Nicolette watched as the men bid each other adieu and walked past her and down the stairs. So it was at the barracks that she would have to seek a private audience with Henri, who was already reaping the rewards of selling her to François.

Nicolette wove her way through the broad court of the bailey, swarming with villeins and servitors as they went about their daily tasks. She swung around a muck pile and then between two pigs and a hen as she passed the carpenter shop where saw and hammer were alreading plying. She had to chase a barking dog from her heels as she approached the well-appointed smithy where she noticed at one ringing forge Alienor's white palfrey being reshod. The master armorer's hammer pounded a new link he was putting into a chainmail suit but she hurried onward to the barracks, merely nodding at his greeting. Her urgency made her feet swift. She raced into the barracks' quarter that would now be Henri's domain.

"Henri!" she called breathlessly as she threw open the heavy wood door. "Oh!" she called out in embarrassment. For it was Michel, the arrogant squire who had purposefully muddied her yesterday. He sat with his boots raised upon the plank table set upon wooden horses.

Michel smirked. "Your esteemed brother has not arrived yet. But I hear tell you are about to become a fine lady. Apparently Sire François found your charms most bewitching last night, Nicolette." She paled as his words registered. So they all knew about last night and already the news of her marriage had spread through the castle. "I knew you should live to regret denying yourself my kisses." His grin grew more mocking, and he rose and menacingly walked toward her as they stood alone in the drafty room.

"Michel, I should watch how you address me," she declared with a show of fearless courage. "For if you say another word, I shall tell François. You will find yourself in the *donjon* pleading for mercy tonight rather than at the supper table."

He continued closer. "Will you now, my pretty lady?" He laughed heartily. "Then I shall have to tell him of the embrace I saw you give a strange knight who rode you to the back gates of the castle yesterday. What would your sire say to that? Did you fool him into thinking you a virgin last night? For the embrace was that of lovers."

Dear Lord, where had Michel been—how could he have seen?

SONG OF THE ROSE

"Your blush flames your ivory cheeks most becomingly," Michel said as he reached out and caressed her neck. "I ask for only one kiss from your ruby lips and you will have me in your confidence for life."

One kiss it would never remain, Nicolette knew. She had to brazen him, for even if he did report to François, François' outrage would find vent on him as the bearer of the news. Even if François believed him. Michel was too clever not to know so himself. He was seeking to bully her with fear.

"One kiss," he whispered as his hand grazed her breast and his mouth sought her lips. Her hard slap reverberated through the room.

"Do not ever touch me again," she said as he rubbed his cheek. "Or you shall be hanged. Mark my words. Now leave at once," she demanded. Michel looked at her with what seemed to be newfound respect and fled the room with nary a word.

Nicolette lowered her shaking body upon a bench. Oh my Davide, she thought. "How much more must I bear, I pray thee?"

"What say you, sister? And what are you doing, sitting here when you should be dressing to wed?" Henri asked sharply. She had not heard him enter.

He stood before her and she flung herself against his legs, her sobs genuine as a torrent of tears broke through her. "Please, my brother. I implore you. I beseech you! I cannot bear more agony. Do not force me to wed François today. Find some pretext—say I have taken ill with a fever—say you anything. When he returns from the Crusade I will wed him as you command me—but please not today. Not after last night—I pray thee—"

SONG OF THE ROSE

Henri shook her harshly, forcing her back to her senses. "Stop, I command you, foolish maid! There is no way I could grant your wish even if I wanted to give you a boon!"

He righted her upon the bench and sat beside her. "I beg for your mercy—"

"It is too late. The baron will not live through the night. It behooves François to make certain all his affairs are in order. He had not intended to ride out on the—I mean to say that he had not expected that his father should deteriorate so rapidly. Besides, the worst is already done, is it not, my sister? Last night he bedded you. You are no longer a modest maiden. Correct?"

She lowered her eyes. She must show nothing that might arouse Henri's suspicions further. For her outburst had brought a crease between his brows that she recognized as an expression of doubt. "Yes, my brother."

"Then you see." He lifted her chin gently and spoke in an oddly caring voice. "You have already suffered the worst, my modest, virtuous sister." His finger ran down the tip of her nose and rested at her lip which he traced. "Did he pleasure you, lovely Nicolette? Come now, you may speak of such things for you are no longer chaste and will be Lady Nicolette, the future baroness, by the time the sun rises to the top of the sky." His fingers traveled down to her collarbone. "And I am, after all, your brother . . . though we did have different mothers. 'Tis that not so? That I am your cherished brother to whom you can confide your deepest intimacies?" Nicolette prayed that their father could not see this moment from his place in Heaven.

"Henri." The tears blurred her eyes. "Please . . ." She lifted his hand from her neck and saw a flash of lustful disappointment play in his eyes.

"Whatever you wish, my lady," he said with mocking obedience. His hand fell to his lap. Her cheeks flamed when she noticed his bulging manhood and Nicolette quickly steeled her eyes upon his face. His smile told her that her discovery had not gone undetected. Surely the fearful infidels could be no more wicked than her "protectors," she thought with a growing rage.

"Henri, my *brother*," she said softly but pointedly. "I ask you but once more—"

"It will do you no good to beg. Dearest *sister*," he answered in turn. "For my hands are tied by François just as they are tied by your virtuousness. All you can hope for is that your dearest, most *devoted* husband dies at the hands of the infidels in Jerusalem. Just as I hope. If you are kind to me, I shall exert my influence to see that you are wed to a valiant count. Perhaps even a duke. One who will be as courtly as he is rich and will love you most tenderly. Perhaps then it will not be your fate to never know the glory of true union between man and woman . . . It would please me to please you. That may surprise you, yet it is true. I do now what I must. Not with intention of bringing you misery but to guarantee our continued good fortune. To prove my heart aches to bring you pleasure, I have already promised you that I will allow *you* to choose little Bruge's husband for her, have I not?"

"You have, Henri," she allowed.

"Moreso," he continued as if he spoke to a small child, "François may have already implanted his seed into your belly. You may be carrying the heir to the barony, sister—"

"'Tis not—" she cried out, but thankfully caught herself in time. "'Tis not proper for you to speak with this intimacy to me, Henri!"

"No, my lady," he said sardonically. "For I *am* and always will be your devoted *brother*. The child would be my nephew." He surprised her with a touch to her stomach but pulled his hand away before she could protest. "Am I not correct?"

"You are correct." There was no hope. She realized now the extent of Henri's scheming. Henri not only hoped for the baron's death but for François' as well. That way, by wedding her to yet another he could further his own wealth and power.

"So go and dress for your wedding, although the sudden turn of events prevents you from having the pomp of celebration you merit." Henri raised her to her feet and brought her into an embrace as his thighs hugged tightly against her and his hands clasped her waist, again in a most unbrotherly manner. "And just remember, should you seek comfort when your beloved husband is fighting the infidels I shall always humbly come to your call. Unless it is the handsome young squire, Michel, built like a bull I hear tell, whom you secretly desire?"

Wordlessly she turned, inured to the further intentional humiliation. How much had he heard, she wondered as she fled the barracks. For he must have been outside when Michel had tried to blackmail her.

SONG OF THE ROSE

No—for if he had heard Michel's reference to Davide he would have tried to use it against her. He must have seen Michel depart, his cheek still red from her slap.

She walked toward the palais chambers stunned and oblivious to the bustle of activity about her. What would you now say, Davide? Her heart, filled with doom, called out for him. But he was not here to help her. The weight of decision rested solely on her shoulders and she was uncertain that she could carry the burden. What if she were to flee the castle? Davide would somehow find her. But she could not leave Bruge behind nor could she endanger Bruge's life in flight.

"Good morning to you," the wizened, kind, kitchen maid Marie offered. "I am most happy for your good fortune, Mademoiselle!"

Nicolette responded to the kind villein's heartfelt smile by taking her hand. She knew this old woman believed her to be as lucky as the ladies about whom the *trouvères* sang their love ballads. Yet the woman's sparkling eyes bore her no envy, only genuine good wishes. "Thank you, Marie. Have you seen the Lady Alienor?"

"Aye. She was walking alone toward the garden. She looked a bit pale, I noticed. Her dear father's illness is the cause, I expect. But I am sure she is joyful to have you as her new sister, you two as close as two peas in a pod."

"Yes, I am certain that is such, Marie. Thank you." Quickly, Nicolette turned in the direction of the garden. She would seek Alienor's aid. For Alienor obviously had heard of the terrible turn of events.

This time she would confess all to her truest friend! But she couldn't— Once again she heard Davide's words, imploring her not to confide in Alienor for Alienor's sake as well as her own and Bruge's. She would talk with Alienor without disclosing more than she had yesterday, except for the news that the sleeping potion had done its work. Perhaps too well.

"There must be something—" Alienor insisted as they walked through the blooming garden.

"Alas, there is not," Nicolette stated with quiet resignation. Tears filled Alienor's eyes but her own remained dry.

Alienor pulled them down upon a stone bench. "I will go to my father! Explain the truth about his son. He will not refuse me my last wish." Gentle tears rolled down Alienor's cheeks. Nicolette knew that Alienor held a place of softness in her father's otherwise granite heart. Alienor had been spared the knowledge of her mother's true plight. Even the most malicious gossips in the barony had apparently held to the carefully woven tale, seemingly unwilling to destroy Alienor's love for her father. Certainly Nicolette knew that she herself could never do so. Just as she was certain that the baron, even on his deathbed, would never grant Alienor her wish and disallow François' intended marriage. She must prevent Alienor from making the gesture, for all that would come from it would be Alienor's disillusionment during the final hours of the baron's life. "You cannot weight the baron with such troubling decisions, for he is said to be so very weak," she softly implored, "is he not?"

"I do not think . . . my father—" Alienor's voice

choked. "He will not see the morrow. Why is everything suddenly so terrible, Nicolette!"

"Only the Lord knows His reasons. It is not for us to question," she answered, hiding her bitterness. Yet she too wondered the same, forgive her, Lord. "You can be of aid in one way, though."

"Pray tell?"

"You must help me pretend a happy countenance for Bruge's sake. Today on her birthday, especially."

Alienor smiled through her tears. "I'd almost forgotten to tell you. Bruge found your chaplet this morning. How her eyes glowed with wonder at your gift. She would not allow either Denise or me to place it upon her head. For this she awaits you. When we received word of your wedding—"

"Bruge did not sense your shock at the turn of events?"

"I was most careful to mask my distress. Both believe you slept in your bed in our chamber last night and had merely awakened early and gone to the chapel. They are laying out your finest clothes for your wedding and are greatly caught up in, forgive me, the romance of it all."

"That is as it should be. We must perpetuate the tale for them. For Bruge. Can you do that, Alienor? Deception is not an aspect of your nature."

Alienor took her hand and squeezed it tightly. "Nor is it of yours." *My life has become more a maze of deception and intrigue than you would ever guess, dear Alienor,* Nicolette thought ruefully. "But that much," Alienor continued, "I can do and will. As odious a task as it is, we must return to my chamber and dress you."

They rose and walked reluctantly in the direction of the palais.

"Nicolette," Crooked Herman, the gruff but dear hunchback gardener, approached. In his hand he held a bouquet of lilies. "A gift wishing you great happiness," he said. He placed the bouquet in her arms and hurried away.

Alienor, Bruge, Denise, and a half-dozen castle maids surrounded Nicolette, arraying her for her wedding. Nicolette allowed herself to be washed and dressed as if she sleepwalked through a dream. Even Bruge had seemingly accepted her uncharacteristic quiet as a display of maidenly nervousness. I am being pampered as if I were a queen, Nicolette thought with despair, when in truth I am a captive. She allowed the pelisson fringed with magnificent ermine, a gift from Alienor, to be slipped over her saffron-tinted linen chemise. The pelisson was being laced so tightly by Denise and Bruge that she could hardly breathe, but she did not protest. Perhaps the lacing would bind her tightly enough to stand before Father Gregoire and Brother Matthew and utter her blasphemous vows.

"Oh, you look as lovely as the finest princess!" Denise exclaimed.

Nicolette felt the elegant bliaut, of green silk with long sleeves, many folds, and a long train, float atop her pelisson. Layers of silk embroidery and elaborate flouncing were added. Then the girdle, which had belonged to Lady Adela and which Alienor herself would wear at her own wedding, was fastened around her waist. It was the fairest girdle she had ever seen, made of many pieces of gold and each set with a good-luck stone—agate to guard against fever, sardonyx to protect against the plague, and such. Not that the girdle had protected Lady Adela. She had died of the fever although Father said she had died of a broken heart and soul . . . Would her own fate be a repetition of Lady Adela's, Nicolette wondered. I must find a way to change it, Nicolette vowed, as the mantle of intricatedly embroidered silk, dyed in royal purple, was placed upon her shoulders.

Alienor stood before her, holding Nicolette's pointed shoes of vermilion leather from Cordova, trimmed with gold-thread embroidery, a gift from Henri. Nicolette took the shoes and slipped them upon her stockinged feet. The slippers pinched.

"Now the veiled crown, Nicolette!" Bruge said as she stood upon a chest and placed the small saffron-colored veil held by a golden circlet, a true gold crown engraved and set with emeralds, upon Nicolette's head. "Ah . . ." Bruge echoed the other voices of approval, "you are a vision . . . truly."

Davide had called her a vision . . . Could it have only been yesterday, she wondered, as she straightened her two great braids of hair weighted over her breasts with an extra intertwining of gold thread. Tears filled her eyes though she tried to fight them away.

"Now, Nicolette," Alienor said mockingly. Their eyes met for a fleeting moment. "'Tis too vain for you to cry at your own beauty!"

Thank you, dearest Alienor, Nicolette thought, as she laughed along with the others at Alienor's saving wit. "You are jealous, methinks, my lady," Nicolette played in turn. "For when Sire Guy sees me, he will challenge François to a duel for my hand instead of yours!" she teased, forcing the lighthearted banter well enough to fool the others. "Now, although it is my wedding day, it is also Bruge's birthday and we have not placed the glorious chaplet I so *expertly* wove, upon her lovely head. I demand the right to do so now. Denise, please fetch the garland immediately."

Her commands were instantly followed. Gently, Nicolette placed the garland upon Bruge's dark, thick hair. "Happy birthday, Bruge. Now just because you are thirteen and dreaming of romance . . ." Bruge giggled and blushed, making all in the chamber laugh. "Do not foster any notion of stealing my husband away from me before my vows, you bewitchingly pretty little maiden!"

"Oh, Nicolette, how you mock me," Bruge insisted, but the glow of her smile belied her words, lifting Nicolette's heart for a brief moment.

Nicolette stood with François, bedecked in his finery of red and blue silk, before Father Gregoire and Brother Matthew. Father Gregoire was officiating at the ceremony, cut short because of the baron's weakness. The baron was propped against pillows in his canopied bed. His eyes closed as Nicolette stared but then opened again and their eyes caught for a moment. Is he remembering Adela's forced vows, she wondered. For although she had avoided looking at François since they had entered the baron's chamber, something in her made Nicolette hold the baron's attention. I no more freely take your son for my husband than did Lady Adela take you, Messire, she thought. For by all that is good and holy I am already wed to a fine young knight who bears a shocking resemblance in stature and face to François but is as loving and noble as your son is vile and debased in body and soul—

"Nicolette Duprey," Father Gregoire said, forcing her back to the odious moment.

"Aye, Father."

"I shall now ask of you the same questions as I have asked of François Perdant . . ."

Numbly Nicolette answered yea to his interrogations: Was she of age? Did she swear that they were not within the forbidden degree of consanguinity? Did her brother consent to her marriage? Had the banns announcing their betrothal been published?

"Do you, Nicolette Duprey, freely give your consent to this marriage?" Father Gregoire asked.

I cannot say so before God, Nicolette thought as her heart beat wildly. Her head pounded and she wanted to flee from the room no matter the consequences. Her eyes roamed for a moment but then fell upon Bruge's face. Bruge met her eyes and then frowned darkly, biting her lip. I would do anything to save you, my dearest sister, she thought and took rein of her emotions, smiling at Bruge until Bruge smiled in return. "I freely give my consent to this marriage, Father," she softly lied.

Nicolette, still in a daze, sat at the table prepared in haste for the wedding banquet. She remembered little after she had given her assent. Wringing her hands hidden beneath the table, she felt the cold metal of the thin gold band on the third finger of her left hand.

This is not a wedding ring, she thought bitterly, as the castle *jongleurs* performed merry song with flutes, harps, and rasping viols before her. This is not a wedding ring but instead a chain as brutal as the irons that tie men to the walls of the bloody prison in the basement of the *donjon* that rose high and harshly beside the palais wall.

"Some wine, my wife?" François said and brought his chalice to her lips as he had the night before. She drank submissively for the wine helped to further blur all that passed around her. "You are more beautiful than the most noble queen, my dear Nicolette." François smiled with pride and an attitude of rightful possession. An expression of unbridled victory shone in his eyes, sickening her as deeply as his arrogant, vile lust had the night before.

"Thank you, François," she replied and brought his chalice to her lips again. A queen, she thought bitterly. She would be a drunken queen, one he would wish to abandon. Annulment, she thought. Quickly she lowered the goblet, cursing herself for her fogged mind! That would be her redemption! When Davide returned and Bruge was protected, they could appeal to the bishop, explaining the circumstances of her forced consent. If he refused, they could go to the pope himself! A marriage forced by terror and unconsummated could never be seen as binding in the eyes of the Lord. How very stupid her fear had made her! Oh, Davide, my love, she thought. We will be saved!

"How brightly you smile, my lady," François said. "You are happy then?" he asked.

"I am very happy, Sire," she replied. So filled with joy was her heart that she withstood his hand that caressed her shoulder and his mouth upon her lips in a chaste kiss.

"I shall make you even happier then, my beauty." He leaned and whispered in her ear. "We shall retire to my chamber—our chamber now. I shall thrill you with kisses before I mount my horse—" He turned her face to his and smiled with lust. "I shall mount you once more before I mount my proud destrier."

Nicolette blushed for he no longer whispered in her ear and she could feel Henri, seated beside her, leering.

"I shall mount my proud wife and then my destrier," he repeated, laughing at his own ribald joke. "And I shall ride you as well, if not better." His hand slipped to her knee and he began to fondle her thigh. Her revulsion rose.

"But my lord," she replied as evenly as she could manage. "Have you not to still prepare to leave for your long journey?"

"My squires and your brother will see to that while I am seeing to you." He reached for her hand as he laughed, pulling her from her seat.

"Sire, come quick," Michel, his first squire, said. He clasped François' shoulder. Michel's normally ruddy countenance was pale. He gave her no notice, uncharacteristically, Nicolette saw. "The baron—"

"Has he—" François asked.

Oh dear Lord, no, Nicolette silently prayed. Keep Messire alive until they have ridden or else François will have his excuse to remain at the castle!

"No. But he wishes to see you and he is agitated."

François dropped her hand. "I shall return for you, my wife, as soon as I can."

SONG OF THE ROSE

"Sire," a knight dressed in his mail suit of armor called, as he approached. "The Count of Champagne's men have come. We must leave with them within the half hour if we are to arrive at the count's camp before sunset."

François' face grew more sullen. He raised his chalice and downed his remaining wine. "I must see my father and then I will meet them at the barracks. Offer them now the hospitality of food and drink befitting St. Aliquis in the name of my father, myself, and my bride. Go now."

Nicolette forced the joy of her reprieve from her eyes as François gazed at her. "I will go and attend to your needs, François," she said. "Unless you wish me to join you in the baron's chamber?"

"No. I do not wish that, Nicolette. And I am afraid that there is no time for you to attend to my needs after all. But I do want you to wait for me in my chamber. Upon my bed, for I shall steal a few moments for a quick farewell, my wife." Suspicion narrowed his blue eyes.

"I will do according to your desires, my lord," she sweetly replied.

"That you will," he said petulantly and turned abruptly, following Michel out of the room.

Nicolette sighed deeply in relief.

"Nicolette," Alienor said as she slipped into François' empty chair. "I intentionally overheard. I shall go with you to François' chamber. For I, his loving sister, want to bid him adieu and godspeed." Alienor smiled so innocently that Nicolette quickly brought her hand to her mouth to suppress her smile at the expression that would appear on François' face when he found his sister in his chamber as well.

"Why do you grin?" Alienor pretended indignation. "Are you so selfish a bride that you would try to steal away the last few moments I could share with my brother?"

"My lady," Nicolette replied with feigned shock. "I would not dream of keeping you from your brother."

"Good. Methinks we should bring Bruge with us. And Denise, for she has always had a fancy for François."

"Aye. Make it into a veritable surprise celebration. We can bring a pair of the *jongleurs* to sing and play. I will have the maids prepare wine and fruit!"

"'Tis getting better by the moment, don't you think, dear sister! Do you think François will be properly surprised?" Alienor asked with a lilt to her voice as they rose to action.

"Very, methinks, Alienor . . . Very!" Thank you, Mother Mary, Nicolette thought, for turning the fates. You do hear my prayers. With your mercy I shall not despair. For soon you will send Davide back to me!

Nicolette and Alienor stood at the castle gate watching François, mounted astride a magnificent destrier, ride off in the lead of thirty-odd knights from St. Aliquis and the count's men. The count's red pennons and their own blue banner of St. Aliquis fluttered in brilliant color beneath the bright sun in the cloudless sky.

I do not wish you to come to harm, François,

Nicolette thought . . . For I cannot help but feel pity for your character, which will cause you to burn in hell. You tried to hide your rage at finding your chamber filled and the *jongleurs* playing merry songs of battle. I know you meant to frighten me into submission when you roughly pressed my hands and whispered that you would return and fulfill your "husbandly obligations" sooner than I might think. But what you will not know until it is too late is that my *true* husband will return before you and take Bruge and me away. Never shall you touch me again, François, nor be a danger to Bruge. So ride well and stay safe, for with freedom in sight I can again feel mercy. . . .

Chapter Six

"NICOLETTE, YOU APPEAR SO PALE AND WEARY. ARE YOU ailing? Is it your womanly time?" Bruge asked, brushing the sweat from the heat of the August sun from her brow.

Nicolette fanned herself. "No. I am well. 'Tis the wet, heavy heat that oppresses me. The garden is no cooler than the palais."

"Aye, but the roses are beautiful, are they not?"

"Aye," Nicolette agreed. How she used to pleasure in the roses. Now their sight brought only pain. Try as she might to wash Davide's song from her mind, she still heard his strong baritone voice singing to her, she still saw his loving eyes, his adoring smile of that day an eternity ago. Over three months and she had heard not a word from Davide. Received not a sign from him. Yet she had been handed four notes from François.

Each night she lay awake in torment trying to explain to herself, trying to deny the truth. Davide had never intended to come for her. As in the *trouvère's* song, her love was "a greater folly than the foolish child who cries for the beautiful star he sees high and brightly above him." She was more foolish than that child in the song. Davide, her heart cried. Davide—she thought bitterly. She knew not either his real name or his origins. Messengers brought reports from the bloody battle in Jerusalem. So many had already died. But Davide lived. This she felt in her bones.

"Nicolette, you haven't listened to a word I've said!" Bruge complained.

"I am sorry. The heat makes my mind wander. Perhaps we should return to our chamber and I will take a rest before going to chapel."

"Will you tell me your account of Gervais Grieves before you depart then, or not?" Bruge demanded.

The glow of infatuation shone in Bruge's bright brown eyes. Gervais was a varlet, a fourteen-year-old neighboring noble's son, being "nourished" by the baron. Messire miraculously still clung to life all these months, leaving poor Gervais, in reality, to the mercy of Henri. "I find Gervais quick, polite, and most handsome. And I suspect he has taken a fancy to you, little sister." Nicolette pulled at her braid and laughed as Bruge's cheeks blazed with excitement.

"Do you really believe so, Nicolette? You are not teasing me? I, too, thought he fancied me!"

"Bruge, what has become of your shy demeanor

and maidenly modesty, you vain creature!" Only Bruge's happiness saved her. For it was a joy to watch her sister bloom into womanly beauty more glorious than the finest roses surrounding them in the garden.

"I am so happy, Nicolette!" Bruge exclaimed. Her smile lessened and she grew pensive. "But you are not, Nicolette . . . Won't you confide in me?"

"I hold no secret from you, Bruge. I have merely been tired, for I have not been able to sleep as soundly since we moved into François' chamber. I had become accustomed to sleeping on my pallet and the fancy bed is still foreign to me, I suppose."

"You are holding back," Bruge said, suddenly unwilling to be placated by her excuses, Nicolette saw with alarm. "But I know the *truth* . . . You miss your husband, do you not! You should sleep well if you lay in his arms."

Nicolette breathed more easily. Bruge must never even suspect. Miss my husband, she thought, as she studied Bruge's face. Yes, I agonize each night for my Davide, though you will never know of his existence. "Aye . . . I miss my husband. One day you will know the rapture love can bring. I pray you never know the sorrow."

"Nicolette, I had held my tongue but I never thought you to be in love with François! I imagined Henri somehow *forced* you—"

"Do not speak of our stepbrother in such a manner! For he is of our father's blood and you must not disparage him so openly!" She had to protect Bruge from not only the truth, but from Henri. For he had always shown a genuine affection for Bruge that she had never seen him hold for another. If Henri suspected Bruge her confidante, his heart would harden against her. He might no longer show Bruge any greater mercy than he had her, Nicolette feared. For although Henri had never touched her again since her wedding day, Nicolette saw the way he looked at her when they were alone. She did her best to avoid finding herself in his singular company but sometimes she could not avoid it.

"I meant nothing—" Tears of hurt welled in Bruge's eyes from the harsh reprimand, but Nicolette could not retract it. "I love our brother. He is very kind to me. I only thought—"

"Bruge, you are still as much a child as you are a maiden! I fear you have been listening too keenly to the romances Alienor reads aloud nightly! You have always had a vivid imagination." Bruge's certainty dissolved to mortification, just as Nicolette intended, so shocked was Bruge at her uncharacteristic display of anger. Nicolette brushed the tears from Bruge's cheeks. How it hurt her to bring pain to her sister, but it was for Bruge's safety.

Nicolette glanced down the garden path, for she could not gaze upon Bruge's wounded face. "Stop your tears, for your handsome varlet fast approaches, my foolish sister. Smile, or he shall take one glance at you and decide to seek out Marjorie instead," she teased.

"Oh, no," Bruge exclaimed. "You don't believe he fancies that vain maiden, do you? She always smiles so boldly at him!"

Before Nicolette could answer, Gervais stood before them, a shy smile on his face. "Good day, Lady Nicolette, Mademoiselle Bruge."

He spoke with an air of assurance that his blushing cheeks belied, which pleased Nicolette. Gervais was a fine boy and would mature into a most handsome knight. Perhaps he would eventually ask for Bruge's hand. But there was much time for that. In the meanwhile Nicolette could rest assured that he would not try to steal Bruge's chastity. For how easily the head of a foolish maiden can be turned! Who should know better than herself, she thought with shame. "Good day, Gervais."

"Gervais," Bruge offered shyly in return.

"I will take my leave from you two, if you will excuse me." Nicolette smiled as Gervais gallantly offered his hand. She accepted it and rose. "Sit down, Gervais. 'Tis too hot for you to stand there in the sun," she said. "I shall see you after my rest, dear sister." Her smile said that all was forgiven and Bruge's face brightened. Nicolette maintained her smile until she turned her head and started down the garden path toward the palais.

It is more dreadfully hot than I'd thought, she said to herself, as she found each step forward surprisingly unsteady. Suddenly her knees buckled and all went black around her as she felt herself helplessly sink to the ground.

Nicolette awoke to find herself in François' canopied bed, the physician, Sire Foretverte, checking her pulse. She raised her head and saw Alienor and Bruge standing before her, pale and anxious. The dizziness overcame her again. She felt dreadfully ill. "Sire—"

"Hush, my lady, for you are still weak and lightheaded. Though it is no great cause for alarm." The stout, bald physician broke into a kind smile. She didn't comprehend—what did he mean? "For many mothers-to-be do the same. My lady, you and Sire Perdant have been blessed. You are with child. Did you not suspect?"

"That cannot be—" Nicolette raised her head so abruptly that the room spun her into silence. Blessed silence, for she had almost given herself away! She dared not look at Alienor's face, so shocked must be her eyes.

The physician laughed. "Aye, but it can. For even one night with a virile husband can produce this result. When did your woman's blood last flow, my lady?"

Nicolette had assumed that her state of hidden fear had affected nature's flow. For the sleeping potion had tricked François and saved her from his attack. A baby—oh, sweet Mother Mary. She and Davide were going to have a baby! How wonderful. Painful tears filled her eyes. Davide had taken her more heartlessly than François ever could have! For she had given Davide not just her body, but her mind, heart, and soul! And now a child! She tried to stop her tears.

"'Tis no reason to try to hide tears of joy, my lady. But I am concerned by your general health. You are slighter than you should be, if I am to assume that the seed of this babe was deposited in you the night before your wedding," he said most matter-of-factly. He was a physician, not a priest.

"Aye," she whispered. "In May. The twenty-first of May."

"Then I am correct. The babe will be born by the end of the first month of our new year or the beginning of the second. To ensure its good health you must eat well, sleep soundly, for Bruge tells me you have not slept well since François' departure, and rest much, in order to regain your strength. I must give the baron his bleeding now, but I shall return before supper to examine you. Lady Alienor and Bruge will remain with you. But I have instructed that they must not excite you and must leave you to rest in a while. Your maids will stay in attendance. They wait outside your chamber."

"Thank you, Sire Foretverte," Nicolette forced herself to say as the physician walked to the door and Alienor and Bruge came to her side. Her eyes felt so heavy she could barely keep them open.

"Don't fight your weariness, Sister," Alienor said, stroking her forehead. "Sleep now and Bruge and I will speak with you later . . ." she soothed.

Gratefully, Nicolette accepted their kisses and felt herself mercifully drift away.

"'Tis five already?" Nicolette asked sleepily, as Simone, her plump handmaiden, placed the supper tray before her. Alienor again sat at her bedside.

"I would not have awakened you, but Sire Foretverte said you must have the nourishment. You may sup with Bruge and the others, Simone," Alienor said, dismissing the *pucelle*.

"Yes, my lady," Simone answered. "I shall return quickly, Lady Nicolette."

"There is no need for you to hurry, Simone, though it is kindly of you. I shall stay with Nicolette through the evening. I will send for you, should you be needed." Alienor began to arrange Nicolette's tray.

"Your color is returning. Do you still feel light of head?" Alienor wiped Nicolette's face with a cold, wet cloth. The coolness enlivened her.

"May I have some water?" Nicolette asked as she sat herself upright. She took the goblet from Alienor and drank greedily, for her throat was quite parched. "Ah, I feel better." But with a glance at the tray filled with soup, bread, fish, and vegetables her stomach turned. "Please, take it away, Alienor. To look at the food torments my stomach."

"You must at least eat some soup. It is dried peas and bacon water, your favorite. Do you intend to force me to feed it to you?"

"No." Nicolette laughed and took the bowl from her. After the second spoonful, she no longer had to force the tasty soup down. Indeed she was hungry. She forced herself to eat very slowly. For while she ate, Alienor chatted castle gossip of the day, delicately avoiding any reference to her pregnancy. Yet the strain showed itself in Alienor's tight lips, always a sign of her upset. As Nicolette pretended interest in Alienor's chatter she rapidly tried to decide what to tell Alienor.

Davide had sworn her to secrecy and how deeply she'd believed he meant to protect them all. But could she believe anything he had done or said—but for the life in her belly? She must confess her shame to Alienor. Alienor would understand, for she too knew lovemaking. Nicolette herself had helped her with her plan to slip away with Sire Guy for an afternoon, shortly before they were betrothed and many an afternoon after. Sire Guy had also ridden with his father's knights to the Crusade. He wrote long letters, of passionate devoted love, which Alienor allowed her to read. Alienor would understand, though she might be initially hurt that Nicolette had held the truth from her for so long now. "Alienor," she began after she finished the last of the soup. Tears filled her eyes and her throat knotted.

"Don't cry, Nicolette," Alienor said. She placed the empty bowl upon a small carved table beside the feather bed. "For I now know your painful secret."

Nicolette felt shock transform her face. "You do?"

"Aye. At first I was vexed that you had not trusted me to share your burden. Then I realized that you had only meant to protect me."

How could she have learned about Davide? Had Michel told her before he rode out with François?

"The potion you slipped into François' chalice that terrible night did not take effect. You have tried to spare me the knowledge that my brother took you against your will, haven't you?" Alienor fought back her own tears. "But still, the babe is a blessing and it shall have all your goodness, shall it not?"

How she longed to correct Alienor and be done with the lie. "I must tell you something very important," she began. Suddenly, Davide's voice played in her ears. *Trust me with all your heart and soul, Nicolette*, it pleaded.

"Are you dizzy?" Alienor asked with alarm. "You have turned so pale again."

I do trust you, Davide. Even if it shall be my undoing. We are going to have a child . . . but then you know, don't you, Davide? Somehow you know. Perhaps the Virgin Mother has told you in a dream . . . You will *come back for us, Davide. I am sorry I* doubted you these past months. Forgive me. Nicolette sobbed with relief as her store of bitter tears broke, cleansing her soul.

"Oh, Nicolette. Please don't cry so, for it breaks my heart." Alienor embraced her as her sobs slowly subsided.

I am sorry, Alienor, to continue to keep you from my confidence, she thought. I do so only because it will prove to be for your sake as well as mine and Bruge's. Though I don't guess in what manner it will unfold. "Alienor, it does pain me to speak of what you know. But aye, I will love this babe with all my heart."

"Perchance François will reform when he learns he is to be a father," Alienor responded wistfully.

"Perchance he will," Nicolette agreed, perpetuating Alienor's hope, though she already knew that François would never see her babe. For Davide would return and take her to safety, where their child would be born. "We shall pray for his redemption each day, Alienor."

"Oh, how I wish that I too were with child." She smiled dreamily. "Even if it should be born before my vows to Guy. I miss him most dreadfully!"

"He shall soon return. For now, you have his letters of love to carry you. And my love as well."

"Ladies." There was a loud rap upon her chamber door.

"Entrez," Alienor called to the deep male voice they recognized as Sire Eustace's. He appeared distressed. Alienor rose in alarm. "Is it Father?" she demanded fearfully.

"No, my lady. He is awake and feeling stronger. But he wishes to see you."

Alienor's fright turned to laughter. "Thank the Lord. Sire Eustace, you gave me quite a fright with your stoic expression! I shall visit Father in a while, after I have seen to it that Nicolette eats her supper, pray tell him."

"I am sorry, Alienor, but I must insist you come now."

Despite the evenness of his tone, Nicolette saw the reflection of her own alarm reappear on Alienor's fair face. Alienor's blue eyes darkened. Nicolette started to rise. "I shall go with you."

"No, Nicolette," Alienor said. "The physician insisted that you remain in bed until the morrow. I shall go and quickly return to you."

They both looked at Sire Eustace but knew better than to try to pry information from the loyal seneschal.

Bruge appeared at the door, her smile fading as she quickly sensed the distress in the chamber. "Are you all right, Nicolette?" she asked with alarm.

"I am feeling much stronger and am glad to see you, for Alienor must visit with the baron for a time now. So you shall keep me company, will you not?"

Bruge glanced at Alienor's worried face but refrained from asking for the information no one offered her, Nicolette saw.

"I shall return as soon as I am able," Alienor called as she hastily left the chamber, followed by Sire Eustace.

Bruge sank upon the feather bed. How she loved

the softness, Nicolette knew, for many a night Bruge slipped into the large bed and slept beside her. "What has happened, Nicolette?" Bruge asked.

"I do not know," Nicolette replied honestly. "But it does not portend well. Perchance we are all overly sensitive today. For I know how my faint frightened everyone as well as myself."

"Aye. How thrilled I am that I shall soon become an aunt, Nicolette! Are you happy for the news?"

"Very happy! And what do you hope it is, boy child or girl child?"

Bruge cuddled against her and gently touched her belly. "I'm certain that François will wish it to be a son, so that he, too, can become a gallant knight. But I hope it is a girl child. Our own little princess. Have you thought of names yet? Can you feel it inside of you?"

Nicolette laughed. "It is far too early for me to feel the child and I haven't even thought of names until you mentioned it. Would you like to play a game of names?" Nicolette asked. "You say a girl's and I a boy's. Then we switch. I go first. What think you of Davide?"

"Davide? 'Tis beautiful. What means it, do you know?"

"Aye, I do. It means beloved . . ."

"Methinks with that bright smile that plays on your face that you have *already* decided what it will be called if it is a boy child. I prefer the name Aimery for a boy child since Henri is already named after Father. For a girl I would choose but one name."

"And what name is that?" Nicolette asked already knowing it was one and the same as was in her mind.

SONG OF THE ROSE

"Doreen. For our mother whom I never knew." Bruge's eyes clouded. "Tell me again what you remember of her..."

"I remember her as in a dream." Nicolette rested her hand upon her belly, wishing she could already feel the life within her. She smiled at Bruge. "Mostly I remember her large, deep brown eyes smiling at me. Eyes so much like your own. And her hair. I remember it thick, dark like yours, and so sweetly redolent..."

"Aye. Father always said I looked like her. How I still miss him each day! He truly loved Mother, didn't he, Nicolette?"

"He worshiped her. I remember him telling friends that he could never marry again after losing Mother, though he was still a relatively young man, about thirty I presume."

"Father's marriage to Henri's mother had been arranged, had it not?"

"Aye. Our mother was his one and only love..." And that is why Henri, who also knew, so hated Father and me, she silently remembered. For although Father loved Henri, he showered his love upon me and then you. He would watch you sleep as a babe. In your sweet face and dark brown hair he saw Mother again. Then he would bring me upon his lap and hug and kiss me, tickling me until I laughingly pleaded for mercy. More than once I saw Henri, a plain and slight but clever boy of nine or ten, watch with hard eyes of jealousy. I remember plainly although I was just past three. But I cannot tell you any of this, Bruge.

Suddenly Bruge clung tight. "Nicolette, you are the

only one in the world who truly loves me. Promise me you'll never leave me."

"Henri loves you too. He just does not show his feelings easily. But I will never leave you, Bruge. I swear." She stroked Bruge's glossy hair. "In fact, when some fine knight asks for your hand I will probably object, wanting to keep you always for myself," she teased. "Which reminds me. Did you have some time to pass with Gervais after my frightful faint?"

"Aye . . ." Bruge's face lit as she sat herself upright. "I did. Shall I tell you everything we did and that he said!"

"Every word!" Nicolette insisted. As long as I live, you shall remain safe and protected, my loving sister, she thought. Oh, how Davide will adore you. I do so wish I could tell you about my beloved. But in time you will know!

"What time is it, Simone?" Nicolette asked of her maiden, as she laid down her needlework.

"It is nearing eight." Simone folded a bliaut and put it into the chest.

"I wonder what keeps Alienor? Bruge," she called to her sister who sat at her loom, weaving and singing merrily. "Would you go find Alienor, or Denise if Alienor is not in her chamber?"

"I will." Bruge rose with a smile.

Bruge's face was pale and her eyes red when she reappeared. Nicolette laid her needlework down and rose with alarm. "What has happened? Is it the baron after all?"

SONG OF THE ROSE

Bruge rushed to her. "No. 'Tis Sire Guy. The baron received word that he was killed in a fierce battle against the infidels!" Bruge sobbed. "Poor Alienor! She was taken to her bed after they revived her from her faint— Where are you going, Nicolette? You are too weak to leave your bed!"

"Nonsense, Bruge," Nicolette said as she fastened the girdle around her bliaut. "I am fine. Alienor needs me."

"Then I'll come with you!"

"No. You stay here. I shall send Denise for your company." Nicolette's feet were unsteady but still she fled from her chamber to comfort Alienor.

The knight rose from his place at the bonfire and walked toward the dark edge of the plain surrounding Acre. He gazed up at the heights of Mt. Carmel wherefrom the mighty warriors of the sultan Saladin looked down upon their camp.

How weary he was of battle, blood, and death! Three weeks before he had lost his recent but dear friend, Guy, whom he had grown to love as a brother. Unknowingly Guy had also remained his connection to his beloved. For the fates had it that Guy had been betrothed to Alienor, François Perdant's sister and Nicolette's dearest friend, as she had told him on their one day three months ago. How long ago it seemed that he had loved and been loved! That they had taken one another for husband and wife. How he longed for her.

François had never recognized him. Not even on the day they met but a week after their initial encounter, which suited the knight's plan perfectly. They had

SONG OF THE ROSE

been introduced by their suzerain lord, the count, who immediately commented on how they looked to be brothers. The knight had pretended cordiality from the first, and since the cowardly, boastful François could claim no true friends, François had quickly taken him into an early confidence. "Pierre Delise," François had said almost each day for the past months, "you are to me like the brother I never had."

So eager François was for a confidant, that he never seemed to notice Pierre's reticence in speaking about his own life. Or if he noticed he did not seem to care, which was more the likely. For each night François had a fresh list of grievances ranging from the food and constant heat to some slight or insult he'd received from an "arrogant knight." Even his own knights from St. Aliquis received no kind word from him, excepting his equally vile but more cunning squire, Michel.

Neither Pierre's knights nor those from St. Aliquis understood why he spent his time with François. When they questioned him on occasion, Pierre answered simply that he had great sympathy for François and greater fear that he would be killed by one of his own knights or another from their own forces rather than meet his death at the hands of the Saracens. "Aye," his friend Guilbert had responded over a flagon of wine one evening. "Especially since François has managed to evade most of our battles." Pierre had not been able to keep himself from laughing heartily with Guilbert.

For Guilbert had spoken the truth. Pierre walked past the royal pavilion. The lights filtering through the cloth of the tent made it look a grayish-white cloud clinging to the ground. There rested his king and most probably François. For François had ingratiated himself first to the Count of Champagne, then to King Philip Augustus himself. He had cajoled the king into appointing him liaison of communications, and therefore rarely left the plains of the desert or ventured beyond the foothills that led to Saladin's mountain stronghold. A knight from St. Aliquis had informed another, who had informed another, until all the encampment knew that François anxiously awaited the news of his father's death so that he should have an excuse to return home.

Pierre walked further on until he came to a large sand dune upon the empty desert. The late evening air held a chill, as it always did, despite the heat of the day, when the temperature boiled them beneath the scorching sun. Pierre pulled the sleeve of blue silk from beneath his mailed jacket. He brought it to his face. At first Nicolette's perfume had clung to the material, filling his senses with her. His sweat in battle had long since caused the perfume to vanish. But nothing could steal away his memory of Nicolette. How he longed to kiss her cherry lips, to caress her face and hair and breasts and belly. How he longed to feel her writhing beneath him, crying out in pleasure again. Or to feel her cuddled against him, chattering or sweetly singing.

When he learned of her forced marriage to François, despite their plan, he had wanted to die in despair. He had wanted to cut François' throat when François boasted, to anyone who would listen, about the "charms" of his new wife. Pierre had been so certain the sleeping potion would work, yet François had bragged about how he had "ridden his fair, feisty wench" and had "broken her in as expertly" as he had his destrier.

Pierre had wanted to flee that night from the campfire, but knowing he had to learn whatever he could, he'd endured. The drunker François became the more coarsely he bragged. He began to describe Nicolette's body shamelessly, and just when Pierre could not bear another insult, François went too far, thank the Lord. Far enough to display himself as the despicable liar he was, even if only to Pierre. For he provided the bawdiest of his fellow knights with a blow-by-blow description of Nicolette's supposed lovemaking. Pierre knew it to be pure fabrication. The woman he described bore no relationship to his Nicolette. The sleeping droplets *must* have worked as planned!

Not that they saved Nicolette from dreadful humiliation. For François described her lovely body, albeit in the coarsest, vilest terms, too well not to have glimpsed it at close hand. But otherwise he had no more taken Nicolette that night than he intended to lead his knights into battle. Yet their plan had gone awry with François' surprise wedding, but an appeal for an annulment to the bishop would rectify that travesty. Surely before the eyes of God, Nicolette and he were wed, Pierre thought.

If only he could have contacted her sooner, he wished desperately again. But with all communications passing through François' hands it had been impossible until the mournful death of Guy. An emissary of the count had been sent to bring personal word to Guy's father. For the baron was wealthy and had contributed heavily with money and knights in their war against the infidels. Pierre had decided he had to trust young Matthew, the emissary. He had saved Matthew from a deadly arrow of fire just days before and Matthew had sworn allegiance to him for life, although Pierre had never dreamed that he should have to call upon it.

All he told Matthew was that his note had to be delivered in person to Lady Nicolette at St. Aliquis in complete secrecy. Matthew asked no questions but swore upon his father's life that he would gladly do as asked. Any day, Nicolette should receive his letter. His poor darling. Had she believed that he had deserted her? Did she doubt his vows of love and devotion? He would understand if she had begun to think he had intentionally disappeared from sight with nary a word. Or did she believe him dead, and mourn? It would be another three weeks to a month before Matthew returned with her reply. It seemed like an eternity.

"I love you, Nicolette," he whispered into the lonely, dark night and kissed the blue silk sleeve. "Please God, let her keep the faith in her heart that her Davide worships her until she receives my letter." He had signed the letter "Davide, your beloved." For he could not yet chance her knowing anything that could endanger her until he removed Nicolette from the barony of St. Aliquis and had her safe within the walls of his father's castle.

"Guy swore to me that he would return! He said time and again, 'Surely you know, my precious Alienor, that not even the savage Saracens, not Saladin himself, could keep your devoted Guy Brouilleaux from returning to you—" Alienor held fast to Nicolette as another wave of wracked sobs broke through. Nicolette stroked Alienor's damp hair and allowed her to cry. "Now he is returning," Alienor's voice choked. "Returning from the foreign battlefield of Acre. In a box in the bowels of a dromond—"

The dromond, a small but swift sailing ship, would leave Sire Guy's body at the southern harbor of Marseilles. The Baron Brouilleaux's men-at-arms would ride to meet the ship and carry Sire Guy home to his father's barony south of Provins. A ride that would take days. Sire Guy's funeral would not take place for at least another week then, Nicolette calculated. She had to find some words of solace she could give to Alienor to see her through the ordeal. But she could think of none. Sire Guy, just twenty-one, dead. Surely the Lord could find a better way for man to honor him. So many dead and more each day . . .

"How I envy you, Nicolette. How I wish it were I who carried my love's child!" Alienor wept more fiercely. "I am sorry, please forgive me?"

"There is nothing to forgive. I understand."

Alienor raised her face and gazed at her. "Do you? But how could you? You rightfully despise my brother, so can you understand?"

Nicolette didn't speak. I know better than you could ever imagine, she thought. For I, too, have denied that my Davide, like your Guy, could have been stilled in battle. Dead. He could be *dead* all this time. 'Tis easier to think he has abandoned me and his unknown child with intention than to think him in a box in the bottom of a dromond. Should I tell you, my grieving friend? Would it help you to know? I cannot see how, for your burden is heavy enough without adding more for you to grieve.

"Nicolette? You do understand, don't you? I see in your eyes the reflection of my misery. May Mother Mary forgive me, but I curse this Crusade that has taken so pure and beautiful a creature as Guy from this world! Too soon! Far too soon! How can his death be a tribute to God? I deny it!" Alienor dissolved into a fresh torrent of tears that Nicolette felt seep through her chemise as they mixed with her own.

Please, Mother Mary. If my Davide still lives, protect him, even if it means that I shall never set my eyes upon his face again, Nicolette silently prayed.

Chapter Seven

'TWAS LATE AFTERNOON WHEN NICOLETTE SAT BESIDE the grieving Alienor with whom she'd stayed since learning of Sire Guy's death the night before. Fighting to keep her eyes open, Nicolette listened to Sire Matthew Tregere, the young knight who had traveled from Acre personally to deliver the news of Guy's death. He had arrived a few hours before to speak with Alienor and had been telling them stories of gallant Sire Guy's last days.

Alienor had wept intermittently since Matthew's arrival, as had Nicolette. But now, through her tears, Alienor smiled as Matthew recounted a tale of how Guy saved the life of a particularly effeminate young knight from Burgundy only to be burdened with the knight's undying love and devotion as strong and passionate as any damsel's. Matthew was a fine storyteller, making Bruge and Denise giggle and Alienor laugh despite herself.

Nicolette was amused but too weary to laugh aloud, for she had not slept during the night, even when Alienor drifted into exhausted oblivion. Nicolette had lain awake, thinking about Davide, and the child she carried. Thinking about François and Henri and Bruge and her departed father; thinking about Guy and Alienor and what fate would befall Alienor now that Guy was dead and the baron dying, thereby leaving Alienor to François' mercy. Thank the Lord, Alienor was thus far too overwhelmed by her immediate grief to look to her future. Nicolette closed her eyes for a moment as the voices receded.

"Nicolette," Alienor's voice called gently. Goodness, she had fallen asleep. "I am sorry. I seem to have—" Nicolette straightened herself against the back of the chair.

"Denise, see Nicolette back to her chamber, for she is exhausted but too stubborn to say so," Alienor insisted. "Have Simone put her to bed until supper."

"Truly, I am not sleepy, at least not terribly. There is no need. I apologize, Matthew," she said. A yawn she could not suppress embarrassed her further.

"Matthew, Lady Nicolette sat by my side through the night though she is most drained herself. Not only by Guy's—but she just learned yesterday that she is carrying her first child."

"Most good wishes, my lady," Matthew said with a kind smile, but something she could not read flashed

SONG OF THE ROSE

in his eyes for a moment. Surprise? Dismay? Perhaps it was nothing but her weary imagination. She should take her leave and rest, for the sake of her babe, if nothing else.

"Thank you." Nicolette rose. "I will rest but I do not need Denise to see me to my chamber. I can do so quite ably on my own, thank you. You will be at supper, then, Matthew?"

"Aye, I have been most graciously invited to stay. But I must take my leave soon after, for I must return to Baron Brouilleaux's palais. The roads have grown most dangerous, I am told. With so many of the knights and men-at-arms away from the kingdom, it is said to be dangerous to ride singularly past dark."

"This is so," Alienor agreed. "Sire Macaire, our provost, and his men chased down two bandits yesterday. Maitre Dennis, my father's executioner, has been forced to put more robbers, culprits, and the like to the rack in the past months than in many a year. It seems every other day another hanging takes place."

"Only last week a band of discharged mercenary soldiers invaded a village in our barony," Denise added. "They stole the peasants' corn, pigs, and chickens, insulted their women, fired many cottages, and set upon three *jongleurs* bound for the castle."

"Aye, they had robbed the *jongleurs* to their skin and stabbed one of the three to death when Sire Macaire's party of men came upon them, managing to seize two of the sturdy scoundrels," Alienor continued. "They were put to the rack and Maitre Dennis forced them to say where their comrades hid. Then they were hung. The provost and his party of men have been out since morning searching for their lair in

SONG OF THE ROSE

hopes of capturing the other bandits. 'Tis a sad state of affairs."

"Indeed," Matthew agreed as Nicolette approached the chamber door. "My lady," he said to her. "Since you are departing, would you be so kind to point me the way to the garderobe, for I must heed nature's call," he said with a frank laugh.

"Certainly. I will show you the direction gladly, Matthew. Alienor, I will rest and return for supper in the great hall unless you are not desirous to sup there."

"If you will stay with me, I should prefer to remain in my chamber. I'm not ready to—" Tears filled her eyes again.

Nicolette crossed the room and kissed Alienor. "I understand. We shall sup here then, for you must eat something—"

"As you must as well," Alienor said and clung to her for a moment. "Go, for when nature calls as it does for Sire Matthew, one must pay heed. You will return, Matthew?"

"In just moments, my lady, if it pleases you," Matthew said with a courtly bow. He followed Nicolette to the door.

Henri turned the corridor to Alienor's chamber when he saw Nicolette exit with an unknown young knight. Quickly he hid behind a curtain, for they had not seen his approach.

"The garderobe is down this hall." Nicolette pointed in the opposite direction and the knight's eyes followed her hand. Henri observed. "You turn—"

"My lady," the knight whispered and led a surprised and weary-looking Nicolette away from Alienor's chamber door until they stood just feet from Henri's hiding place. "I do not have need for the garderobe. I had to speak with you in privacy," he said. He removed a sealed parchment from within his jacket. Nicolette's expression changed from shock to excitement as she observed the sealed letter. Once again providence has brought me to the proper place at the correct moment, Henri thought, as he clearly observed the ensuing intrigue.

"'Tis for you, my lady. I was asked to deliver it. I can say no more, but that I vowed that I would deliver it to you and carry your reply back to Acre. We must not risk being observed in further private communication. You may send a maid to me with your return message. But whomever you send, they must speak the word 'rose' to me and then I shall know that all is accomplished. The word 'rose' *must* be uttered . . . perhaps in the sentence, 'Are not the roses lovely in full bloom, Sire?' Do you comprehend, my lady?"

Nicolette's hand shook as she took the letter from his hands and slipped it beneath her yellow bliaut. "Yes, I understand. And I thank you, Sire Matthew," she whispered tremulously, "from the depths of my heart."

The knight kissed her hand and strode toward Alienor's chamber, while Nicolette fled past Henri in the direction of her own.

Henri waited until the knight entered Alienor's chamber and then hurried down the hall. Nicolette surprised him by appearing at her door, embroidered purse in her hand, which she attached to her girdle.

SONG OF THE ROSE

Henri darted from sight before she saw him, for she spoke to her maiden. "No, Simone, I must have a moment alone in the garden to refresh myself before I can rest. The odors of the castle I find more offensive than usual."

"Where may I find you should I need to, my lady?" Simone asked.

"At the bench by the roses. In its restful seclusion I can breathe the air and not be bothered with having to make pleasantries with anyone. You may have the hours until supper for yourself, Simone, for I shan't be needing you."

"Thank you, my lady. I shall take leave of your chamber as soon as I've finished my tasks. I know you sleep so lightly that you will rest the better in solitude when you return."

Nicolette smiled with affection at the stout, red-haired maid. "That is most thoughtful of you, Simone." Nicolette walked gracefully down the hall, to the stairs.

How easy you make it for me, dear sister, Henri thought as he waited until he no longer heard her footsteps. You think you shall be alone in the garden, but I shall be there with you. For I must learn from whom the knight brought your message. And what it says. Then I shall know how to proceed. Are not the roses lovely in full bloom, Sire? Henri silently repeated to himself, memorizing the code he might need.

If anyone should happen by, they would think Nicolette in calm repose amongst the roses. But her heart beat wildly and her fingers trembled as she carefully unsealed the letter she'd removed from her purse. It had to be from Davide! Why else the secrecy and caution that Matthew took? She looked about once more. There was no person near and she had passed Crooked Herman on his way to prune the hedges by the garden entrance. "My beloved," she read, and tears of joy and relief filled her eyes, blurring her sight. Quickly she brushed the tears away and continued:

Forgive me for leaving you so long with no word. It has been impossible. Through François' hands all communications pass and I dared not trust anyone until I met Matthew Tregere. I cannot write most of what I long to say for Matthew leaves momentarily. I love you more than life itself and nothing has changed my promises to you. I shall come for you as soon as I'm able, just as I said. For you, Bruge, and poor Alienor, should she need my protection now that Sire Guy is dead. Do not worry that I believe your "marriage" to be anything other than the sham it is—I understand that our plan *worked* despite what seems. You are the only wife I shall ever have as I am your true husband, and one day soon all the world shall know that we are rightfully joined. I will easily arrange an annulment of your marriage and we shall be wed in grand celebration.

I caress and kiss your silken blue sleeve each night. Each day it remains against my heart and has kept me alive through many a bloody battle. There is so much to say and no time! Feel my kiss upon your lips and lie with me in your dreams each night, as I do with you. It will not be long until I hold you in my arms again. I pray each morn to the good Lord and ask him to keep you safe and well until my return. Continue to write to François, but tell him of your daily comings and goings, for you will be filling *my* heart with joy—I can say no more that could, in any manner, endanger your safety. *Burn* this note as soon as you've read it and continue to carry me in your heart as I carry you.

"Davide"—your beloved.

Henri watched from behind a bush as Nicolette read and then read again, brushing away tears, though she smiled with a glory he had never seen. Still she uttered not a sound. I must see this letter that you kiss so lovingly, Henri thought. My saintly sister involved with a lover? Surely that could be the only explanation. But who? When?

"Davide..." Nicolette whispered. "My beloved..."

Davide? Henri silently urged her to whisper again, but the wench cried into her handkerchief instead, as Henri watched impatiently.

"Davide..." she whispered again. "You do live... I love you so..."

Henri had heard enough. He must set himself in hiding in Nicolette's empty chamber before she returned. Somehow he would read the letter himself, then he would know what needed to be done.

Again providence had been with him, Henri thought, as he hid at the side of a massive wardrobe in the corner of Nicolette's chamber. He could not be seen but had full view of the room he had easily entered. He had no fear for his exit, for the uncomely, fat, redheaded Simone would be his unknowing ally. How clever he had been to win the plain and slow girl's affection shortly after she'd arrived from a small village in the seigneury where her father was a petty noble. It sickened him each time he took her bulk into his arms, brought her thick lips to his and between kisses whispered promises of marriage as soon as François returned. Simone lapped his lies as hungrily as she lapped food and drink in virtual serf fashion. Only when she thus lapped his manhood, kneeled before him, and he did not have to look upon her but could dream it was Alienor who did so, did he enjoy the dull girl.

Henri warmed as he thought of Alienor. He had loved her from afar since they'd first arrived at St. Aliquis. Even then she was to be betrothed to Guy. Had she not been, she still would not have smiled kindly upon him. For Henri had no doubt that it was Nicolette who had poisoned Alienor's mind against him. Guy's death filled Henri with joyous hope. He would bargain hard with François until he consented to wed Alienor to him. No longer would he have to court the Baron Harcourt's dark, skinny, old-maid daughter, Sabine. Before the dawn Nicolette herself would become his unwilling ally, for he would have in his hand the ammunition he needed against her. That letter! He wished she would stop weeping and retire to her chamber. While she slept he would go about his business.

Where was she? He'd been certain she would return to write a response to her "Davide." How he hated Nicolette! How he had always hated her—his "virtuous" stepsister who had outvied him for his father's attention just to spite him. She had been a fair and sweet babe but had grown into a willful, coy child who bewitched Father after his stepmother Doreen's death. Only the babe, Bruge, had shown him any smiles and kisses. He still held the maiden in fondness and it had saddened him to have to threaten to use her as a pawn to obtain Nicolette's compliance. But use her again he would if Nicolette forced him.

The haughty, virtuous beauty Nicolette! He still remembered the softness of her skin, the feel of her hips against his thighs, his hands around her tiny waist, that brief moment on the morning she wed François. He had thought he could never take her—for he dared not satisfy his lust if it could lead to François' disfavor and he had not been convinced that Nicolette would remain silent if he pushed further. He ran his tongue across his dry lips. Now providence had made it possible that he might yet have her before François returned. Have her before she became fat with François' child in her belly. The idea pleased him greatly as he played with it while he waited in the empty chamber. Nicolette would pay for her transgressions. She would obey him, with glorious abject humiliation, for she already had that babe growing in her belly and therefore nothing but pleasure for him could result in his taking her. Nightly if he chose, while he meanwhile courted the grieving Alienor!

"Simone?" Nicolette called as she entered her chamber and closed the door. Thank you, Mother Mary. Simone was gone and Bruge still busy with Alienor. Hastily Nicolette walked to the planked table before the window and sat to write the letter to her beloved Davide she'd composed in her mind as she'd sat beside the roses. "My beloved, Davide," she whispered softly as she wrote the words.

Henri watched her from his corner. My beloved,

SONG OF THE ROSE

Davide, he silently repeated. 'Twas as bad as he suspected. And as good for him as he had hoped, he thought as he watched her write.

Nicolette laid her quill on the table and read her short letter through:

There are no words to describe the joy your letter brought me. I had feared that you had abandoned me or worse yet that you had been killed. Now my heart and soul, so weary from months of worry, can rejoice. I in turn will not say all that I would tell you were I lying beside you, for I hear your words for caution even as I write. You were correct as to your assumption about our plan. I am yours and remain yours only. I have news I must tell you, for if I do not I am afraid you may come to the wrong conclusion. You are to be a father, my beloved. The end of January or beginning of February. I pray that you will be with me before the blessed event, for surely the battle will not continue endlessly? What is endless is my love for you, Davide—I write your name and kiss it. Come for us as soon as you can, my angel.

Your Beloved

Nicolette blotted the last word, for her tears had fallen onto the paper and blurred the ink. She folded and sealed the parchment, then rose and placed Davide's letter and her reply beneath a pillow on her bed. She pulled back the covers and wearily began to disrobe.

Henri felt his manhood throb as Nicolette stood naked before him, her rosy nipples begging for his caress as she stretched, unknowingly presenting herself in full view before him. He gazed with mounting desire at her blond womanhood he had so accurately imagined, for he had not seen her naked since she was just a small child. She bent, her apple breasts jutting most pleasingly, as she massaged her calves. His heart pounded as she walked toward the chamberpot, and so caught in his passion was he that he felt distress when she turned and climbed instead into her bed. She removed the letters from beneath the pillow at her side, kissed them, and hid them away again. Her face rested against the pillow and Henri silently willed her to alter her position or she would foil his easy task of removing the letters once she slept.

Henri did not have to wait long for his wish, for Nicolette fell into a quick, steady slumber as he remained hidden—it was almost too easy. Stealthfully he crept from behind the wardrobe until he reached her bed. Her succulent mouth was slightly opened as she breathed in sleep. He resisted his urge to touch her. Instead he deftly slid the letters from beneath the pillow upon which her arm rested. His ardor for Nicolette's body diminished as the sense of the power he held in his hands increased. He stole back to his spot and soundlessly sat and read the letters.

Henri smiled to himself as he read them again. 'Twas better than he could have hoped! Not only did she have a lover but the babe in her belly was his, not François'. He tucked Davide's note into his chausses, securely beneath his girdle. Again he crept to Nicolette's bed and replaced her letter beneath her pillow. He took a risk at keeping the first letter, he knew. But Nicolette had appeared so weary that she might readily assume that she'd put Davide's letter somewhere for safekeeping until she could burn it, as he'd cautioned.

Nicolette stirred and Henri ducked from sight until her breathing assured him she still slept. He peered carefully from behind the backboard of the heavily carved canopy frame. Sleep she did. But in her movement she had revealed one pert creamy breast. How he hungered to suckle it. But he would have to wait until later tonight. He would roam her body with abandon then, he consoled himself. Now he had to retire to his own, smaller chamber and devise his plan, leaving no room for mistake, for Nicolette was more cunning than he'd thought. But he would show her what cunning was. Tonight, he thought, as he closed the door carefully behind him.

Chapter Eight

"Damnation!" Henri muttered and tore to pieces the well-scripted letter he'd intended to substitute for Nicolette's loving reply. For it suddenly occurred to him after almost an hour's labor that Davide might know Nicolette's handwriting. Why had he not thought such an hour ago? This situation bedeviled him. He would have to alter his plan for he would need to force Nicolette into writing a farewell to her lover that Davide would believe came from a change of heart. How well did Davide know Nicolette? Well enough to give her his seed, he thought, chuckling to himself. He needed Nicolette's cooperation but could he be certain that she would grant it? Or would her knowledge that her lover was indeed alive make her even more proudly intransigent than before?

Despite his exasperation, Henri loved the game almost as much as the win. Few could beat him at chess and this was much like a high-stakes game against a worthy opponent. He held the advantage. With sweet little Bruge as his pawn he could not lose. Nicolette would do anything to protect Bruge, for to her the sun rose and set on Bruge . . . Pretty little Bruge . . . He hoped for her sake that Nicolette did not force his hand. For it would pain him to see Bruge betrothed to Count Bompart, a whoring drunkard, who had sent two previous young wives to the grave far too painfully and slowly.

Henri recognized the timid knock at his door. It was Simone, whom he'd sent his varlet to summon, telling the boy he was then dismissed for the evening. His varlet, Damon, went most happily. *"Entrez,"* he said as he hid Davide's letter in his Bible. Henri rose, fixing a passionate smile upon his face. "Simone . . ." he said to the girl who nervously filled his doorway. He took her hand and bolted the door behind them. "I am so pleased you were able to slip away, for I have missed you deeply! It is almost a week since we have been alone. Did your mistress suspect, my lovely?"

"Oh, no. My lady sleeps, for she was up all night with poor grieving Alienor," she said mournfully.

"Aye, my heart goes out to Alienor, to have lost her gallant knight. Her love."

"Oh, Henri." Simone broke into sobs and ran into his arms with such uncharacteristic intensity that she almost caused him to lose his balance. "I am so grateful that I have you! I thank Mother Mary each morning!"

"No, 'tis I who is grateful, my lovely," he said as he

stroked her red hair. "Come, let us comfort one another," he said with feigned despair tinging his voice. He led her to the bed. He sat and she stood before him, his thighs spread wide to embrace the girth of her hips as he reached beneath her chemise and fondled her pendulous breasts. She kissed his face wetly like an eager puppy. Henri sighed with pretended passion.

"I love you so, Henri," she whined pathetically, so repulsing him that he didn't know how much longer he could stand to touch her flesh. "How can I bring you comfort, my love?" she asked between kisses.

"I will show you, my blooming flower," he whispered and lowered the bulk of her to her knees. He had trained her well, for soon his sighs were no longer feigned.

She lay beside him, naked, on his bed. "Simone, my love—oh how I yearn for the day we can be wed!"

"I too," she answered placidly.

"I have a boon I must ask of you, my little chicken."

"You know I would do any favor in my power for you, Henri," she answered earnestly.

"I know I am the most blessed man on this earth because of you, Simone." He planted a kiss on her snub nose. "I must have a serious meeting with your lady, my sister Nicolette. For she has many a heavy weight upon her with Sire François fighting valiantly for our Lord and she just learning that she carries his child. The baron is dying and Alienor is deep in mourning. Nicolette has written a letter to François that will put him in danger. For when he reads of Lady

SONG OF THE ROSE

Nicolette's strife, he will worry *so* that he will not give full mind to his own safekeeping. Battlefields are not the place for such selflessness. I fear he could come to the same end as Sire Guy because of her letter."

"'Tis terrible! Can you not stop her? Talk with her?" Simone pleaded, playing into his hand as he knew she would.

"That is what I intend to do, with your help—I am so glad I can find a sympathetic ear and good counsel in you, my lovely!"

"What can I do?"

"Nicolette will ask you to deliver this letter in *secrecy* to the knight Matthew who brought the devastating news of Sire Guy's death to us. He will be returning to Sire Guy's family tonight and leave for Acre on the morrow. Since we do not wish to alarm the court, or worse yet those simple villeins who depend upon St. Aliquis for their survival, Matthew, Nicolette, and I decided to give no one cause for speculation. Thus the secrecy is vital. You know how some of the maidens and knights gossip! So, Nicolette will tell you to slip the letter to Matthew when you go for supper at five. She will tell you our *code*—but you must vow you will *never* allow Nicolette to know that *I* have made you privy to our most private family affairs. She would be most angry, for as I told you, she does not approve of our intended betrothal, though she hides it well from you, does she not?" Henri watched as her face contorted in heartfelt pain, hardening into quiet anger.

"She hides such so well that if I did not know you and trust you so completely I would not believe it.

SONG OF THE ROSE

Her smile is always warm and her words rarely sharp. She is so beautiful. I do wish she approved of me. I always do my best to make her feel kindly toward me, Henri!" A tear trickled from her eye and Henri kissed it away.

"I know, my beauty. At bottom, Nicolette is kind and loving. It is only because she rose in rank so quickly that she has forgotten from whence she came, as I've told you before."

"Aye . . . So you wish me to do what with the letter?"

"I wish you to bring it to *me*. Then I wish you to summon Nicolette to my chamber. Tell her it is urgent. Then you go back to her chamber. I want you to return here precisely at seven. By then I will have been able to reason her into writing her dear husband a most *comforting* letter that will leave his heart filled with joy rather than dread! Nicolette will send you back to the great hall where you shall *then* secretly deliver the letter to the knight Matthew. Your code will be, 'Are not the roses lovely in full bloom, Sire?' You need not try to memorize it now," he said, as he saw her lips mouth the words. "For Nicolette will expect you not to have heard it before. Later you shall eat here with me, when we have accomplished our mission and have the late hours for ourselves."

"I understand, Henri, and will do exactly as you ask. But what if Bruge or Alienor seek my lady, as they surely will? You would not wish for them to know of your private talk with Nicolette, methinks."

"I had almost *forgotten* to tell you that part!" he said, sincerely distressed. He playfully bit at her nipple. "You are a clever damsel. As clever as you are beautiful, my sweet! You must *first* go to Alienor's chamber and report that Nicolette still sleeps and that she wishes to sleep through the night. Alienor, who knows how light a sleeper Nicolette is, will instruct that Nicolette not be disturbed. Bruge should perhaps spend the night with Alienor as *you* will be with your sleeping lady through the evening." He gave her an intimate, conspiratorial grin. "Is that not correct, my lovely Simone?"

Simone giggled in response, happy to be needed by him, as he'd thought. "I shall indeed stay in the chamber, *undetected,* after I have seen that Nicolette arrives in your chamber. For if anyone comes to the door I can step outside and say she is still asleep. But they will all be at supper until the entertainment ends. Aye?" She smiled happily as if they were children playing a game. "My white lies are all for my mistress's benefit, are they not, Henri?"

"Indeed. And what I wish most, for *our* benefit, is to make passionate love to you again." He ran his lips from her chin to her large belly, making her giggle again.

"Henri, there is no time. For surely I must dress and awaken my lady before anyone comes. It is nearing five."

Henri rose, giving her a false sigh and a frown. "Your succulent body makes me forget my duty. For when I look at you, caress you, Simone, all I can think of is *our* pleasure. But I cannot gainsay you. I must deny myself in order to help my sister think clearly and act accordingly. If only she were as easy as you to

SONG OF THE ROSE

talk with. I am so fortunate to have won your love and respect, my angel, Simone!" He gave her a passionate kiss and smacked her bottom to get her moving. To get her out of his sight and doing his bidding.

"Where is Davide's letter?" Nicolette whispered to herself as she frantically searched beneath her bed's massive frame. "It has to have fallen, somehow—'tis not here." Her puzzlement quickly changed to alarm. Could someone have taken it while she slept? 'Twas not possible, for she slept so lightly she would have heard the door open—although she *had* slept as heavy as death itself this afternoon. But if someone did, why did the person leave her reply? That could not be! For no one knew she'd received the letter except Matthew and herself! Perhaps in her weariness she had hidden it somewhere else and forgotten? 'Twas not like her . . . but possible.

Nicolette walked to the table where she had written her reply. She then looked inside her Bible and romance book that sat on her bedside table. Again, nothing. She searched her empty purse once more. Why had she not burned the letter immediately as Davide instructed! She had meant to do so but couldn't part with the very parchment Davide had touched. It had to be somewhere! She looked beneath her pillow where *her* reply still lay singularly. It had to—

"My lady! I thought you should still be asleep," Simone said. Nicolette appeared distressed. Had something happened that could foil Henri's plan? How Henri loved his sister! He was willing to act against his purest character to prevent Nicolette from completing an impetuous action she would otherwise come to regret.

"Oh!" Nicolette uttered. "You gave me a start! I didn't hear you enter." Nicolette tried to compose herself. She would find Davide's letter later. Presently she had to give Simone her reply to bring to Matthew and the sentence she must utter so he would know all was well.

"I'm sorry for startling you. I did not knock for I thought you to be asleep, my lady. But you are awake and dressed."

"Simone, I can very well dress myself. After all, but months ago I was a maiden-in-waiting just like you. I too was a *pucelle,* for my father was a petty noble as yours is. I am *not* a delicate princess of noble blood over whom you must fawn, as I've told you before."

"Yes, my lady." Simone studied her. She would take Nicolette as sincere if she did not know better. For if Nicolette thought herself no better, why would she so strongly object to Henri wedding me?

Why did Simone appear to be studying her? "Simone, did you enter my chamber while— Never mind. Simone, can I trust you? Do I have your loyalty and confidence?" Nicolette watched Simone's face carefully. If she detected the slightest hesitancy or felt the slightest flicker of doubt, she would take the note to Matthew herself. Perhaps she should do so anyway. Just as she should have burned Davide's letter immediately after reading it.

"Of course. I am your loving and loyal maiden."

Simone's face was filled with quiet devotion. She had no reason to doubt. But she would take no chance. She would deliver the letter to Matthew herself. "That pleases me deeply. Thank you . . . I believe we should leave for supper now."

Simone was careful to give nothing away. Henri would be vexed, but what could she do? She would have to pretend to use the garderobe during supper and run to Henri's chamber to inform him. "Aye. Would you prefer me to bring your supper here? You still look pale and tired." Simone told no white lie on that account.

"No. But thank you for your concern. I am still tired, though I slept quite soundly. I . . ." A sudden wave of dizziness attacked her as her stomach rose and fell. Nicolette sank onto the bed and lowered her head into her hands.

"My lady, you are ill! I fear you may take a faint again." Simone hurried to the washbowl for a damp cloth.

"I am not ill," Nicolette said, as she felt the comfort of the cool, wet cloth that Simone used upon her face. "The physician said I could feel the dizziness from the babe for some time."

"And he told you you must rest, did he not?" Simone asked with genuine concern. "Yet you stood awake all last night. That cannot be good for the babe."

"Methinks you are correct, Simone." Nicolette reached beneath her pillow. "Listen to me carefully, Simone. For I do need your aid and complete confidence."

"Simone, one more thing," Nicolette called as she rested upon her bed, still fully dressed.

SONG OF THE ROSE

Simone walked from the door to Nicolette's side. "I do remember the code, my lady. 'Are not the roses in bloom lovely, Sire?' " she softly said.

"You are a quick maiden. I do not doubt that you shall say it properly. But I almost forgot that I was to sup in Alienor's room. I do not wish Alienor nor Bruge to be alarmed by my condition. So would you go by Alienor's chamber? Tell her that I was sleeping so restfully that when you awoke me for sup I told you that I wished to continue to sleep. That later I would eat some cheese and fruit that you would bring to me. Tell Bruge I suggested she spend the night with Alienor. Assure them that I am fine and was sleeping like a babe when you left me. And that you will spend the evening at my side after you've supped."

"I will." Simone could not believe how Nicolette had unintentionally saved her from Henri's anger. For he had struck her across her face some weeks ago when she had failed to overhear a conversation between Alienor and Nicolette. But that was the way of men when they became troubled, her dear mother had taught her. Nothing to hold against them.

"Good." Nicolette sighed with relief. "Go quickly, Simone."

Simone hurried from the room. She tried to keep all her orders straight. She would have to tell Henri to go to Nicolette's chamber, for her lady was too weak to be summoned to his. As she walked down the narrow hallway a thought struck her, causing her great distress. How was Henri to account for the fact that she had delivered Nicolette's letter to him rather than to Matthew? Nicolette would have her flogged or *worse* for her disloyalty! But Henri was so clever. He must

SONG OF THE ROSE

have thought of something! Still, she would have to know before she handed him her mistress's letter, she decided, as she knocked upon Alienor's door.

"You are wonderful," Henri whispered as he opened his door and pulled Simone into his chamber. "You have the letter?" He strove to appear calm. "How does my dear sister feel after her rest?" He feigned concern.

"She is not well—'tis the babe has made her dizzy again. She rests now in her bed and gave me the letter. For a time she mentioned nothing about it and seemed to have decided to deliver it herself. I cannot, in good conscience, summon my lady to your chamber, Henri. You must slip into hers to speak with her, methinks."

Henri repressed his delight. *So my dear sister lies in bed.* The image of her splendidly naked body filled his mind's eye. "I shall do as you request. Nicolette is fortunate to have such a loving, devoted maiden-in-waiting as you. Someday soon you shall be her sister as well, my lovely chicken." He kissed her quickly. "Hand me the letter, please." She pulled away and looked at him with doubt, surprising him. *What the devil was wrong with her?*

"Henri. You have not told me how you will explain to Nicolette why I delivered her letter to you instead of the knight, as she ordered me." Simone reeled from the blow to her shoulder, dropping the letter in her hand to the floor. She felt her girdle rip as he tore it off and her purse fall to the floor. She raised her head and caught a slap that made her cry in pain and shock. "Henri! Why—"

"I am sorry, my sweet, loving beauty." He pulled her into his arms and stroked her hair and face. "It pained me to hurt you more than it did you. I thought it best to catch you by surprise so that your recounting would ring from painful but unavoidable truth."

Simone looked up at his face. Though her cheek still stung and her shoulder ached, the regret she saw in his eyes, so deep and sincere, thrilled her. She did love Henri so. "Aye . . . I see now—"

"I will tell Nicolette that I passed you in the hall and asked for the letter. You refused and I had to cuff you a few times until I could retrieve it. Then I slapped your face for your disobedience to me and threatened you further a beating until you told me what I demanded to know of Nicolette's plans for the evening. I ordered you to remain in my chamber and repair yourself until seven, when I commanded you to return to Nicolette's chamber. I threatened you by saying I would accuse you of trying to rob me of my best jewels otherwise. Does that ring true?"

"It does, but it makes you appear so harsh and devious, Henri! How will your sister believe you could act so?"

"She will believe I was so worried that I acted with desperation for her benefit—once she comes to her senses. She will feel she bears the burden of my actions. Next time she will listen to wise counsel more easily, do you not think, my lovely?"

"Aye . . ."

"I must take leave, though it is always difficult for me to let you from my sight," he said and kissed her again. "Damon and my servants have been dismissed for the evening so no one should disturb you, dearest.

Amuse yourself quietly and be sure to appear exactly at seven. After you deliver Nicolette's letter return to my chamber. For Nicolette will dismiss you for the evening. I will see to that. You see, I think I have paid less attention to my dear sister than I should have these last weeks. I want to sit and visit with her. Bring her comfort and relief."

"How very dear you are, Henri."

"I try, my pet. I do try."

"I will not write one word you tell me, Henri!" Nicolette, long over her shock, spat at him. "Matthew will know something is amiss if he does not receive my reply. He will come to find me. If you prevent such, he will report what has happened to Davide! And I will expose you tonight to the baron. I will tell him the truth of everything and he will have you hanged!" Nicolette rose from the table where Henri had parchment and quill waiting. She started for the door.

"Still pronouncing your righteousness though you are a whore and liar! You deceived and cuckolded your husband. But you, ever the saint, would indeed go to the baron and tell all, Nicolette?"

The resignation in his voice made her stop and turn to him. Perhaps she had addled him sufficiently to cause him to concede. "Aye. I will do so immediately."

"I daresay I admire your plucky courage. I'd feared no threat I could make would deter you."

"You feared rightly," she said, meeting his eye with all her unveiled contempt.

"That is why I foresaw to have Bruge waiting with Simone in my chamber," he lied evenly, watching with satisfaction as her face paled and her shoulders sagged. "Sit down," he ordered amiably as he laid her scripted letter open. "You will want to add a postscript to your valiant lover. Telling him of your sister's marriage to Count Bompart on the morrow."

Nicolette sank upon the bench. "You could not—you would not do that to the innocent child! I know you are genuinely fond of her. You love Bruge, Henri—"

"Aye, it will pain me to know that sweet little Bruge will be at the mercy of that lecherous old drunkard. I hear tell that he treated his previous young wives with less than love and respect. But *you* will force me to do so. For if you do expose your own transgressions to the baron, Bruge will no longer hold me in esteem. My little sister will no longer love me once she learns what I have done, will she?"

Nicolette stared into his beady dark eyes. She could suffer anything but this. Henri was as clever as he was depraved. For she had intended to go *not* to the baron but to take Bruge and appeal to Matthew Tregere to ride them to safety. But Bruge was at Henri's mercy. Even the baron, if she did go to him, could not easily prevent the marriage, for Henri was Bruge's guardian by law and could marry her to whomever he chose unless consanguinity could be proved. But Bompart was no blood relation. She didn't doubt that Henri would use her as a threat to receive Bruge's required consent to the marriage. He had won. She fought back her tears. She would not give him that satisfaction. Somehow she must keep her wits about her and find a way of making Davide know that what he would read was all lies!

SONG OF THE ROSE

"Well, Sister?"

"I will do what you say. For I love Bruge as much as I despise you."

"I am truly injured at your words, my sweet sister, Baroness Perdant," he said, mocking her. He handed her the quill. "Quickly now, I want you to write what I say. No. Better yet, I want you to tell him that you do not love him in your own words. That you judged François unfairly. That you love your husband and carry his child. Plead with him sweetly not to expose your dalliance to François for your child's sake. Bewitch him with words as you did all those weeks with your body," Henri said. He ran his fingers gently across her cheek and down her neck, knowing she dared not push him away now.

Nicolette was too happy for the *first* mistake Henri had made to feel his bony fingers. He *had* believed her story about Davide after all! How they had been lovers for *weeks* and that she had gone to the forest to meet him that afternoon when François appeared. For she had not risked denying the encounter in fear that François *had* told Henri how Davide had come to her aid. Henri had told her he was pleased to hear her finally speak the truth, so she had guessed that she'd been correct. But Henri was such a practiced liar it was hard to know. But he had just said "those weeks"! If she innocently passed the information to Davide he would immediately know! Nicolette dipped the quill into the ink and began to write.

She handed the brief note to Henri and watched as his brow wrinkled above his hawklike nose as he read it carefully. He looked up at her and smirked with satisfaction, then read it again.

SONG OF THE ROSE

"My sister. You are as talented as you are beautiful. You have a gift in your way with words. Perhaps you should try your hand at writing love songs? This letter will both break his heart and silence your poor Davide forever. Do not cry with such unhappiness, Nicolette! For I will always be here to comfort you."

Nicolette let her tears of rage and relief flow, for Henri would become suspicious if she did not show abject despair. She forced herself to endure his kiss upon her neck and his arm around her waist, his fingers like the legs of an ugly spider. "How do I know you will not marry Bruge to Bompart despite my acquiescence?"

"You are so distrustful, lovely Nicolette." He laughed. "You have my word, is that not enough?"

She glared at him but said nothing.

He laughed harder. "I see 'tis not." He reached for the quill and paper. Quickly he wrote and signed a note to the baron. He dated it and handed it to Nicolette. He watched as she read his request for the betrothal of Bruge Duprey to the fine squire Gervais Grieves.

"But you could make this request invalid whenever it suited your purposes." Did he really think her that gullible?

"Aye. Once again Bruge's happiness will rest in your hands. If you treat me with the respect and affection I demand." He ran his finger across her chin and slowly down to her waist, enjoying her cringing but helpless acceptance of his caress. "Then Bruge shall be wed to Gervais after he is knighted. Let us see, that will be in four or five years, will it not, my obedient sister?" His hand boldly stroked her breasts.

He could feel her nipples beneath the layers of clothing he would soon remove. He kissed her mouth, and although she gasped she did not fight him. He felt his groin heat in anticipation.

The knock on the door angered him. But then he was grateful, for as soon as Simone took the letter and returned to tell them it had been properly delivered he could glory in his victory! He could take her at his leisure, *whenever* he chose. For years, if he didn't tire of her. She would live at his mercy as he had been forced to live at hers when he was but a boy.

Simone stood timidly before them. "I am terribly sorry, my lady. He forced me to—" Simone began to cry. Henri noticed that her cheek was still reddened from his slap and her girdle had been tied back together but was most obviously tattered.

Tears filled Nicolette's eyes. She looked from Simone to Henri. Silently he demanded that she say what he had instructed to the poor maiden who had become one of his victims because of her. "Simone. 'Tis I who am sorry. For had my dear brother not been so angered by my lack of considered reason he would not have struck you." Poor Simone's cheek was as red as her hair. Would Matthew suspect something was amiss? Although it was still light outside, she remembered how ill-lit was the great hall. The flickering candlelight would cast enough shadow upon Simone's face to mask the mark. "Would you please deliver this letter immediately to Sire Tregere. Do you remember the code?"

"Aye, my lady. Are not the roses in bloom lovely, Sire?"

Nicolette felt Henri's eyes studying her. She forced

a smile. "Very good, Simone. Return as soon as he has accepted the letter."

"Aye." Simone curtsied clumsily and left, the letter secure in her purse.

Henri sauntered to the shelf where he'd placed the wine and grapes he'd carried in over an hour before. He filled one goblet and drank the red wine down. He filled the goblet again and then the other, which he carried to the desolate figure of Nicolette. "A toast to our sweet Bruge's intended marriage." He watched as she drank the wine. "Another toast to François' child—a son I am sure—the future Baron of St. Aliquis."

How she wanted to throw the wine at him! Instead she silently drank until there was no wine left in her goblet.

Henri examined the room while she sat in silence. He played a moment with her pet falcon. Abruptly he turned. "I almost forgot." He removed Davide's letter from his jacket and carried a standing candle to the unlit fireplace. He lit the parchment and tossed it gleefully into the hearth.

Nicolette looked away, unable to watch as the letter became ashes. Davide will know we are in danger. He will come for us, she soothed herself. But what if he did not? Or couldn't come? How long would she have to allow her stepbrother's loathsome advances? Surely now that she carried a babe Henri would not expect to— Oh, dear Mother Mary. He would! For he would have no fear of planting his seed in her now! She wouldn't let him touch her again—but how could she stop him and keep Bruge safe? For all she knew Henri would threaten to rape his little sister if she did not accede to his lust, Nicolette realized with horror.

Simone knocked quickly and immediately entered. "I have delivered the letter, my lady. It went well. Sire Matthew has left the castle. Is there anything else?"

"Thank you, Simone. You may take your leave and go back to Henri's chamber until Henri returns," Nicolette said as Henri demanded. "Please give my love to Bruge," she added, unable to stop herself.

"Bruge?" Simone looked from Nicolette to Henri. He was correct. Nicolette was not herself, for it was not like her to speak with such confusion. "My lady, Bruge is with Alienor. Remember you asked me to tell her to stay there for the night?"

"She has not been with you in Henri's chamber then?"

"No, my lady. I have been there alone."

He had tricked her into believing! She dared not look at his gloating face. "Aye. Of course. You may go, Simone."

"If I pass anyone who inquires, should I say that you are asleep in bed, my lady?"

"That is exactly what you are to say, Simone. That Nicolette is well tucked into her bed. Now off with you." Henri bolted the door after her, then strolled toward Nicolette, who stared into the distance.

Henri stood pressed behind her, stroking her hair. Nicolette was numb. She would take no more chances. On the morrow she would take Bruge and flee. No! She would not trust Henri even that long. As soon as he was done with her she would awaken

Bruge. Despite the dangers of the road at night. For there could be no greater danger than her stepbrother who now boldly grasped her breasts as he breathed like an animal and rubbed himself against her.

Henri led a defeated Nicolette to her bed. He took her into his arms and kissed her deeply as he felt his manhood cry for release. Nicolette did not return his kisses but lay as still as a pretty doll. 'Twas good enough, at least for the moment. But his hatred for the frozen beauty drove him to toy with her. "Do I not kiss you as well as your lover did, sweet Nicolette?"

Taking her body was not enough for Henri, she saw. How much like François he was. Were all brutal men the same? She thought of Davide, so gentle and loving a man, and her heart shattered once more. For once they fled he might never find her! She had no choice.

"I asked you a question, Nicolette. Answer."

"Aye."

"Look at me."

Henri had risen. He stood before her with his trousers unfastened, his manhood, long and as slender as his bony fingers, erect before her. Her stomach turned again and she had to fight her nausea back.

"Am I not as big and hard as Davide, Nicolette?" he asked in a choked voice.

She could not bring herself to respond. Angrily he yanked her from the bed and brought her to her knees before him.

"Answer me, whore." He chuckled malevolently. "Or perhaps you must sample it first to answer? For you are too virtuous a damsel to lie, aren't you?" he taunted as his hand caressed the top of her head and forced it down slowly. She resisted, unable to stop herself. "Perhaps you do not love Bruge as well as you pretend. Perhaps you would rather it be she who kneels before my manhood, leaving you to dream in peace about your lover? Convince me otherwise, Nicolette. For her sake. It is a long time since I have taken a virgin. And Bruge is so sweet and innocently compliant. Perhaps she will be more to my liking . . ."

The tears poured from Nicolette's eyes as she silently lowered her head—

The loud rap upon the door startled them. "Henri? My lady, are you in there?" Nicolette recognized Sire Eustace's deep voice immediately. Praise the Lord for his delivery of the baron's seneschal to her door, Nicolette thought, as she quickly rose and fled to open the door.

"Sire Eustace, come in, please. We were playing with my falcon," she said, trying to explain the delay. Sire Eustace did not seem to hear. He looked dour and impatient.

"Sire," Henri said as he approached. What crisis had driven the seneschal to this door at his moment of triumph? He saw an expression of relief spread across Nicolette's face. No relief, Nicolette, he thought. Just a reprieve. I will make it worse for you than you could imagine, as soon as he leaves.

"Henri, you must come with me at once to the baron's chamber," the seneschal said with stern urgency.

"Has the baron taken a turn for the worse?" Henri asked.

Nicolette noticed that he had managed to fasten his

pants. For his manhood had begun to shrivel rapidly from the moment of Sire Eustace's loud knock. So the baron was again ill. Why did Sire Eustace look at her that way?

"The baron is dead. Sorry for speaking it so abruptly, my lady."

"I understand. I am truly sorry. Henri, go with Sire Eustace at once. I shall go to Alienor and Bruge and bring them to the baron's chamber. You have not told Alienor yet, I take it?"

"No. I hoped you, her friend and sister, would do so, for women have a way with such things."

"I will." She looked Henri in the eye. *Now it is you who have no choice. For as soon as it is learned that the baron is dead, St. Aliquis will be subject to invasion by greedy neighboring barons who know François is fighting the infidels: you, Henri, as commander of the men-at-arms must make immediate plans for protection of the barony. I, as the new baroness, may give the orders until François returns.* She knew Henri read her thoughts.

"We will see you in a few moments then, dear Sister?"

"Aye."

"I count upon it, in this moment of distress," he said and turned down the hall with Sire Eustace.

Nicolette closed the door behind them and leaned against it, almost collapsing with relief. *May you rest in peace after all, Simon Perdant. For you have saved Bruge and me in your death as you never protected us while you lived.* Tears streamed down her face but she had no time for them. She brushed them away, adjusted her clothes, and ran down the hall to Alienor's chamber. Her poor Alienor. First Guy and now the father she innocently, deeply loved. And I won't be here to bring you comfort. But I have no choice. I will try to contact you once we are safe, my dearest, kindest friend.

Bruge clutched Nicolette's hand as they watched Alienor say her tearful goodbye to her father. Alienor collapsed into sobs and Sire Eustace lifted her.

"I will carry her to her chamber. Henri, go alert your men. I will meet you immediately, for we must act quickly. Even Macaire and his men are gone, still hunting for the bandits. So we do not have our provost to help us until the morrow. We must send two of your men to find Macaire, tonight," Sire Eustace ordered, as he reached the door with Alienor in his arms. "Nicolette, would you and Bruge come with me and care for Alienor?"

Nicolette did not look at Henri. "Of course," she said as she pushed Bruge in front of her and followed the seneschal out the door. Henri would be occupied for many hours, providing them with the time she would need to enact the plan she'd been devising since Sire Eustace appeared at her door.

Nicolette sat beside the weeping Alienor, stroking her hair, when Henri appeared just as she'd expected. His smile told her that he was satisfied that she was still his prisoner. Henri turned to Bruge, who sat on the other end of the canopied bed, reading Alienor's favorite section of the Bible to her.

"Bruge," Henri called, and Nicolette's heart

pounded in terror. "Come here and give your brother a sweet kiss and hug, for he is going to be working a long hard night."

Nicolette watched as Bruge innocently complied. Henri's sardonic smile directed at her was not lost upon Nicolette. She received his message only too clearly. Henri patted Bruge's head and turned down the hall. You will burn in hell before you ever touch her—or me—again, Henri! I make this vow in my dead father's name, Nicolette said silently as she felt the terror in her heart give way to a steely-cold, grim resolve.

Chapter Nine

MERCIFULLY, ALIENOR HAD SLEPT FOR THE PAST HOUR, allowing Nicolette time to concentrate freely on the details of her plan of escape. She glanced at Bruge, also asleep upon her former pallet beside a slumbering Denise. The antechamber, where Alienor's maids slept, had grown silent as well. Nicolette studied the notched tallow candle on the fireplace mantle used to determine the hour. 'Twas almost eleven.

During the past two hours she'd devised and rejected many plans. At first lingering terror and fury had addled her brain, driving her to rashly decide that she and Bruge must escape on foot, as soon as Alienor fell asleep, and hide in the nearby village until morning. That village and others close by were part of the barony. Their faces would be known by villeins—serfs who were bound in allegiance to the baron—and therefore would provide them no safe harbor once word had been spread on Henri's orders. Moreover, Nicolette had soon come to understand that Henri, apparently uneasy that she and Bruge were beyond his grasp tonight, intended to be sure that they remained captive. For he had first sent Damon to Alienor's chamber under the pretext of concern for Alienor's condition. An hour later Gervais appeared, unknowingly a tool of Henri's determination to use him as a second pair of eyes. Gervais, obviously believing his instructions benevolent, offered that Henri had instructed him to visit them upon each hour.

Henri's orders, meant to intimidate her, had produced the opposite effect during the elapsed hour. Nicolette had settled into cold, clear reason, bringing the power of her position and its possibilities to the forefront of her mind. She, as François' wife, the baroness, was now, after the baron's death, François' "jure"—the holder of his pledge to protect St. Aliquis. It was she who was, by right, in command of the castle until François' return from Jerusalem.

True it was custom to allow a baron's advisers to command in actuality, although she had heard tell otherwise. All knew that King Richard the Lionhearted's mother, Eleanor of Aquitaine, had not only astounded the world by deserting King Louis VII, father of their reigning King Philip Augustus, and wedding Henry II of England, but had ruled England as Henry's consort when he fought in the last Crusade. Nicolette had no thought of presuming to interfere in military matters but she intended to wield her conferred power in order to save herself and Bruge.

The only question that remained unresolved was whether she could leave Alienor safely, albeit sadly, behind. For now. Would Henri be a threat to Alienor? As cunningly vile as Henri was, Nicolette doubted that he would attempt to harm her in any manner. For François would be returning within weeks of receiving the news of his father's death. No doubt Henri would be on shaky ground when François learned his "wife" had fled. Henri could not risk any action that would increase François' wrath, although Nicolette suspected that Henri had always dreamed that he should have been betrothed to Alienor. But despite his fancy for Alienor—obvious to all except Alienor herself, who despised him—and his abiding quest for power, Henri was too clever to act against his own best interest. Alienor should remain safe until François' return. François, unlike her own brother, held his sister in loving esteem. He would act accordingly and find Alienor a husband to her liking.

Nicolette looked at the notched tallow candle again. It was time for her to act, for Gervais should appear at the chamber door in a moment. Nicolette rose and crept soundlessly to the thick wooden door which she opened as quietly and narrowly as possible. She slipped into the hall when she heard Gervais' footsteps.

"My lady," he said with a slight bow, "do you require my services? I would have thought you and the others asleep."

SONG OF THE ROSE

"The others do slumber, Gervais," Nicolette whispered. Was she correct in believing that Gervais so loved Bruge that she could count upon his unqualified allegiance? She gathered her courage, for she needed to sound him out if her plan was to work. If he engendered any suspicion of doubt, she would have to resort to her second, more dangerous plan. "Gervais," she began in an urgent whisper, "I require your frankness. Do you love my sister?" His eyes lit as brightly as his face reddened. Before you have spoken, dear Gervais, you have given me my answer, she thought.

"Aye, my lady. I am but sixteen and will not be knighted until four or five years have passed," he whispered earnestly. "But I have planned to ask my father to arrange for my betrothal to your sister if you and the baron—Messire François now—will give your assent."

"Bruge loves you deeply and she has picked well, Gervais, for I can not think of another squire, another knight, baron, count, or even duke, who could outshine you," she whispered with a smile that quickly faded as she realized she had to press ahead. "'Tis imperative that I speak to you in my chamber." She saw Gervais perceive the urgency of her words. Without a word, he glanced in each direction of the hall and then took her arm as they hurried to her chamber, undetected. For except for those who met in the barracks, the folk in the castle had long retired for the night.

As they stood before the fireplace in her empty chamber Nicolette wondered where Simone might be.

SONG OF THE ROSE

She had assumed that she would have to awaken Simone and send her from her pallet to the antechamber to sleep with the maids. Could Simone be having a secret romance with one of the servitors, she wondered, remembering now that Simone had been acting rather peculiar in the past weeks. So she was in love, Nicolette thought. I bid you well, Simone, for you are a loyal, sweet girl who deserves her chance at romance. But I must get to more urgent matters, she thought, as she saw Gervais waited silently but in obvious disconcerting darkness. "Gervais, I know my behavior appears queer, but you shall soon understand all," Nicolette began. His face held such caring concern that Nicolette knew that she must tell the gentle but brave squire the complete truth.

Gervais took her hand in a loving, brotherly fashion as they sat upon a bench in the far corner of her chamber. Nicolette, weary from repeating the horrors while forcing her tears away, glanced at her pet falcon, Corbet. Corbet slept peacefully upon his perch. Regaining her composure, Nicolette turned back to Gervais.

"I am sorry, my lady, for the ghastly indignities you have had to endure. I only hope that I shall be half as courageous as a man and knight as you are. I pledge to you my life! I will do *anything* you desire to protect you and Bruge. I only wish that I had sought your audience before. For I have long suspected Henri to be full of trickery and deceit, though I cannot say that I could have imagined him to be as heinous as I now know him to be. I had thought some of the stories

Damon, Henri's varlet, confided to me exaggerated by the youth, for he much hates Henri—with good cause I now see."

"What stories does he tell?" Nicolette asked, anxious to learn of any of Henri's schemes she might not know.

"Damon is but eleven and has years before he will become a squire. He is a quiet and kind youth. Apparently so quiet that Henri sometimes forgets the boy is at his side. Damon has told me that he heard Henri say that he hoped Baron Harcourt would attack St. Aliquis when Baron Perdant died, for his defense of our barony would cause Sire François to reward him greatly. Damon overheard Henri speaking to himself this morn, saying now Lady Alienor would most certainly be his. Even though he courts your maiden, Simone, with promises of their betrothal. She is besotted with him and is at his beck and call, poor maiden."

"Simone?" Nicolette repeated, shocked. How could that be? "I don't understand, for Henri has always ridiculed her stoutness and derided her stupidity, as he calls it."

"Aye. For Damon says that when he sends Simone back to you, after their evenings of intimate pleasures, he rants at her repulsiveness and how she sickens him. He prays that he will be able to rid himself of her as soon as her usefulness has passed. Damon knew not what he meant. I suspected, though not the depth of depravity or harmful intent!" Gervais dropped to his knee before her. "Pray forgive me for my stupidity," he beseeched. "For I had believed that he used Simone to learn what he could from you about *Alienor*. I was afraid that if I told you, you would doubt me! Yet I see now, from what you've told me, that he cajoled her into conspiring against you today."

"Rise, dear Gervais, and sit once more beside me. You had no cause to think other than you did. I truly know so, better than most. I am thankful that you told me what you knew. For it will help us now. I can count on you now to help us to safety then?" she asked, already knowing his response.

"I will do everything within my power, my lady. Tell me your plan."

Nicolette kissed him on his cheek. "Thank you. I shall and you must help me to rethink quickly. For your information causes me to alter it. I cannot trust poor, foolish Simone. Also, I do not believe we can leave Alienor behind. Henri's rage and lust seemingly know no bounds. But one more question first—is there a man-at-arms whose loyalty we might depend upon? One who knows Henri's true nature?"

Gervais chuckled wryly. "There are many who know his true nature, for they have felt his blows firsthand. But aye, Herbert de Leon has taken a liking to me. He speaks openly to me of his hatred of Henri, for it was Herbert who should have risen to the position of commander. Indeed it is Herbert de Leon who does command, in fact if not in name. For I know I can speak freely now. Your brother is incompetent and lazy. He much prefers his wenching and drinking to work. It is actually Sire Eustace and Herbert de Leon who now make the plans to defend St. Aliquis, for they are certain the Baron Harcourt has planted spies in the castle and will know within hours that Baron Perdant is dead."

"I'm afraid what you have told me leads me to think that Herbert must hate me as well. For I am François' wife and Henri's sister."

Gervais' cheeks flamed again but he held her eyes steadfastly. "Forgive me, for I do not wish to bring you further humiliation, but Herbert tried to tell me—though I thought him wrong—that he was certain you had been forced to bed and then wed François. He holds great sympathy and tenderness for you, for he has always despised François, though he has been clever enough to hide his feelings in order to ensure his position.

"Just this evening he told me that he feared for Alienor now that Sire Guy and the baron were dead. He said most certainly Henri would try to force François to wed her to him—using blackmail if necessary. The blackmail being you and François' babe you carry." Gervais blushed but continued. "Herbert said that although François was fond of his sister, his fear of the humiliation of losing you and his child, when he learned you were carrying his heir, would hold greater weight than his brotherly affection. I have no doubt we can rely upon Herbert's sympathy and aid. He is very clever, for he has managed to cause Henri to believe him his most trusted and loyal servant."

Nicolette sought to absorb all Gervais had said as she sat quietly for a moment. "Then we must enlist his aid, Gervais. And he is in the strongest position to help us. I will tell you how. For we must act quickly

SONG OF THE ROSE

and should anything go amiss, then I am afraid we are doomed."

"Pray tell me then," Gervais replied, his body alertly erect, his beautiful blue-green eyes bright and clear.

Nicolette shook Alienor gently but firmly to awaken her. She had to act quickly now for Gervais was secretly preparing the suits of armor she and Bruge would later need. How grateful she was that Father had taught her and Bruge to ride as well as any young men. Nicolette was also grateful to Gervais, for he had openly disagreed with some aspects of her plan and had the good wit to suggest a far better approach.

Though the new plan would greatly rest on Alienor's ability to playact, Nicolette agreed that if Herbert responded on cue it would not only work but leave Henri frustrated but unsuspicious until it was too late. By the time Henri discovered what had truly occurred, Herbert would step in, if need be, and further outwit Henri. With hope Matthew would agree to ride her and Bruge with him until they were safe under Davide's protection.

Alienor shifted and muttered but stubbornly slept on, until Nicolette shook her more firmly and whispered into her ear. "Alienor . . . you must wake . . . Pray wake for me, Nicolette . . . Alienor . . ." The sleeping drops the physician had given her had worked too well. Nicolette hoped that Alienor would not be too drowsy to act once she was awake.

Alienor's eyelids fluttered and her eyes slowly opened. Alienor looked at her and gave her a befuddled smile as she rubbed her eyes and yawned. "I am awake," she whispered and yawned again.

"You must dress and come with me at once," Nicolette whispered in her ear. "It is urgent. Can you do so?" Alienor studied her face in response. She rose somewhat shakily.

"Go where, Nicolette?" Alienor whispered.

"To my chamber where we may speak."

Alienor nodded and lifted herself off the bed where she stood most unsteadily though Nicolette held her arm. "Help me with my chemise, Nicolette," she whispered.

Nicolette had already laid out her raiments and reached for her chemise with her free hand. Nicolette helped her slip it over her head. Alienor seemed to hold the ground more steadily. "Are you able to stand now on your own?" she asked.

"Aye." Alienor took the awaiting pelisson and slipped that over her head as well. Then came her ruby-colored tunic. Nicolette tied Alienor's girdle around her waist and smoothed the ruby tunic. Alienor sat back upon her bed and slipped on the stockings Nicolette gave her. When Nicolette handed her riding boots rather than slippers Alienor looked with surprise but quickly put them on her feet with Nicolette's help. "We are riding someplace?" she whispered. "Do I not need my mantle?"

Nicolette smiled at Alienor for her sleepy but unquestioning acceptance. "We shall return for that and other things later. Can you walk now?"

Alienor took small steps, testing her balance. "Aye. Let us go then, wherever you are taking me."

"To my chamber," Nicolette whispered. She

hugged Alienor quickly and kissed her upon the cheek. "Walk very quietly," she warned. "For the maidens can't be wakened just yet."

They scurried down the hall, Nicolette continuing to help support Alienor whose steps were slow and less than steady. Finally they reached her chamber and Nicolette quickly sat Alienor in the straight-backed, armed wooden chair which was François'. Alienor yawned again but Nicolette did not worry. She knew that once she told Alienor the vile story, her revulsion and fright would cause her blood to course rapidly. How she hated to add to Alienor's misery but now it was for Alienor's safety as well as her own and Bruge's.

"Nicolette, you appear so distressed. Pray tell what has given you cause to bring me from my bed—though I do not doubt your reason was grave."

"Alienor, if I could spare you from further grief and unhappiness I would do so. 'Tis not possible, I fear. I have been less than completely truthful with you these past months, more for your sake than my own. Now you must know all the terrible truths and make your own decision upon hearing them."

Sleep fled rapidly from Alienor's face. "What time is it?" Alienor glanced at the notched candle.

"'Tis almost midnight. We have little time. Alienor . . . Bruge and I are in immediate danger. I cannot say how long you, yourself, shall not be inflicted with it. Remember the day I went to the forest to make the garland for Bruge's birthday present?"

"How can I forget it? Worse yet the night that followed."

"'Tis even worse than you could guess."

SONG OF THE ROSE

Alienor paled but said nothing as she waited for Nicolette to continue.

Shortly past midnight came Gervais' knock which Nicolette and Alienor expected. Gervais bowed and appeared pleased yet serious, showing Nicolette that Gervais took their plan not as a game but with the seriousness it demanded.

"Providence was with us, Lady Nicolette. I did not have to invent some excuse for speaking privately with Herbert, for he was approaching the castle when I walked through the inner ward toward the barracks. We spoke in utter secrecy. As I'd hoped, he was outraged at the story that confirmed his worst suspicions. His message to you both is that he will take an oath, if you require, to proclaim his allegiance to you ladies. He believes the plan will work and told me to hurry back to tell you so. He will prepare the suits of armor for you and Bruge should you require them," he informed Nicolette. "Herbert believes that Sire Eustace, out of the goodness of his soul, will unknowingly support our plan and will insist you have a parchment of safe conduct."

"'Tis wonderful, Gervais, thank you! I do believe we shall all be safe and well before the morrow. Alienor has done much to give me further courage in the past quarter of an hour. No one could be blessed with more devoted a friend than she."

"Gervais, I must express my gratitude to you," said Alienor. "For we are surrounded by so many enemies and such hideous schemes that it is good we can place our faith in someone as gallant and forthright as yourself. And Herbert de Leon as well, from what you have told us. I always respected Herbert. He taught me to ride when I was but a child and whispered that I rode with greater skill than François. He showed me how to ride not only my palfrey but my first roan which I rode in the hunting party Father allowed me to join." Alienor's face lit as she smiled, lost momentarily in pleasant memories.

Gervais laughed. "Indeed, Sire Herbert told me just what you say many a time." Gervais tried to no avail to stifle a deep chuckle. "The fact be that often he would swear and complain about Henri's incompetence, saying that if François had made Lady Alienor the commander, in two weeks time she would be far more effective than either François or Henri. So you see, my lady, his words were not mere flattery."

Nicolette laughed as she imagined the tall, brawny, handsome Herbert, who had been a knight for over twenty years and whose reputation and demeanor forced respect from men of any rank, curse and rail about her brother and François. Just the other day Nicolette had seen Henri so delicately give an order to Herbert that it sounded as if he made a request that the knight could choose to ignore. Nicolette repeated the incident to the others and consequently laughed as hard as they, tears springing to her eyes. How good it felt to smile and laugh again! But they had to stop for fear that they would arouse someone. Moreover, they had to act quickly. Nicolette quieted and the others followed her cue.

"I think Guy would have smiled had he just seen us, do you not, Nicolette?" Alienor asked with a melancholy smile.

"I do. Although I believe he would have laughed

the heartiest at the story himself," Nicolette replied, pleased by Alienor's chuckle in response. "Are you prepared, Alienor? Moreso, are you certain that you wish to participate in the plan?"

"As certain as I have ever been of anything. I am sorry only that Father is not alive. For surely, if you had gone to him, he would have thrown Henri in a dank cell in the *donjon*, I have no doubt, do you, Nicolette?"

Nicolette had withheld only one portion of her story: the fact that the baron knew that she had not given her free consent to her marriage. For what good would it do to disparage her Alienor's dead father whom she adored? She had not told Alienor of her knowledge about Lady Adela, for that too would devastate her dearest friend to no purpose. Neither had Nicolette told Gervais, for the information added nothing to their plight or salvation. Only she and Henri carried the secret their father had spoken of that night at the hearth. "I am certain you are correct. I hoped not to be forced to burden your father, for he was so weak and . . ."

"I understand, Nicolette," Alienor said and brushed away new tears of loss.

"Are you certain you can go through with this, Alienor?" Alienor nodded as she fought back her tears. Softly, Nicolette continued. "Then we must slip ourselves back into your chamber. As we planned, I will lie upon your bed, pretending sleep, so it will appear that you dressed while the rest of us slumbered. Then you will drop your Bible or whatever and awaken me and I will be so upset that I will awaken Bruge and Denise. I *am* glad you insisted we

SONG OF THE ROSE

take Denise along. For not only will she too be protected—my brother's lecherousness does seem to have no limits as you said—but it will seem more plausible if your first maiden-in-waiting travels with you. I'm sorry. Gervais, I forgot to tell you this, so we'll need another roan saddled for Denise."

"Aye, I agree as well," he answered. "I shall see to that and all the other details. I must go, but I remind you to take your knife, though I pray you will have no cause to use it. Yours as well, Lady Alienor. It will all go well because the Lord watches over the righteous, does he not, ladies? I will see you in the barracks by the hour then." He bowed and kissed their hands. "Let me ascertain that the hall is clear to Lady Alienor's chamber and there I will leave you."

Nicolette and Alienor followed him out the door. Nicolette and Alienor crept into her chamber. With nary a sound Nicolette climbed upon Alienor's bed, fully clothed. She lay curled upon the coverlets, appearing as if she had thus fallen into sleep while attending Alienor. The coverlets on Alienor's side of the bed were turned down and Nicolette watched as Alienor sat herself upon the feather bed and quietly removed her boots, puzzling Nicolette until she heard the heavy boot thud to the floor. Immediately she understood. "Oh!" Nicolette exclaimed loudly. "Who goes here?" she cried as she heard the stirrings of Bruge and Denise across the room.

"Pray calm yourself," Alienor whispered intentionally loud. "'Tis only me, Nicolette. I dropped my boot."

"What is wrong?" Bruge called from across the room in a sleepy voice.

SONG OF THE ROSE

"Are you feeling ill, my lady?" Denise called out drowsily. They heard her rise.

Nicolette sat up quickly. "Pray tell what you are doing with your boot in the middle of the night!" she demanded. Denise, with candle in hand, appeared at her side, followed by Bruge. Both had covers wrapped around their naked bodies.

Alienor did not turn in their direction but fastened her right boot and then proceeded to slide her foot into the left. "I am sorry I clumsily awoke all of you," she said, "for I would have allowed you to sleep until I'd done my hair."

"It is almost one o'clock, the dead of the night. Why are you dressing as if you intended to ride somewhere? I fear your anguish has gotten the better of you," said Nicolette.

"'Tis not so. I wish the three of you to quickly dress as well. We are going to St. Martin. If you do not wish to join me, Nicolette, you and Bruge may remain here and Denise and I will go alone."

"In the blackness of night, my lady? 'Tis not safe!" Denise responded with alarm.

"'Tis not, she is correct, Alienor. What possesses you to think such a notion?" Nicolette asked with feigned alarm.

"I had a dream that told me I should be with Sire Guy's mother. She has become like a true mother to me and only there shall I find the comfort I need." Alienor began to cry, in part real tears, Nicolette suspected.

"I understand, but there is no harm to wait until morn. The roads are unsafe, Alienor. You know so. What with all the bandits and robbers—even worse out there. Even if we rode as four we are but ladies, unable to protect ourselves!" Nicolette insisted.

"Perhaps you are correct . . . Then I will go—we will go to Sire Eustace. He will issue us a parchment of safe conduct—"

"My lady, think you criminals care that we have such a parchment? I heard tell that two village girls were brutally raped, beaten, and left to die shortly after sundown last Thursday! Pray come to your senses, my lady!" Denise pleaded.

Bruge remained speechless in fear and clung to Nicolette.

"I have not lost my senses," Nicolette snapped. "I wish to leave tonight. I will have your brother send a man-at-arms, an armed knight, with us. They will give us the protection we might need, although I do not believe we will, for even robbers sleep."

"Methinks neither Henri nor Sire Eustace will allow us to ride to St. Martin. For it is a goodly three hours upon the darkened road," countered Nicolette.

"They cannot stop me! Nicolette, 'tis you who are now baroness. If you agree, they must obey!" Alienor walked to Nicolette and kneeled in pathetic supplication. "Pray, my sister. You must come with me, for I do not believe that I can far longer stand my grief. You are my most loving friend and sister . . . Bruge, you too are like a younger sister to me . . . Denise, you are dear to my heart, not some mere lady-in-waiting. I beseech you all to support me when I need you most." Alienor rose and wiped the tears from her face.

"If we have protection, we should be safe, Nicolette?" Bruge finally spoke, the softness of her heart overriding her fear, just as Nicolette had expected.

"Aye, I should think Bruge is correct. I will go with my lady if you wish to stay behind with Bruge," Denise loyally offered.

"Either we all go or no one goes!" Nicolette insisted, still feigning doubt. "I believe we should wait until the morn!" she continued stubbornly.

"Nicolette, I am greatly surprised by your stubbornness!" Bruge cried out in anger. "If you had made such a plea to Alienor, you know she would never refuse you! You may stay behind—perhaps you should because of the babe—but I intend to go with Alienor and Denise."

"You would defy me, my sister!" Nicolette challenged, causing Bruge to pale beneath the candlelight but hold silently firm. Nicolette thanked Mother Mary for the first sign of flaming resolve she had seen in Bruge, for later Bruge would need to call upon it. She was taking Bruge from her home into the unknown, and until they found Davide, Nicolette knew not what dangers they would face.

"Dress yourselves," Nicolette said with feigned resignation. "We shall go to the barracks where I believe we shall find Henri and the others. Alienor may plead her case, and if they cannot dissuade her from this rash plan then I shall go with you as well. But I do *not* like it nor shall I change my mind that morning would be a most sensible time to leave!"

"Oh thank you, Nicolette!" Alienor fell into her arms and hugged and kissed her while Bruge and Denise quickly set about dressing.

"Thank you," Nicolette whispered into Alienor's

ear. "You have done better than I could have imagined!"

"I will not hear of it!" Henri declared as soon as Alienor had laid her plea before him, even more frantically determined than before. Nicolette saw his frown of suspicion and met his eyes with an expression of innocence.

"How dare you speak to me with such a tone, Henri!" Alienor responded with indignation.

She turned to Sire Eustace, who stood by the hearth across the barracks room where Henri and two of his aides sat at a table covered with maps of the castle and region. Gervais stood beside Henri and had not spoken nor had his opinion been sought. Herbert de Leon, who sat across from Henri, continued to draw markings on the map, apparently disinterested and annoyed by this interruption. So far all was going as they'd hoped, Nicolette thought.

"Sire Eustace. I was certain you would understand and seek to help me rather than deafen yourself to my entreaties," Alienor said quietly. Sire Eustace did not reply but lowered his head as he stood deep in thought.

"As for you, Henri." Alienor spoke with anger flashing in her eyes. "You are every bit as hard as your sister!"

Nicolette saw the look of surprise register on Henri's face. "As hard as which sister? Nicolette?"

"Aye. For she too is adamant that we shall not travel until the morn. She said she hoped that you and Sire Eustace would deter me since she failed to do so. Well, I shall not be deterred!"

Henri turned to her with lingering suspicion that only she could see, so he thought. "You have tried to convince Lady Alienor of her folly, Nicolette?"

"Aye. The roads are unsafe; I tried to tell her but she would not heed me. She did promise that if Sire Eustace and you forbade her she would desist. For although I, as baroness, could choose to overrule you, I could not do so in good conscience."

"You shall make a fine baroness, my dear sister," Henri said, as pleased as he was surprised. So she had not schemed this as he had first suspected. Nicolette was clever enough to realize, after all, that her lack of resistance to his wishes was all she had to save little Bruge, at least until François arrived home.

Nicolette met his eyes with such sadness that he almost felt a sense of pity for her. Then the memory of her kneeling before him, her mouth ready to take his manhood, drove all pity away as he felt a rising lust. How he wished he could retire to his chamber and leave all this warfare business to Sire Eustace and Herbert de Leon, for it was they who formulated the plans for which he would receive credit. Aye, how he wished to have Nicolette humbled before him, his hands upon her silky hair, her perfume filling his senses, her mouth pleasuring him before he took her, her tears only heightening his fire.

"Henri, do you listen to me!" Alienor continued, bringing him reluctantly back to the matter at hand.

"I do, my lady. But I act only with concern for your welfare and that of my sisters and your maiden." Henri turned his glance at Bruge, wondering again whether *somehow* Nicolette had involved them all in an elaborate scheme of trickery. Bruge smiled at him with love and innocence. His little sister knew naught of deceit. Her smile was as prettily pure and true as always.

"Henri," Bruge said. "As Alienor said, you could send a knight or two to ride us safely to St. Martin."

"You would like me to send Gervais, perhaps? For I dare not spare but one knight. Would that please you, for he would remain with you ladies during the few days you plan to stay at St. Martin?"

Bruge's face turned scarlet and she lowered her eyes in embarrassment. Henri chuckled and turned to Gervais, whose face mirrored Bruge's. There was no scheme after all, Henri was convinced. He did not mind their trip to St. Martin, for if Baron Harcourt did intend to strike, the women would become objects of capture for ransom. A messenger should soon return with news as to whether there was unusual activity in Harcourt's barony. He supposed he would be too busy the next few days to indulge himself in the pleasure of taking Nicolette.

"You may send whomever you think best, brother," Bruge said when she finally found her voice.

"Sire Eustace, what say you?" Henri asked.

Sire Eustace stroked his beard in thought. "They would have to be given a parchment of safe conduct in order to cross the two toll roads and in the event they should run into a provost other than our Sire Macaire . . . We could send Gervais, though he is but a squire, and I suppose we could spare one knight—at least to ride them to St. Martin and immediately return. Perhaps Herbert, if he consents. For sending Herbert as their escort would be equal to sending a half-dozen lesser knights."

"What say you, Herbert?" Henri asked politely.

"Methinks it is nothing but women's nonsense," he said brusquely.

Alienor quickly walked to Herbert and took his rough large hands into her own. "Pray help me, Sire Herbert. You have been nothing but kind to me since I was but a child. You know we will ride well, for it was you who taught me and you have said how well Nicolette and the others ride. It is very important to me . . ." The tears ran down Alienor's cheeks. "For in but two days I have lost my truest loves. My husband-to-be and my dearest father. My mother died so long ago and I need the Baroness Brouilleaux, for we will share our grief together . . ."

Herbert appeared openly uncomfortable. He pulled his hands from Alienor and coughed. "I suppose I could ride them there and return by morning. Gervais could come with us and stay with the ladies until their return. Certainly Baron Brouilleaux will see that his men ride them safely home again. Still, I am not certain—" He looked at Alienor's tearful face. "I will do so only if you stop that infernal weeping, my lady! It will bring neither Sire Guy nor Messire Simon back to the living and is most unbecoming," he said brusquely.

Henri covered his mouth to hide his smile, for Herbert had expressed the sentiments he did not dare to utter. Henri decided to further ensure his hold over Nicolette. "Perhaps you too should stay on with them. You could use the opportunity to ascertain whether Baron Brouilleaux would come to our aid against Harcourt, should he strike. Our best knights are with François. We could use whatever additions Baron

SONG OF THE ROSE

Brouilleaux might offer. You could lead them back when the ladies return. With you at St. Martin I shall also be assured that my sisters are well protected, as well as Alienor and her maiden, Denise, of course."

He smiled at Nicolette, who intentionally showed in her face that his covert message was not lost upon her. "I still believe that we should wait for the morrow," she said. "But if you have decided to allow Alienor her way, there is nothing for me to do but have Simone and one of the maids pack for us and—"

A man-at-arms ran into the barracks, breathing hard. "Sire Henri," he began, obviously trying to catch his breath. "Baron Harcourt does prepare for war! Our spy told me that we can expect the attack at dawn the day after the morrow!"

"Just as we suspected. Herbert, you must ride the ladies to St. Martin, where they shall be safe. I believe they should remain there until we have conquered Harcourt's forces and returned them to Harcourt with their tails curled between their legs! Gervais will remain with the ladies but it is imperative that you return to St. Aliquis by evening. I shall issue their safe conduct immediately," Sire Eustace declared.

"Aye," Herbert agreed reluctantly and rose. "Why do you ladies tarry? Hurry off and pack your things and do not carry too much for we will be riding fast. Gervais and I will ready the roans. I shall ride my destrier, as will Gervais, for he has proven more than an able rider with shield, sword, and mace, has he not, Henri?"

"Aye. Gervais could well have ridden with François to the Crusade except that we needed him here, just for such an event as now befalls us." Henri looked at the ladies. "Off with you, then." Sire Eustace was already headed for the door, and the other men were dispersing. "Oh, Nicolette," Henri called back to her. "Should you see Sire Matthew Tregere, do send my regards to him, dear sister."

Nicolette understood his true intent. "Aye, brother."

"Herbert, I should like a word with you in private before you leave to mount the horses. For I want to remind you of my sister's delicate condition," he said, with a smile at Nicolette to further intimidate her.

Nicolette turned and followed the others. She knew that Herbert would report whatever Henri intended to say.

Henri waited with Herbert until the room was empty. "Herbert. I wish you to keep my sisters in view at all times. I also wish you to remain with them, despite Sire Eustace's instructions. I cannot say why, only that you will be handsomely rewarded. Do you trust my word?"

Herbert grinned. "Implicitly."

Henri clapped him on the back. "Good. You are the one man I trust fully, Herbert. Also, should Sire Matthew Tregere be at the castle—and I expect that he will be readying to leave just as you arrive—I want you to make certain that Nicolette does *not* speak with him in private. As I said, you shall be handsomely rewarded."

"Your word is my command," Herbert answered.

As always he took orders without question. Henri smiled sanguinely. "Although we shall miss you, methinks the plans of defense and counterattack you have drawn up should see us through the siege which we will combat most effectively. Baron Harcourt will rue the day he decided to attack St. Aliquis. He will be forced to pay us a large fief as part of his surrender. I promise that you will profit handsomely from it. I think specifically of his small castle near Bar-sur-Aube. That shall be your gift if you desire it?"

"I do desire it, Henri. I thank you with sincere gratitude." Herbert heartily slapped Henri's slight back and with a chuckle turned to the door.

Simone, who had returned to her lady's chamber sometime during her lady's absence, had been roused from her bed and now helped her pack. Lorraine and Suzette, two of her maids, helped Bruge as well. Nicolette forced herself not to glance excessively at Simone in fear that the stout maiden would report such back to Henri.

After her shock diminished, Nicolette had been furious at Simone's betrayal. But soon her anger turned to pity. For Nicolette understood that Henri had indeed enlisted Simone's aid in preventing Matthew from receiving her first letter. Most likely Henri had attacked Simone only to perfect his scheme. How ruthlessly clever Henri had been, for she had shouldered the guilt for Simone's beating just as Henri expected her to do, never dreaming that Simone had betrayed her. But pity had replaced her rage when she realized the stout, clumsy, insecure girl acted only out of love. She did not doubt that Henri had fed Simone a story that led her to believe she was acting in Nicolette's best interests, for Nicolette clearly remembered that Henri had insisted upon the exact words she say to Simone when Henri held her captive in her own chamber.

"Nicolette," Bruge called. "Shall I take my green bliaut as well as my purple? What about the red? And do we need our fur-lined mantles, for it is so very hot these days but still, the weather could become damp and rainy? And what about my gold slippers?"

Nicolette refrained from laughing. "We are not attending a wedding nor a tourney where you will present your sleeve or scarf to a knight on his fine white destrier, Bruge. It is but a quiet visit to a mourning family. Bring your simplest clothing. And do take your warm mantle, for as you say the weather could turn, or I am afraid to say that if Baron Harcourt's men attack we might be forced to remain at St. Martin's longer than the men optimistically anticipate."

"You are correct, Nicolette . . . though the thought of being away from home for long saddens me . . ."

Nicolette knew once again that she had been wise in allowing Bruge to believe the story they fed Henri. For in part, it had been Bruge's innocent countenance that Henri so carefully scrutinized, just as she'd expected, that seemed to convince him that the demand to leave suddenly for St. Martin had originated from Alienor's grief rather than from her own scheme. Only when they were safe within the castle walls of St. Martin and Matthew had agreed to ride them to Davide would she expose the painful truths to Bruge. Even now, Henri still played his hand close to his chest, Nicolette knew. She had no doubt that he had sought to make Herbert his guard *in absentia*. Henri had made the fatal mistake of thinking himself too clever to be foiled, thank Mother Mary for his excessive pride!

"All your raiments are packed, my lady," Simone said.

Nicolette had almost forgotten what she meant to say to Simone that would surely be reported to Henri. "Simone, I have been thinking. Methinks you should ride with us, for I will miss you dearly. Also, I would feel more assured of your safety, if you understand what I mean," she said, causing Simone's smile to turn to a blush. Of guilt? Nicolette wondered.

"My lady, that is so kind and I too shall miss you. But"—her hands flung in a helpless, embarrassed gesture—"I am not an able rider like the rest of you and I should slow you down. I am afraid that my weight would slow my horse as well even if I knew how to ride a roan." Simone blushed as Bruge and the maids giggled in response.

"Bruge, maids!" Nicolette said sharply. "You are being cruel and I won't have it. Some people are born to be slender and others stout, Simone. That does not alter the kindness of your heart nor your worth. Some men find a well-fleshed maiden most attractive, Bruge, as you well know." Nicolette took in Simone's agreeing smile of what she believed to be true. Nicolette felt only sympathy for the poor maiden who would soon be cruelly abandoned.

Bruge approached and kissed Simone on her cheek. "I apologize, Simone. I was unkind and foolish. You have a most pretty face and lovely red hair, and I am certain many men will fight to win your hand one day."

I only hope that a better man than Henri will do so,

Simone, Nicolette thought. "Bruge is most correct, Simone."

Simone smiled but then her eyes filled with tears. "My lady," she began and Nicolette instantly feared that she intended to confess, which would prove terribly detrimental. She had to stop her. "There is something I must tell you before—"

"Simone." Nicolette stopped her with seeming insensitivity. "There is no time for chatter, for we must leave as quickly as—" Thank the Lord for the knock upon her door. "Please answer the door, Simone." Simone hesitated but then turned away and walked to the door.

"My lady is packed and ready," Denise said, dressed as well in her boots and with her mantle clasped at her shoulder with a ruby brooch.

"We shall be there in a minute, pray tell Alienor," Nicolette answered as she allowed Simone to help her with her mantle. Nicolette turned to see Bruge's progress. Bruge was attempting to stuff something into her large purse. "What is that, Bruge?" Nicolette asked.

"'Tis nothing," Bruge answered quickly.

Nicolette started toward her. "You seem to be having much difficulty stuffing nothing into your purse," she retorted. Nicolette didn't know whether to laugh or cry when she saw that it was Bruge's oldest rag doll. The doll Father had given to her for a birthday and with which she had slept every night since.

"She doesn't take much room, Nicolette," Bruge said with a pleading embarrassment.

"I suppose not," Nicolette said and kissed Bruge's

forehead. Bruge was as much a child as a maiden, she thought again. To think of Henri's vile threats to her innocent sister—he would never see Bruge again, Nicolette vowed.

"Are you angry with me, Nicolette?" Bruge asked. "For you have a most disagreeable expression upon your face," she said anxiously.

"I love you dearly, my little sister. I could never be truly angry with you." Nicolette looked at the doll, Babette, whose head rose from the purse. "I am glad you are taking Babette along. For I should miss the sight of her upon your bed as well. Let us leave now."

Bruge hugged her and gave her a sweet, loving kiss. Then she started for the door. Nicolette, the last from the room, stood at the door for a moment, gazing at the chamber that had brought her nothing but grief and humiliation. She was relieved that she would never set eyes upon it again!

Chapter Ten

A PARTY OF FOUR LADIES UPON ROANS WITH A KNIGHT AT the lead and a squire in the rear rode unimpeded through the darkness of night which was beginning to dissolve into a misty gray predawn. A cool wind had risen and the air felt heavy with the portent of rain but Nicolette did not mind. Each league they traveled brought them closer to safety. Still she fought back her weariness, for her lack of sleep leadened her eyes despite her rising spirits. Although she had traveled these roads many a time with Alienor, she had never done so in the dead of night and Nicolette found the transformation most enticing, each grouping of ordinary trees disguised as creatures in strange shadow.

Bruge, who rode as close to her side as possible,

was unnerved, certain as she had earlier insisted, that fairies and evil spirits lurked at each turn in the road, eager to trick them or worse yet do them harm. Nicolette had not been able to persuade her otherwise and soon stopped trying. *I wish you could know that we are gaining our freedom from those who* truly *wish to do us harm,* Nicolette thought. *Then perhaps the spirit world illuminated in your imagination would not frighten you so.*

"I am going to ride ahead to Sire Herbert, Bruge. For I wish to know when he thinks we should arrive at St. Martin. Why do you not hang back and ride with Gervais for a time?" she said, knowing Bruge would have no objection to her suggestion. Nicolette brought her horse to a gallop and soon rode closely at Herbert's side. They were far enough ahead of the others now that she could speak freely without worry of being overheard.

"Another hour, my lady," Herbert said with a warm smile. "We travel more slowly than by daylight to ensure everyone's safety."

"Aye. I know. I wanted to ask you where you have hidden the suits of armor."

Herbert laughed good-humoredly. "Nicolette, 'tis not possible to pack chainmail suits and helmets in the leather bags that contain your raiments and supplies."

"I know so, Sire," Nicolette responded, slightly abashed that he should think her so foolish as to think otherwise. "'Tis why I ask."

"I am sorry, I did not mean to laugh at you. 'Tis a good question, for once Gervais and I devised our plan we could not find a private moment to tell you.

SONG OF THE ROSE

During the confusion of the farewell, when Henri, Sire Eustace, and most of the others watched our departure from the front gate of the castle, I had Robert, one of the few remaining knights at St. Aliquis who I can depend upon, ride with his brother Gregoire through the back gate in full armor. The guards thought nothing of it, I am certain, for since we expect imminent attack from Harcourt, our knights have been patrolling through the wee hours."

"I am sorry. Perhaps my mind is addled but I do not understand."

"Nor would I expect you to. Robert and Gregoire will be awaiting us at St. Martin. Gervais and I have arranged to meet them and present them with ordinary raiments. Not only are Robert and his brother trustworthy, but they are small statured, which means that should you insist upon riding with Sire Matthew, their suits should fit you and Bruge with a bit of tailoring, methinks. I take it you have never had the pleasure of putting on a full coat of armor?" he asked in a playful manner.

Nicolette laughed in response. "No, I have not. Are they terribly uncomfortable?"

"More than uncomfortable at first. And quite heavy. A good thirty-five pounds or so, and that does not account for carrying the shield or wearing your sword and mace at your girdle. 'Tis one of the reasons it takes so long to turn a squire into a competent knight. Perhaps you may wish to rethink that part of your plan, Nicolette?"

"Perhaps." He had given her reason for consideration. Not so much for herself as for Bruge, who would be wearing armor a third of her weight. Nor could the unaccustomed strain be good for her babe, Nicolette thought. She would seek Matthew's advice. Perchance he would know some safe castle, hamlet, or even one of the growing new towns like Troyes, where he could ensure their safekeeping until he notified Davide as to their whereabouts and circumstances.

"Do not frown so, Nicolette. It shall mar your pretty face," Herbert teased, causing her to laugh. "Nicolette, you have the quick instincts and courage that mark the finest of knights. For in battle, wit is as important as might—sometimes moreso. All will go well. I have grown weary of tolerating such pompous fools as Henri and François before him. The baron, may he rest in peace, though I doubt it, was a scoundrel but at least he had wit and charm to compensate . . . especially in his prime. I was a fairly young knight but I remember clearly.

"After my father died, while I was in battle, the baron rewed my mother to a comfortable and kind count. She lived the rest of her years more happily than she ever had before. For that I owed my allegiance to the baron, and loyal I remained, despite everything—even François and worse your insufferable brother. But the baron is gone and I've got a yearning to see one more bloody battle before I die. So, if you'll have me with you, I'll not let you out of my sight until I see you safe in your lover's arms. What be his name?"

"Davide . . ." Nicolette's eyes filled with tears as she stared at the usually laconic knight who offered his friendship and protection. She knew that if she became effusive she would only embarrass Herbert de Leon. "I would be most honored to accept your friendship and offer of protection. I am most grateful that you are able to see that Bruge and I are not like our stepbrother, Henri . . ."

"Aye, that Bruge is a sweet little thing. She reminds me of a little sister I had—she's been dead for years—died in childbirth, like your own mother I understand. Caron was her name. Prettiest little thing . . . Perchance I should not speak so, but when Gervais told me of your stepbrother's threats to the little one I could have verily cut his throat as easily as spit upon him. I am most anxious to—now I speak out of turn for certain"—Herbert grinned—"for I have forgotten the proper way to converse with a lady, I fear, but never the mind."

"Pray tell!" Nicolette teased, enjoying Herbert immensely.

"No. For I fear you will take my words in the wrong manner and believe I insult you."

"I could never believe such, now." She gave him a gentle smile.

"Remember your words, Nicolette—I should be calling you Lady Nicolette, but I still remember you more as a child when you first arrived than a woman."

"Please do not call me by a title that was forced upon me. You remind me some of my father, Sire Herbert—"

"Herbert," he corrected. "'Tis a high compliment. I fought with your father. He was a fine man. A proud, gallant, virtuous knight."

"Thank you, but you are avoiding speaking what you began and then halted."

SONG OF THE ROSE

Herbert grinned at her. "I began to say that I am most curious to meet this Davide of yours. To win the love and passion of such a reverent and virtuous maid as you—do not doubt that *many* a young knight confessed to the others of his failed attempts to win a simple kiss from you." Herbert chuckled again. "Your Davide must be quite a splendid man."

"Aye, he is the most handsome, tender, and witty man I have ever met!" Nicolette stopped her gushing, suddenly feeling shy to speak so openly of Davide who had lovingly beseeched her to tell no one of his existence. But he had no way to know what had befallen her. Surely he would approve of her actions tonight. Nicolette knew that Davide would be as fond of Herbert as she was quickly becoming.

It happened so frightfully quickly. Hoofs clapped, dust flew, horses whinnied and neighed, voices shouted! Nicolette reined her frightened roan. In the darkness of blowing dirt and night she pulled her dagger from its scabbard. She could see nothing but rapidly moving shadows and heard clanking of steel sword upon sword. A scream from behind sounded like Alienor—or was it Denise? Then she heard another and felt the cold metal of mail as a huge arm tried to pull her from her horse. She stabbed at the hand with her dagger and felt it sink into something soft. A cry that sounded like a cat's howl blared as her horse neighed and reared. "Ride, ladies!" Herbert shouted above the clamor. "Ride hard and don't turn back!"

Another horse approached. She readied her dagger.

SONG OF THE ROSE

"Nicolette!" came Bruge's cry just as Nicolette was about to stab at the shadowy figure.

"Dear God!" Nicolette cried out. There was no time to contemplate what she had almost done.

"Ride, ladies!" came the hoarse shout of Herbert's above the clinking of steel and the dull thuds of mace clubs.

"Alienor! Denise! Ride onward!" Nicolette screamed behind her. She and Bruge galloped hard with the skill their father had helped them perfect.

They galloped down the rutted road for a good league until Bruge cried out, "We've got to stop, Nicolette! My arm pains me so!"

"Just a bit farther," Nicolette pleaded. It had been some time since the pounding hoofs behind them silenced. She and Bruge rode as fast as lightning. The rising dawn slowly transformed the blurred shadows into trees and bushes. They galloped on for another five or ten minutes. Bruge cried but kept pace. "We can slow the roans now, methinks," Nicolette called and they slowed to a canter and then to a trot.

Nicolette saw a cluster of beech trees at the right-hand side of the curve in the road. "In there," she pointed. "We may stop and hide here . . ." They guided their horses carefully down the shallow ditch and up into the patch of trees. Nicolette felt a sharp pain in her stomach but ignored it as she dismounted. Her knees buckled when she stood upon the grassy earth. "We must tie the horses over there," she ordered. Slowly they walked their panting horses to the trees at the bottom of the sloping mound that they had not seen from the road. The horses secure, Nicolette clutched Bruge tightly in her arms. They sank onto the damp grass.

At first Nicolette thought Bruge's shoulder wet. But how could it— With horror she looked closely. She smelled the blood. "Oh dear God! Bruge, you are wounded!"

Bruge fought back her hysteria, Nicolette saw. "I thought so . . . I felt something rip at my mantle and it pained but at first it was a cold, strange sensation. What happened, Nicolette? Where are the others?"

Nicolette worked quickly. She pulled off Bruge's mantle and ripped the sleeve of her bliaut and pelisson away. She shuddered but forced herself not to cry out as she saw the deep bloody cut on the back of Bruge's upper arm. Mercifully Bruge was but able to see the part of her white skin that had only been grazed. Quickly Nicolette reached beneath her shirts and ripped off a section of her chemise. She carefully poured some of the water from her flask onto the cloth and washed the caked blood off the still-bleeding wound.

"Who were those terrible men?" Bruge demanded, her voice sharp with fear. "Where are the others?"

"I do not know any more than you. Sit very still for a moment!" Nicolette raced to her resting horse and found the roll of fresh cloth. Little had she dreamed that she would have to minister to her wounded sister. She ran back and poured more water onto a rag.

Bruge uttered only a small cry as she began to swoon from the pain. Nicolette caught her and rested her sister in her lap. Bruge quaked as Nicolette worked as quickly as she could. Nicolette tied the last of the cloth tightly around her sister's arm, careful not to stop the flow of her blood through her veins. "'Tis finished . . ." Nicolette said, fighting back her own tears.

Bruge lay sobbing in her arms and Nicolette wished to release her own tears but she dared not. "Bruge . . . you must stop weeping. Later you will have time to cry. Pray try to calm yourself. We are safe and your wound, though it hurts, is not dangerous. I have tended it well. We must keep our wits. You must rest here while I hide behind a tree off the road, for I must watch for the others—"

"Do not leave me, Nicolette," Bruge pleaded as she tried to quiet her sobs.

"I will not." Nicolette pointed to a cluster of trees rising up the mound at the edge of the road. "I shall hide there. You will be able to see me and speak to me every moment." Nicolette rose. Again she felt the sharp stab of pain in her belly. Pray Mother Mary, keep my babe safe, she prayed. She walked to Bruge's horse and rummaged through a leather bag until she found what she looked for. Nicolette removed Bruge's doll from the bag. While Nicolette had made light of Bruge's stab wound so as to not terrify her further, she was sickened by the jagged, raw cut. Babette should bring her some small comfort.

"Babette is frightened all alone," she bantered with difficulty. She handed the doll to Bruge. "Methinks she needs comforting as much as we." Nicolette kissed her sister's dusty forehead and crept toward the trees by the road. She kneeled in waiting.

* * *

SONG OF THE ROSE

She watched the dawn swallow the last of the night . . . Had she heard her name being called? 'Twas just her imagination? Then she saw the mounted figure and heard her name again. "Bruge! Nicolette!" She recognized Gervais' voice before his figure became clear to her eyes.

Nicolette scrambled up to the edge of the road. "Here, Gervais! We are here!" she cried. Quickly he rode to her, jumped off his horse, and embraced her. How good it felt, despite the dampness of the steel links of his chainmail hauberk.

"Bruge!" he said with alarm. "Where is she?"

"She is right there." Nicolette pointed to the figure of her sister curled upon her mantle. Bruge lay still in exhausted sleep.

Gervais removed his helmet. His face was white with alarm. "She is not—"

"No, Gervais. She sleeps. She was cut badly. A long, deep, jagged slash from the back of her upper arm to the front. I ministered to it but she must be tended by a physician. She is more in shock than pain and I think it best if she does not know the extent of her wound."

"Aye. You are correct, Nicolette. We must ride her to St. Martin's as quickly as possible. Do you fear the wound might fester?"

"I do. Where is Alienor and the others? Are they safe? Who attacked us?" The strain on Gervais' face and the cloud in his narrowed eyes forced her to prepare for the worst.

"Sit down and I shall tell you all I know . . . There were six men. Two knights and four men-at-arms.

They carried Harcourt's shield. I can only guess that spies somehow told them of our leave from St. Aliquis. Sire Herbert is—he is dead."

Nicolette covered her mouth to drown her cry of despair.

"He fought valiantly. I was knocked from the road and my destrier rode off quite smartly. I ran back into the fray and one of the knights hit me hard upon the shoulder with his mace club. He was about to run his sword across my throat when two of his comrades called to him. Herbert slew one of the men and was fighting two of the others. Two held Alienor and Denise captive. The knight who intended to kill me took a blind stab and thought he left me for dead. He went to the aid of the other two. It took the three to finally still Sire Herbert de Leon." Tears filled Gervais' eyes and his voice choked but he went on. "Immediately, the knight who had tried to kill me was sent to ride after you and Bruge. The others assumed he had already killed me. One walked by me as I lay at the edge of the road. I closed my eyes and pretended I was dead. He kicked me with his boot but I forced myself to neither cry out nor move though the pain wracked me. Satisfied, he walked back to the other men who held Alienor and Denise. Denise cried but Alienor remained proudly silent despite her fear—I could see clearly for they were but feet from me."

"They didn't harm—" Nicolette forced the words.

"No. They were very courteous, actually. They identified themselves and told the maidens not to fear. One man searched their satchels until he found their parchments of safe conduct identifying first Alienor and then Denise. The knight explained that they would be taken back to Harcourt's castle and held for ransom. He said that they would come to no harm as long as they obeyed and tried no trickery. The knight took Sire Herbert's destrier and with the extra horse they rode the maidens down the road from whence we came."

"How did you finally reach us, for you ride your destrier, do you not?" Nicolette found her mind refusing to comprehend all he told her.

"Aye. I rolled down the slope and hid behind some bushes. I knew I could do nothing but wait until I assessed the situation. I was confident that the knight should not have caught up with you and Bruge. For I have ridden with Bruge and she is as agile and swift a rider as any maiden I have ever seen. She told me that you were even a better rider—if that were possible—and that your father had taught both of you to ride bareback in the country village where you had lived. . . . I decided to wait until I saw the knight returning to catch his party, which I was certain he would do. Or if the worst had occurred he would be riding with both of you in captive. I planned to surprise him on foot, for I still had my sword and shield and easily found my mace."

"How did you regain your horse?"

Gervais laughed and his face registered the pain he had thus denied. "My destrier proved as loyal as the finest comrade, for he soon trotted across the field, whinnying gently. He is a fine horse! Soon after, I heard the gallop of hoofs and from my hiding place I saw the knight riding singularly, thank the Lord, down the road. He rode hard—I assume to inform the others that he had not caught up with you. I waited a few minutes more. Then I rode, calling your names until I found you. I passed two peasants but neither man had seen nor heard anyone. I guessed that you had wisely hid."

"Gervais, I am so worried! But we must ride on to St. Martin's. There we can have men sent to retrieve Sire Herbert's body—" Nicolette sobbed in mourning for the knight who had been such a loyal friend. "We cannot tarry for Bruge's wound must be seen by the Brouilleaux's physician. I must be as brave as the most valiant knight . . ." Nicolette wiped her tears away.

"You already are, my lady," Gervais said as he helped her rise. They walked quietly to the sleeping Bruge so as not to startle her. Nicolette kneeled beside her sister and kissed her awake. Gervais stood behind, so as not to frighten the sleeping maiden.

"Bruge . . . you must wake. We are safe. Gervais is with us!"

Bruge rose and grimaced with pain. "Gervais? Where? Where are the others?"

"I am here, my sweet Bruge," Gervais said as he kneeled before her and took her into his arms. He glanced at Nicolette and she smiled silent approval. Gently he kissed her lips. "I will ride you on my destrier and Nicolette will be right at your side . . ." He stroked her hair as she began to cry. "You shall be fine. We are safe . . . try to calm yourself, Bruge. I love you so that it crushes my heart to see you in such pain."

The shy youth has become a man, Nicolette thought, as she wiped her own tears from her eyes.

SONG OF THE ROSE

"I love you too . . ." Bruge said between sobs. "But you *must* tell me where the others are."

Gervais looked at Nicolette. She nodded. As Gervais gently began to repeat the story Nicolette mourned as she watched the horror rip through Bruge more painfully than the sword had cut her tender flesh. Nicolette knew this was not the final hurt she would have to endure before the sun had set. For once they were safe within the castle chambers of St. Martin, Nicolette would have to tell Bruge the rest. Oh, Davide, she thought, shall this nightmare ever be over?

Nicolette kneeled and crossed herself as she began to pray to Jesus and Mother Mary to protect Alienor and Denise as well as the three of them. She prayed for Sire Herbert's soul and knew that he was at peace in Heaven. The sharp pain in her stomach assaulted her again and she prayed that Mother Mary watch over the babe she carried. Nicolette crossed herself again and wearily rose.

Gervais had finished speaking. "We must ride now," Nicolette said, mustering all the determination she could find. They had to reach St. Martin before Matthew departed! She would not allow the fear that he had already left consume her. She could not. She turned from Bruge and Gervais so that they would not witness her grimace as another sharp pain struck her.

Chapter Eleven

THE CASTLE OF ST. MARTIN LAY AT THE JUNCTION OF two rivers. The smaller of these tumbled down from the hills, cutting a gorge through the dense beech forest until it ran beneath a precipitous slope, then dashed into the greater, more placid current of the Loire. At the triangle formed by the converging streams rose an abrupt plateau practically inaccessible from the banks of either river. It could be approached only from the third side, where the land sloped gently. Here rose some jagged crags marking out the place as a natural fortress, Nicolette thought.

They approached the castle as the morning mists were lifting from the rivers. Nicolette saw through the dispersing fog the mass of towers, walls, and battlements of gray and brown. Here and there she saw a bit of green, for where a little earth had been allowed to lodge a few weeds shot forth. High above all soared the mass of the great central tower, the *donjon*, from the summit of which Baron Brouilleaux's orange banner now idly trailed.

They rode down the road that took them over the tollbridge across the Loire past the exercise ground where last spring's tournament had been held. Today they passed but a few knights practicing martial exercises. The road was filled with many peasants from the village they had earlier passed just west of the river. A prior on a mule bid them greetings as they quickly passed him. Soon they approached the barbican—the high sharply pointed palisade almost identical to that of St. Aliquis. In fact, except for the arrangement of the palais and chapel, St. Martin was close to a duplicate of St. Aliquis.

A whole crowd of folk were waiting for entrance through the heavy wooden barrier of the main gate being thrown open by a rather sleepy porter. He checked their parchments of safe conduct and waved them through, though he required others to leave their weapons in his custody. They proceeded onward to the inner gate and Gervais rang loudly on the heavy metal gong hanging there. In but a minute a squire appeared. Gervais identified himself and his ladies. The squire welcomed them and sent another squire to summon Messire Brouilleaux to greet them. Then he helped Nicolette dismount while Gervais lifted Bruge from his destrier and carried her in his arms as the squire quickly led them to the great hall.

Bruge, whose pain had worsened, cried and rubbed her reddened and swollen eyes. "We are safe now,

Sister," Nicolette said, trying to comfort her. Baron and Baroness Brouilleaux hurried into the hall, Marguerite, Guy's sister, right behind. Their orders flew so rapidly and Nicolette was so heartsick and in such secret dizzying pain, that one moment it seemed that they were seated in the great hall and the next they lay in a chamber, she and Bruge, as the physician ministered to Bruge's wound.

A maid was washing Nicolette when such a sharp pain jolted her that even clamping her lips could not stop her cry. Marguerite rushed to her side.

"What ails thee, Nicolette?" she asked. "You are as pale as death, beneath the grime of the road."

"'Tis my babe, I fear," Nicolette cried, giving vent at last to her pain and fear. She forced herself to speak, realizing that Marguerite could not yet know that she carried a child. She clutched Marguerite's hand as another pain cut through her and slowly the room went dark. She could not faint. Not now. "Matthew," she whispered through the darkness. "Sire Matthew . . ."

"He rode before dawn, Nicolette."

He was gone? . . . He could not be gone. "He cannot . . . I must . . ." Nicolette's words were lost in another stab of pain and suddenly she was floating away.

"'Tis what time?" Nicolette whispered weakly as the blurred figures around her became more clear. "Where is Bruge? Gervais? I must speak with Matthew at once . . ."

"My dear, you must rest. You have been ill," the woman said in a kind tone. At first Nicolette did not recognize her but as the fog that filled her mind lifted she knew it was Baroness Brouilleaux who held her hand.

"My lady," Nicolette insisted despite the great difficulty she had in uttering the words. Her mouth was dry and her tongue felt swollen. "I must speak to Matthew. 'Tis imperative. I must speak to him before he takes leave for Acre." Nicolette glanced from the baroness to Marguerite, who sat beside her. She turned and saw two maids, but she knew neither by face. Where was her sister? Had someone fixed her wound? It was such a jagged, deep cut! Had Bruge not been lying on a feather bed beside her? "Bruge, why is she not here?" Nicolette asked with increasing alarm.

"There, there, Nicolette. You are still confused by the fever," the baroness said as she patted her hand.

The pretty maid laid a cool cloth upon her forehead. 'Twas so warm in the chamber; the coolness of the cloth so soothed that Nicolette closed her eyes for a moment. She was weary. She wished to sleep. Just a short rest and she would come to herself again, she thought . . .

The chirping of the black birds outside her window woke her. The sun poured through the windows of her room with uncharacteristic brightness. "Simone?" she called and turned toward Bruge's bed. She cried out as the pain shot through her. Suddenly two maids ran to her. Two maids she had never seen. Why were they in her chamber? Her eyes darted across the room, taking it in. This was not her chamber, nor Alienor's. Where was she? "Bruge!" she cried out.

"Fetch the baroness and the physician, Daphne," the fairer maid called to the other.

The baroness? . . . She remembered. They had arrived at St. Martin just past dawn. She'd been resting upon this bed when the knifelike pains increased. Yet it was morning—no, it had been gray and dark and now the sun shone. She must have slept through the day. "Pray tell me what day 'tis?" she asked the maid at her bedside.

"Friday, my lady," the maid answered.

"Friday? That cannot be. 'Twas Tuesday morn that we arrived. It must be Wednesday," Nicolette insisted.

"No, my lady. You were fevered for days. 'Tis why you are confused."

Friday . . . memories, like fragments of dreams, fluttered through her mind. Much blood—Bruge's wound—but more . . . Herself. She had bled. The babe—she had bled from the babe. A short, bald man with a soft voice. He had told her she might lose her child. She remembered burning and freezing at the same time. And so terrible the pain. Carefully she touched her belly, finding it tender to her fingertips. Did the babe still grow inside her? Where was Bruge? And Gervais? Where was Sire Herbert? Men on horses in the night—clanking of steel and screams . . . The face of the maid blurred as memory flooded her. Sire Herbert was dead!

"Nicolette, my dear." The baroness kissed her upon her forehead, then took her hand. "You are better, now, my child." The baroness's smile reminded her of her mother's smiling eyes. How blessed Alienor was to have found another mother—Alienor!

The last pieces of her lost memory fit themselves into place. "Alienor! Is she here? Have they brought her home?" Nicolette asked anxiously. So much she needed to know.

"I shall answer all your questions. Sire Gerson, our physician, said you would awake befuddled. Your fever was so high." The baroness felt her forehead. "You are much cooler now. 'Tis an answer to our prayers. Bruge prays now for you in the chapel. You did not lose your child, though you lost much blood. Sire Gerson tended you night and day. There, there, do not weep. You must save your strength," the baroness soothed.

"Alienor?" Nicolette watched Baroness Brouilleaux's face darken.

"She and her maiden are still held by the truculent Baron Harcourt. We received a message from your brother, Henri, yesterday that leaves us sanguine. Though St. Aliquis is besieged by Harcourt's men, they already negotiate for Alienor's release. Thus far, we are told, Harcourt's men have not been able to penetrate St. Aliquis. The archbishop has intervened in the count's name. By the by, we learned that our Crusaders took the city of Acre a few weeks ago and move now toward the Holy City."

"Sire Guy? His body?" Nicolette asked and saw the baroness's face age before her eyes.

"My son should be returned to us by the start of the new week. I pray that Alienor will be freed in time to see him laid to rest. Alienor is like a daughter to me . . ." She wiped her eyes with a green scarf. "But there is more I must tell, to rest your mind," she continued.

"Bruge's arm pains her but less so each day. It heals cleanly and in a few weeks the fillets that bind it should be removed. Fortunately 'twas her left arm, so she gets about with less trouble than she might otherwise. She has been a brave maiden, though she has been sick to death with worry for you. When she returns from chapel she will be thrilled to see you awake and alert. She loves you dearly!"

"And I her! . . . Gervais?"

The baroness smiled and her eyes twinkled with laughter. "He stays by her side like a shadow. They remind me of Guy and Alienor a few years past." She smiled. "A pair of lovebirds, verily." Her eyes darkened. "'Tis not for us to question the Lord's ways . . .

"I have news that should cheer you greatly," the baroness continued. "Soon after your arrival the other morning, we sent a knight to find Sire Matthew. He did so. Sire Matthew will carry the news to François that you and Bruge will remain at St. Martin's until his return. Our knight told Matthew of the baron's death, so François should be returning within weeks. I do not fathom that the war between Harcourt and St. Aliquis will continue that long. I'm certain François will be much heartened when he learns you carry his child and are safe with us, do you not agree?"

'Twas all over . . . François would return and she would be held captive once again. Of course Henri had made certain that François be told of her babe . . . She had not been able to reach Matthew. Oh, Davide, her heart cried out, I pray you know the falseness of the letter he carries to you! Even free of Henri's undaunting vigilance she could not send another, for to whom could she address it? Did she dare confide the truth to the baroness? She could not risk doing so, for without Alienor to corroborate her story, the baroness might doubt her. She would have to discover where Robert and the other men had hidden their suits of armor. But even then how would she carry forth her plan? They knew not where to find Davide now. Bruge would be lame for weeks and she had almost lost her babe—

"Nicolette?" the baroness said. "You seem so far away. Are you drifting from us again?"

"No, my lady. I was lost in thought," she replied, trying to force a smile. "For there is so much you have told me, and—"

"Good! Finally my patient is awake. I see a hint of color returns to your cheeks, my lady," the physician said. "May I introduce myself, for I fear hitherto I was little more than part of a ghostly dream to you." His bright smile matched his lively speech, so different in disposition was he from her physician, Sire Foretverte. "I am Sire Gerson." Nicolette returned his smile the best she could. "I should like to check you once again, my lady." He felt her head and took her pulse. His smile broadened. He gently explored her belly. "Bring the chamberpot," he ordered the maid. "I want to be certain that your bleeding has stopped, my lady."

Nicolette felt a sudden shyness overcome her. She sternly reminded herself that she was not a maiden and that the physician was interested only in her health and the welfare of her babe. She submitted and quickly 'twas over.

"Good!" Sire Gerson exclaimed. "I believe the

babe is well. But you must remain in bed for at least three weeks. I implore you that your delicate feet must not even *touch* the ground during this time, Nicolette."

"But I cannot—"

"If you want to birth a live child, you can do nothing other than what I say," he stated severely, his good humor tempered by her resistance. "You will remain with us till the babe comes."

"Aye, Sire . . ." she weakly replied.

"Nicolette?" Bruge, her left arm and shoulder swathed, called, as she came to her side. "You are awake finally! Oh Nicolette, my prayers have been answered!" Bruge showered her with kisses and clumsy hugs.

Nicolette's heart filled as she brushed her sister's tears away. "I am well. So is the babe." There was a bruise on Bruge's forehead that Nicolette had not noticed before. But then, her sister had been covered in grime. "And you look well, though you remind me of the little sparrow with the broken wing you mended a few summers past."

"Oh, Nicolette! When I first looked upon myself I thought much the same thing," she said and they fell into soft laughter at the happy memory. For a moment Nicolette was spared from her worry of the future.

Chapter Twelve

"'Tis unjust, I declare!" Bernard, a knight of St. Aliquis, drunkenly bellowed at Pierre Delise. "François prepares to return to St. Aliquis with his lapdog, Michel," the knight spat out, "leaving the rest of us to rot on this desert. Or to have our throats slit by Saladin's warriors."

"Aye, he speaks rightly," added Alain. "François' hands remain as soft and lily white as a lad's while I will have to plow my fields with this." He waved the stump that had once been a strong hand at them.

"Truly François is a mewling coward, we all know," Samson interjected more quietly. "But 'tis right that he leave, for with the baron dead and St. Aliquis under siege—"

"François will not command his men. Hitherto Sire

SONG OF THE ROSE

Herbert de Leon, may his valiant soul rest in peace, commanded us in fact, if not in name. He and the honorable Sire Eustace. 'Tis only due to his sister's marriage that the shifty, pernicious Henri wormed his way into the position. Though my heart goes out to Lady Nicolette. She is a fine maiden. So beautiful and gentle a soul," Bernard said in a softened voice. "To think the poor maiden was forced to bed and, worse yet, wed François. I have a daughter but a few years younger than she."

"Do you say you would not have wed your daughter to François had he wanted her? Made her a wealthy baroness, living in the splendor—" Alain taunted Bernard.

"I should never make my daughter into a whore!" Bernard hotly declared. "Rather she live simply but happily! Do you gainsay me?"

"I gainsay! You would have sold your daughter for a large fief and easy days the rest of your life!" Alain yelled. He dipped his flagon into the steaming caldron of heated wine and downed the contents quickly.

Bernard rose to his feet drunkenly. He pulled his sword from his scabbard. "Retract or I shall be forced to slay you!" he bellowed as he stood in an unsteady open-legged stance.

Alain had risen and stood likewise. "I shall not retract!"

Pierre jumped up, kicked the pail of wine away, and stood between them. The six or seven other knights, all of whom had been sitting around the bonfire amiably just moments before, chose sides. Only Matthew came to Pierre's aid. "My dear friends! The drink and the irritation of these long weeks of battle have gone to your heads. Is it not enough that Saladin's warriors disfigure and kill us, King Philip Augustus' loyal lieges? Need you thin our ranks further with this foolishness?" Matthew asked.

"Put down your swords, my good friends," Pierre added. "For if you should duel and Bernard should fall, who would entertain us with stories of the glories of past battles?"

Despite himself, Bernard smiled reluctantly, Pierre saw. "If it were Alain who fell, who would have us roaring with laughter at his ribald stories of fine wenching and carousing?" Pierre continued.

"A toast to my comrades: Bernard and Alain. Alain and Bernard!" Matthew raised his flask.

Quickly Alain and Bernard held flagons high as well. They toasted and sat peacefully upon the ground once again. Pierre gave Matthew a quick wink. Matthew smiled knowingly.

"Did I ever tell you men of the time when I was a young knight sent to Provence to deliver a letter to lady . . . eh, what was the wench's name?" Alain began.

Pierre strode across the white desert sands. He had been walking for a good half hour. He had left the carousing group at the bonfire with no need for explanation. By now his friends accepted his nightly solitary walks as they accepted his reticence in speaking of his own life. Less easily did they understand his friendship with François and his protection of their lord. Alain declared, good-naturedly, that Pierre was far more Christlike than his greedy bishop and wenching abbot. Pierre laughingly assured him that he was far from a saint, as many a damsel in Champagne could attest. His remark and much backslapping appeased Alain who had not raised the subject again.

Pierre's smile at the remembrance faded when he thought once again of his plight. For weeks he tried to decide the best course of action. He was stunned at first by the letter from Nicolette. He had read it through three times before his wit cut through his shock. How slow he had been, missing the allusions to "the long weeks of their love" that ran through the brief note claiming she neither loved him, nor ever wished to see him again, that told him she was carrying her husband's child. Mercifully his torture had been as brief as it was wracking. Nicolette had managed to tell him all she could not write.

Later that night, Pierre had taken Matthew into his confidence. He questioned Matthew slowly and methodically, helping the willing Matthew to recollect each action, each particle of information, each expression on Nicolette's pure face, each intonation of voice.

Between them they had pieced the probable events together. Somehow Henri had discovered his letter to Nicolette. From what Matthew reported as to the lateness of his receiving Nicolette's response, the nervous condition of her maiden—who Matthew said most definitely wore the imprint of a harsh slap upon her cheek—Nicolette had indeed answered his letter, which Henri somehow intercepted. This accounted for the maiden's condition and the lateness of the reply. Henri somehow forced Nicolette to write what he wished her to say. As quick in wit as she was pure in heart, Nicolette managed to satisfy Henri and still let Pierre know that not only was her disavowal a forced lie, but that he, Pierre, was the father of her child, the babe François boasted of as his "son and heir, the future baron of St. Aliquis."

They were less certain as to whether Nicolette had engineered their flight to St. Martin in the dead of the night. Matthew suggested that she must have taken Lady Alienor into her confidence. He assured Pierre that after the hours he spent with the lovely, brave, and loving Alienor, Nicolette would have been quite correct in doing so. Matthew had a sense he couldn't prove that Nicolette had intended to find him to send a message to Pierre. For over some flagons of wine at the inn at which the knight from St. Martin had found him, the knight told him of the plight of the party that had arrived from St. Aliquis at dawn. He said a maid who helped care for Nicolette said she had called out Matthew's name in her delirium. The knight assured him that the physician expected Nicolette to recover and the babe to live, though he had been less confident about the latter. He said that Bruge's wound was tended and that a party had been sent to recover Sire Herbert de Leon's body.

Because of their reencampment, Henri's departure had been delayed by three weeks. 'Twas expected that he would leave with his squire, the carefully clever scoundrel Michel, on the morrow—the first of October. No word had yet arrived as to whether the siege of St. Aliquis had been successful or deterred. Nor had there been word as to Lady Alienor's release.

For the past two weeks Pierre argued hard with an equally stubborn Matthew. Pierre insisted that he should go to the Count of Champagne and explain that he had to see to urgent family business. Matthew argued that such a move would be futile. First, even should the count grant him leave, which they both doubted since their ranks had been mightily thinned by the Saracens, his sudden leave would arouse suspicion. They did not know what Henri had reported to François. Perhaps François hid his knowledge behind a mask of arrogant, talkative stupidity. But even if Henri had written all he knew, Nicolette's lover went only by the name Davide.

Moreover, even if Pierre appeared at St. Martin, Matthew advised, if Nicolette had not lost their babe she would be confined to bed until the babe was born. Pierre could not ride her to his father's castle so many leagues away. Pierre had to comfort himself with the gossip that King Philip Augustus debated about withdrawing his troops and returning to France. Word had it that, indeed, Richard the Lionhearted and their king were greater enemies than either was to Saladin. This could mean that they, the French knights, would return home by Christ's birthday. Matthew promised he would ride with Pierre to St. Martin. Together they would find a way to save Nicolette and Bruge.

Impotent fury took hold of Pierre once more as he strode across the desert. His beloved needed him and he was helpless. He dared not risk sending word. For he knew not what spy Henri might have enlisted within the palais of St. Martin. Perchance a maiden or maid who waited upon Nicolette?

Please Lord, Pierre kneeled and prayed... Mother Mary, let her know that I understood her hidden message. That I pray each night for Nicolette

SONG OF THE ROSE

and our babe. Pray keep them well and safe. Each day apart is like a year and the weeks like an eternity. Pierre crossed himself and rose. He wiped away his tears.

Pierre hurried toward the tent François and Michel shared. On his thoughtful walk to the edges of the desert a divine inspiration had been given to him!

On the morrow François would begin his return to St. Aliquis by way of St. Martin. François had requested of Pierre that he become his vassal while remaining the count's as well. Over their months of "friendship," Pierre knew that François assumed him a brave, loyal, albeit poor knight of "petty noble" origins. Pierre had let François embroider this tale. François now offered him a large fief and a small castle. Pierre had neither accepted nor declined.

Tonight he realized that he must accept. For in order to protect Nicolette and Bruge he must insinuate himself into the core of castle life at St. Aliquis. Alienor would require his aid as well, for François had confided that he seriously considered rewarding Henri with his sister's hand in marriage if Henri conquered Harcourt's forces in his absence. He would accept François' offer. Then he could carry forth the plan he had so carefully devised.

He smiled as he pictured himself and Nicolette safely ensconced in his father's castle. Their babe would lie sleeping in a crib in the corner of their chamber while he and Nicolette lay entwined upon the pillowed feather bed, the curtains of the canopy drawn as he held her tenderly. He pictured her pert breasts, swollen enticingly with milk for the babe. He imagined the sweet taste as he suckled one breast and then the other.

His pace slowed as he fell deeper into his fantasy. He could hear Nicolette's sweet sigh deepen as he tasted and fondled her. "Now," she sighed. "Now, my beloved," she pleaded, as she opened her thighs further, pressing her calves more tightly around his back as he adored the delicate throne of her womanhood, ruby red and full now with desire. "I want to feel you in me, my beloved," she moaned and pulled him to her, laughing with exultation that changed to wordless moans as he entered her, slowly at first, then driving harder and harder, bringing them both to a frenzied state of passionate union . . .

The hardness of his manhood pressed against his chausses brought him back to the moment. If he continued he would have to relieve himself, a gratification inappropriate to the moment at hand. He broke into a run toward François' tent in an attempt to expend the tension he'd built within himself.

Just as he was about to enter François' tent he heard a muffled cry and a sharp whisper of warning to François. Pierre stealthily crept around the back of the tent and peered through a crack. The torch held by Alain burned dangerously high, thus accounting for the odor of smoke. There were three knights with Alain but Pierre could not make out their identity as they stood in the gray shadow by Michel's cot. Michel writhed so and his cries were muffled, leading Pierre to guess that he too had been bound and gagged.

"We have given you not only our lives but the sweat of our toil all these years, François. Now your father is dead. We will give you less allegiance than a wallowing swine, you pompous bastard! You shall die a hero after all, François." Alain chuckled as he withdrew his dagger. "You will die like the swine you are. But do not fret, for we shall carry back the story to St. Aliquis that you died a hero's death. We shall tell them how you single-handedly slew a half-dozen mighty Saracens before you fell! And you, Michel, loyal to the end." He laughed sardonically. "It shall be said that you died trying to save your liege lord."

Pierre heard enough. He drew his sword and darted to the front of the tent. Matthew approached and appeared as if he was going to call out a greeting. Pierre instantly clamped his hand over Matthew's mouth. "Alain and three others. They are going to murder François and Michel," he whispered into Matthew's ear. He released Matthew who quickly drew his sword.

They leapt into action. Pierre felt his cheek slashed by a dagger as he cut François free from his bonds. From the corner of his eye he saw that Michel was freed. Pierre's sword swung mightily against Alain's. A quick turn saved him from the sword that came at his chest from another knight. He swung his mace hard at the man's head and heard the crack of his skull. Pierre turned but he was too late. For Alain severed François' neck. Pierre sailed his weapon through Alain's chainmail suit. Alain fell to the ground. Pierre pulled the sword from Alain's heart.

The knight Pierre now recognized to be Jerome was about to lunge his sword into Matthew's chest. Pierre's practiced lunge stopped him in midmotion. Jerome's mouth flew open, blood pouring from it. He clutched his heart and fell to the ground. Pierre saw the eruption of fire from the torch that had fallen onto François' cot. "Fire," he cried out to Matthew, the flames spreading as rapidly as his words. The murdering knights were dead. François was dead.

Matthew ran to a wounded but breathing Michel. He lay unconscious. "I'll carry him out," Matthew called. "You get François."

A wooden pole fell upon François, torching his dead body. Pierre tried to lift it but suddenly the entire tenting cloth fell upon them, a fiery curtain. Smoke choked Pierre's lungs. He couldn't save François' body. He felt Matthew pull him from the inferno.

As they lay upon the ground, choking, they heard the clamor of knights running to the burning tent. "Are you all right, François?" Bernard asked. "And you, Matthew?"

Pierre nodded, still choking. He tried to say he was not François but Pierre, but the smoke strangling his lungs barricaded his words. "I am not . . ." he managed weakly.

"Good," a distracted Bernard said and ran to help the others extinguish the raging fire.

Pierre felt a choking Matthew pull him away from the tent. What was he doing? Had the smoke addled his brain? Not having the strength to protest, he followed to the caldron of drinking water yards away. They drank with a thirst Pierre had never known, though the water burned his chest as he swallowed. Pierre felt something drip down his chin. He thought it water but when he wiped it away he saw it was dark blood and remembered the gash upon his cheek. He tore at his chemise, wet the cloth, and held it upon the aching wound. He brushed back his hair and his hand came away with stinking scorched clumps of hair.

He found his voice. "I cannot believe that I should have tried so hard to save the life of the man I most despise. Yet I sorrow that I failed. François is dead, can you believe it?"

"No. François is not dead. Pierre Delise, who tried to save him, burned to ashes in the fire. You are François." Matthew spoke as forcefully as he did quietly.

"Have you gone mad, Matthew!"

"You are Baron François Perdant. Husband of Nicolette Duprey, though she will have to grow used to your face, for that cut will leave a permanent, nasty scar, I am afraid. So much for your pretty countenance, my friend François," Matthew said.

"You have gone mad! I cannot use François' murder—"

"Who better? You tried with true courage to save the life of the man the others murdered. The man who has been the bane of your existence. The man—I shall say it plainly now—who forced the woman you love, the mother of your child, to lie with him, as if she were a common whore. Then worse, with the cooperation of her despicable brother, forced her to wed him, using a sweet child like Bruge as a threat. The man who intended to marry his grieving sister to Henri, fully knowing his character, or should I say lack of it. The man you stopped from raping Nicolette the day you first saw her. Pray tell, need I continue?"

Matthew was correct. And there was more, much more even Matthew did not know. It had to be God's will. For surely the Lord's ways were mystifying to mere mortals. He could not countenance the idea, had he bloodied his hand in ending François' life. But it *was* so that he had tried to save François as valiantly as if François had been a brother or a dear friend like Matthew. He looked hard at Matthew for the slightest indication of a second thought. He saw none.

"Aye . . . I am François Perdant. Baron of St. Aliquis. Pierre Delise died valiantly. He saved my life. On the morrow I shall return to my home. My loyal squire died as well in the fire, for he fought your efforts to carry him out in his half-conscious condition."

"Aye. He struggled for he was dazed. He believed I tried to kill him rather than save him. I did my utmost to save him, as much as I despised him, Pie—François."

"Aye, Matthew. I saw through the smoke." He clasped Matthew tightly on the shoulder. "As I began . . . since my loyal squire is dead, and I am somewhat wounded, more than I'd thought . . ." He pointed to his thigh, where his chausse was ripped and blood dripped to the ground. "I shall ask that you travel home with me, if that be your desire."

"It would. I am sick of this hellhole. I have seen enough severed heads and limbs detached from dying bodies to last me quite a time. I shall be content to fight the gentlemanly wars of greedy barons, counts, bishops, and abbots for a long time to come! It will be my honor to swear my allegiance to you, François Perdant, my liege lord." Matthew bowed. Pierre held Matthew tight as they embraced.

"I am François Perdant, Baron of St. Aliquis.

Husband of Baroness Nicolette Perdant who carries my child. Perhaps, dear Matthew, if you are tired of wenching and can win my beautiful sister Alienor's consent—for she must freely give her consent!—you may become my brother by marriage. But always you shall be my brother by heart and soul, no matter the course our lives take." François Perdant, Pierre thought. He could hardly wait to see his father's face when he told him the news. It only tore at him that for now his dearest father would have to think that it was he rather than François who died in the fire. As for Nicolette, he wondered how quickly she would realize that it was Davide who returned to her and their babe?

Chapter Thirteen

WRAPPED IN HER FUR-LINED MANTLE, ALIENOR WALKED slowly about the inner bailey of St. Martin. The castle grounds bustled with great activity, just as St. Aliquis always had in late autumn. 'Twas the last Thursday of October, the season when supplies and foodstuffs were busily being stored for the approaching siege of winter. Many peasants who did not work daily at the castle swarmed through the bailey. They carried in, on mule or their sturdy backs, sacks of vegetables from their own gardens and fruit from their orchards, part of their yearlong payment to the baron for his protection. In turn they exercised their customary rights in the seigneur's forest by gathering firewood and shaking down acorns and beechnuts to feed their hogs. St. Martin's provost and his men watched carefully for poachers and settled minor disputes among the childlike villeins and serfs.

Yesterday Bruge had ridden out to the fields with Gervais and Lily, Marguerite's first maiden-in-waiting, with whom she had become fast friends. Bruge returned to tell how they watched the grapes being trampled in vats and the fermented wine transferred to huge casks. 'Twas also "blood month," the time of the slaughtering of livestock, which Bruge had refused to observe, so soft in heart was she.

Nicolette listened to Bruge's prattle with less than full attention, for her thoughts lay elsewhere. Despite the slowness of their gait, each step was heavy for her. She felt her babe kick and rested her hands over her large belly. At least the babe was healthy and full of vigor, Nicolette thought, as she felt the pleasantly sharp kick again. They neared the garden. "Bruge, let us sit for a time," she said.

"Are you certain you are well enough to be out, Nicolette?" Bruge asked. "Sire Gerson was displeased that you refused to remain in bed any longer."

"Aye, I am well, just weary," she said as they sat upon the bench. A cool wind blew, making the last of the gold and red leaves in the garden's trees flutter gently to the ground.

"Nicolette, I do worry so about you. You have not been yourself since we arrived at St. Martin's two months ago. 'Tis more than you keep saying. Alienor has been safe at home for a week. I felt sure that her arrival any hour now, would cheer you considerably. And François should return soon. Your babe grows fatter each day, despite the fact that you seem to eat little enough to nourish yourself! You constantly insist on knowing my whereabouts each minute of the day and night, as if you suddenly distrust me—"

"'Tis not so, Bruge." Nicolette had worried that Bruge would think her vigilance thus. But now that St. Aliquis was no longer under siege, she could not help worry that Henri would try to steal Bruge back to the castle. Each of his letters, sickly sweet with pretended brotherly concern, held a subtle but sinister warning that he considered her still at his mercy and still used Bruge as his weapon to assure her submission. "I not only trust you, but already I love Gervais as a brother. When François returns"—she tried to keep her feeling of dread of his imminent arrival from her face—"I will have him immediately arrange for your betrothal. I know I have not been myself, but it is only due to all the events that have passed and my worry that I might lose my babe. I am most excited that we shall soon see Alienor, and it comforts me that she will remain with us until the babe is born."

"You forgot to mention Simone. Are you not pleased she will be with us as well?"

"Aye. She is a sweet maid. And so loyal." To our vile brother, Nicolette thought wryly. Once again Simone would be Henri's eyes and ears but she could not rid them of the poor, lovesick maiden.

Nicolette heard the blare of horns and her heart skipped. Did it announce the joyful arrival of Alienor and her party or the dreaded return of François?

"Oh! I wonder who has appeared at the gates?" Bruge's eyes sparkled with excitement. Nicolette knew she wished to run to the courtyard to see who came.

"Go on, Sister," Nicolette said. "I see how you can barely stand the suspense."

"No, Nicolette. I cannot leave you," Bruge said with reluctant obligation.

"Certainly you can. If it pleases you, fetch Daphne or Blanche to sit with me, for I have not the energy to go with you."

"Are you certain?" Bruge silently debated, Nicolette saw.

"Aye." Nicolette laughed. "Be off with you!"

Bruge kissed her upon the cheek and began to run. "Walk . . ." Nicolette called after her in vain. "Ladies do not run, Bruge." Nicolette laughed and thought to herself, Run all you wish, Bruge. Enjoy each moment of your blessed freedom.

Nicolette glanced about. She was alone. Quickly she withdrew the letter she had received early this morning from the Count of Reims. Thank the Lord it had been secretly delivered to her by Jehan, a squire from the count's domain, who was being nourished by Baron Brouilleaux. 'Twas providence that had allowed her to learn of his presence at St. Martin last week. Jehan had become a friend to Gervais. Through Gervais, Nicolette learned that he was returning to Reims for a short visit. She had taken Jehan into her confidence—telling him only of her need to send a letter in secret to his liege lord. Jehan had proved his loyalty, as she'd hoped. The count's reply was intentionally vague, as Nicolette had cautioned, for Henri's interception of Davide's letter had taught her a lesson only too well. But it still conveyed the response she'd prayed for.

The count would be sending his emissaries to the baptismal celebration when her child was born, "in respect for her host, Baron Brouilleaux." This meant the count remembered her father's aid and would come to Nicolette's rescue. The count was willing to risk a war with François, an inevitable war when François learned that she, Bruge, and her babe were safely living in his castle at Reims. Months ago, Nicolette would have been ecstatic at the news of their certain salvation. But too many plans had gone awry for her to allow herself more than guarded, fervent hope that this time her plan would not be foiled.

To ensure no repetition of her previous mistakes, Nicolette tore the parchment into tiny pieces which she would toss into the flaming fireplace in the chamber she and Bruge shared.

"My lady," said pretty Blanche, the maid who had waited upon her, along with Daphne, since their arrival. Always cheerful, Blanche's face glowed with excitement. "I have glorious news! Your husband has returned! Sire Perdant just rode into the castle. He asked for you immediately!" Blanche offered her hand. "Come quickly, for we must dress you for your husband—why are you so pale, Nicolette? Are you ill? Sire Gerson was afraid such would happen when you refused to heed his warning. Oh, my lady!"

"I am not ill. Just weary and overcome with the surprise." Nicolette forced a wan smile. The moment had come. She felt almost a resigned relief. For now she would have to face what she had long dreaded. Davide, please help me through this sham! How I miss you, my beloved, she thought. Nicolette rose. "Aye, let us return to our chamber," she said softly. "So that you may prepare me to greet François." She could not force herself to utter the word "husband."

"I told you your fears were groundless," Matthew whispered to Pierre in a moment of privacy. They had been greeted with much welcome and soon taken to the chamber that had been Guy's. There they had washed the grime of the road from their bodies and changed into fresh clothing. Pierre had dismissed the servants. "'Tis been almost six months since François was last seen. Time and the healing wound upon your face makes you appear as much like him as if you had been his twin," Matthew continued. "You always did appear uncannily similar, even before. Except your body was more muscled and your hands more roughened. François pampered himself like a maiden and his drinking and eating made him flabby before his time. But six months at battle could toughen even a François, and surely the tale of his 'heroism' shall soon run from the mouths of the knights seeking to forget their comrades' 'attempt' to murder him. There is nothing you do not know about François' life. He regaled you nightly with stories of his life from the moment of his first steps, as you told me."

Pierre chuckled heartily, though the wound ached with any strong facial movement. "You are right once again, Matthew. My nerves are raw with the joy and fear I feel at knowing that I shall see Nicolette in just moments. I know I will want to take her in my arms and tell her her Davide has returned...." Tears filled his eyes. "Yet I quake with fear at the expression of unvoiced hatred I will see in her eyes when she looks at me and sees François. I must be very careful not to upset her more than I'm certain she already is, for our babe's sake. Even the discovery that I am Davide," he whispered, "could be too much. You heard the physician's caution, when he took me aside to warn me that he was deeply worried about her frail state."

"Pierre, you will know what to do when the moment comes. For the Lord has seen fit to allow you two to be rejoined. Certainly he will not fail either of you now." Matthew hugged him tightly. "From this moment on, I shall never call you by your rightful name again. You are François Perdant."

I must tell Matthew the rest, now! Pierre thought. I have hated so to withhold from him the truth that—

"Sire François," the young squire, Jehan, who had led them to the chamber said. "Your lady awaits you. I shall show you the way."

"Thank you, Jehan," Pierre said, pitching his voice, as he had done since he was mistaken for François after the fire, to mimic François' slightly higher, louder tone. "Let us go now, for I long to see my sweet, lovely wife," he said with a lusty grin, falling once again into the role of François so well that it made him feel as if it had been Pierre Delise who died in the fire. That 'twas François who now wore Nicolette's blue sleeve close to his heart.

* * *

Nicolette's chamber echoed with the happy chatter of maids and maidens as they gleefully finished dressing her. Bruge had begged to be allowed to fix her hair and Nicolette now sat quietly as Bruge finished entwining blue and gold strands of thread through her thick pale braids. Nicolette wore a loose pelisson of blue silk, embroidered with gold and trimmed with white ermine. Too well she remembered the other morning, that sad May day when she had been dressed to wed François.

Marguerite entered the chamber. She looked at Nicolette and smiled. "You are more beautiful than anyone I have ever seen," Marguerite said softly. "Your husband awaits your permission to enter. He is well and robust, but I did want to warn you that his cheek is badly cut from a wound he suffered at the hands of the Saracens. Do not be frightened by its flaming color, for Sire Gerson said it will eventually heal and be a proud mark of François' bravery. His hair is also cut short, for his bangs were scorched in a fire when François tried to save his squire, Michel, and his knights from a fiery death."

"Michel is dead?" Nicolette asked with surprise. Lord forgive her but she could not mourn his passing. "Daphne said that François arrived with a young knight?"

"'Tis Matthew, the knight who brought us the tragic news of Guy's death. He has taken an oath of fealty to François. It is Matthew who also waits outside your chamber."

Nicolette could not believe it. Was there no end to the treacheries? She had never believed that Matthew would betray her and Davide! Nicolette bitterly wondered what size fief and how large a promise of riches had bought Matthew?

"May I allow François and Matthew to enter?" Marguerite asked.

Nicolette forced a smile. She no longer trembled inwardly, for with this knowledge of Matthew's betrayal she had neither the heart nor energy for even fear. "Aye."

Marguerite walked to the hall. The maidens politely backed into the far corner of the room and Bruge leaned down and kissed her upon her cheek. "I am so happy for you, Nicolette!" Bruge said with innocent joy.

"My lady," François said as he stood at the entrance of the chamber, the traitor Matthew at his side, boldly smiling as well.

"My lord and husband," Nicolette replied, softly. She was shocked, despite herself, by the scarlet battle wound that cut jaggedly across his right cheek. He appeared robust though thinner and more rugged, as if he had been toughened by war. He wore the same sardonic grin, yet she could see it pained him to smile. Nicolette stared at him. Suddenly her head went light, for as she stared she saw her beloved Davide before her. Her mind was playing tricks on her! She fought back her tears.

"Your lady weeps with joy at your return, François." Matthew spoke quickly, seeing that Pierre was too stunned at the presence of his beloved to speak. "Methinks we should leave the two of you alone. Do you agree, my lady?" he asked Nicolette with forced boldness, for her pain hurt him too. He remembered the joy that had filled her bright blue eyes when he handed her Pierre's letter so many months before.

"Yes. I wish to be alone with François—my husband," she said through the knot that pained her throat. Though she tried to rein her mind, her senses still filled with the vision of her Davide. She had to control herself—for her babe's sake. Nicolette wiped her eyes with her gold scarf. In a moment only she and François remained in the sunlit chamber. She gazed at the crucifix that hung between the arched windows of glazed glass. Give me strength, Mother Mary, she silently prayed.

"I fear my return has unsettled you, my lady," Pierre said as he cautiously moved toward her. "I have missed you."

"I am still weary from the fever I suffered," she lied.

"Does the cut upon my face offend you, sweet Nicolette?" he nervously asked, brushing his short hair from his forehead. "I am delighted that our babe is well," he continued and brushed at his forehead once again.

His voice was François' but something—*something* nagged from her memory.

"I am weary too, the truth be known," Pierre said and quickly strode to the table upon which he spied the wine and glasses. With his back to her he quickly poured himself a full goblet of wine. He turned. "Wine for you, my lovely Nicolette?" he asked, hearing in his voice the echo of François'.

"Aye . . ." What was it that her mind was trying to tell her?

Pierre turned away from her again. Quickly he

downed the wine and poured himself another. Then he filled a goblet for her. He turned back to Nicolette and the sight of her sad beauty almost overcame him. He steeled himself harshly. He brushed his hair from his forehead. "You look more enticing than ever," he said with François' crude, lusting tone.

Nicolette clutched the arms of the carved chair in which she sat. It had come to her! She thought she would swoon in joy and her heart pounded so rapidly in her chest she believed he could hear it. Her babe began to kick and she brought her hands to her belly, thinking that now her babe knew joy for the first time. She prayed she could restrain herself for but a moment. Just one moment for then she would have all of the rest of her life and eternity. "I have missed you too, François," she said, lowering her eyes in pretended shyness. "I fear you will not find me desirable now, already so heavy with our sweet babe," she said.

Pierre's heart shattered. She believed him François and she spoke with a shy, but loving intimacy! Did she do so for show or—

"Would you come to my side and kiss me, my husband?" she asked and raised her face, staring directly into his eyes. Her eyes were filled with true longing. There was no pretense in them. He stood, unable to move as his life crumbled about him. "For I have missed you *so desperately,* my Davide," she whispered. It took a moment for her words to seep through his addled brain. "Davide . . ." she whispered and opened her arms for him. Tears streamed down his face as he rushed to her.

Nicolette wept now with joy as she had not allowed

herself to weep in sorrow or terror. They held each other tightly, each desiring never to let go.

Nicolette lay in Davide's arms upon her bed, which he had carried her to an hour or so before. "The babe kicks wildly again, quickly, feel," she said as she pressed his hands upon the silk material of her pelisson. "Do you feel it, Davide?"

"Aye! I do. I feel my son!" His face shone with heavenly delight. "Does his kick pain you?"

Nicolette laughed. "'Tis a wonderful feeling! But I did not know how wonderful until now!"

"I am still astonished at how you knew 'twas me," he said as he gently rubbed her belly, though the babe had quieted again. "I never realized that I had the habit of brushing back my hair, but I thank the Lord that I do! For I did not know how nor when to let you know 'twas me," he said again.

"And I thank the Lord as well. For I *instantly* knew that 'twas not François who stood before me but you. Yet my brain told me I was plainly and quickly going mad!" She brought his mouth to hers and luxuriated in the long gentle kiss. She pulled herself upright with some difficulty, causing Davide to laugh, but she caught his laughter with another kiss. This time a deep, probing kiss that made them sigh with pleasure as they explored each other's mouths.

Nicolette kissed his forehead and the tip of his fine nose and then softly brought her lips to the jagged wound on his cheek. He started to turn his head away. "Don't, Davide. Do you think this wound that marked the moment you could return to us could ever be anything but beautiful to me?" She kissed each inch of his right cheek and then found his lips once again as his hands caressed her body.

"Nicolette, I want you so. Did the physician say whether we could be together, with the babe, I mean?"

"He spoke to me yesterday, when his assurances only brought me greater pain." She smiled so gloriously that Pierre thought he still must be dreaming. "I fear, though, that I shall be less agile than I was before," she said with a shy laugh.

"Good!" he teased. "For I quite remember you were going to be the death of me that afternoon! Until our babe is born you will be forced to show me mercy then, you wench!"

He rested her back upon the pillows. He removed her clothing between kisses and caresses, layer by layer, until she lay naked before him. Her body was so profoundly beautiful, her breasts fuller and nipples taut and beckoning. He traced the taut rise of her mound of belly to its gentle slope at the fair triangle between her alabaster thighs.

How she had dreamed each night of this moment, she thought, as she watched him remove his clothing. He stopped for a moment and reached into his chemise. Wordlessly he handed her a piece of faded blue, ragged material. 'Twas the sleeve she had given him that day in the woods.

"It never left my heart except for the moments each night I would remove it and kiss it. Holding it close to my cheek until I could hold you again," he said softly. He rose from the bed and started toward the roaring fireplace.

"No, Davide," she whispered, "don't burn—" Then she realized he was right. They didn't need the symbol of their separation any longer.

He returned to her quickly and stood before her as he lifted his chemise above his head and tossed it onto the bedframe. How beautiful he was, she thought, as her eyes feasted upon his body. "Davide!" she said in alarm when she saw the scar on his right thigh. "You did not tell me you were wounded further!"

He laughed. "'Tis just a surface wound. It does not pain me at all. I tend to forget its existence ... Perchance you could find another part of my body to gaze upon which would bring you more pleasure," he teased. She grinned as her eyes boldly rested on his manhood and he laughed, remembering again her open, loving lustfulness.

"I think I have," she said with intentional coyness that turned into a giggle. "Come closer so that I may see better, for the light is dimming rapidly."

"Is it now, my lady?" he said as he climbed back into the bed. "Can you see better, my love?" he asked as he straddled her belly carefully and moved closer to her face. He fondled her breasts, teasing her rosy nipples as she touched him with her silken fingers. "Closer still, my lady?" he asked. She nodded in answer, her eyes smoldering with the passion that throbbed through him from the touch of her fingertips and coursed through his entire body.

Nicolette clasped his strong, heavily muscled thighs as she teased the tip of his proud manhood with her lips. She writhed as the pleasure she had almost forgotten went through her like shock waves when his hand gently nudged her thighs apart and his fingers slid to the spot of her pulsating desire. "Oh, Davide, how I love you!" she moaned.

How exquisitely she pleasured him with her mouth. He could hardly stand to tear himself from her but he wanted to feel her deep inside. He needed so to be inside her! He withdrew from her mouth and showered it with kisses. He reached for two pillows and placed them beneath her hips.

Nicolette cried out as he kissed and teased her, his head nudging her thighs further apart, his tongue bringing her to a fevered pitch. "Now, Davide, I pray thee!" Before she could cry out again he entered her, filling her to her core. She cried with love and pleasure and knew that each tear washed away the memory of the indignities she had suffered at François' and Henri's hands. She responded to each wonderful thrust with unbridled passion. Clamping her legs tightly around his strong back, she rode the undulating waves that carried them away together.

He felt her draw him deeper into her and smiled into her eyes until he could no longer see; then, as his body was wracked with pleasure and boundless love, he cried out her name.

Nicolette sipped from the goblet of wine he brought to her lips as they lay warm beneath the coverlets. "Davide, I fear we are corrupting our babe. For he kicked with such joy when you were inside me."

"Did my son do such?" Pierre responded with mock alarm. "I *pray* that does not mean he favors men, like some of the knights I have seen!"

Nicolette punched him in the stomach. "How can

you say such!" she complained but then broke into giggles.

"I see you have not lost the power in your arms," he teased. "At least you have not kicked me in my groin yet," he said and laughed as he quickly grabbed the knee coming his way. "You still have the litheness of a feline, despite your growing belly," he teased. He leaned over and kissed her belly. "Your mother, the Baroness of St. Aliquis, has the spirit and strength of a lusty wench, my son," he said. Nicolette pulled away and scrambled upright. Her eyes darkened and she frowned. "How did I upset you, my angel? I was only jesting," he said with alarm.

She kissed him gently, sorry for the moment of discomfort she had brought him. "'Tis not that," she began. "I could not stand hearing you call me the Baroness of St. Aliquis! Oh, Davide! We must escape! Please say you'll take us away! Tonight!" So quickly had the real world again intruded that she could not stop the tears that flowed from her.

"Cry, Nicolette. Let the tears drain from your heart. Then we shall talk," he whispered as he held her against him tightly.

"Oh, Davide." She laughed and cried at the same time. "Those are much the same words you said to me in the woods, the first time you held me. Do you remember?"

"I remember," he answered softly. Too soon, but of necessity, she had made him begin to think again. He realized that she would cry even harder when he explained that never again could she call him Davide. She did not know him as Pierre Delise, yet she must begin to call him only François. At least until they were safe at his father's castle. Then she could call him whatever she chose.

How to begin, he wondered. For he had told her only of the events that brought him to St. Martin as the conquering hero, François. He would not tell her about his father, or any of that, for it would be more than she needed to cope with for now. Convincing her to pretend he was François, the man who had so coldly misused her, would be difficult enough for now. Her weeping lessened and her body stilled as he held her tight. She looked up at him with reddened eyes, and as he wiped the tears from her cheeks, she smiled.

"I am ready to talk now methinks." She broke into a grin. "No. I am not ready to talk yet," she said as she brought his mouth to hers and traced her fingers bewitchingly down his neck.

"I believe I have said this before, but I see now I will be saying it for the rest of my life," he pronounced lightly, as her mouth played at his chest. "You shall most definitely drive me to an early grave with your insatiable lust, Nicolette. But oh, how happily I shall die! Ouch!" he cried. She had bitten his shoulder playfully in response, his plucky, lusty woman. "'Tis unseemly for the woman who carries my child to behave such!" he exclaimed. She went for his shoulder again but this time he was prepared and pinioned her arms as she shook with laughter.

"'Tis mad! I cannot play such a charade!" Nicolette vehemently declared, in the same manner he himself had done before Matthew helped him to see the logic and necessity of assuming the identity of François.

"You convinced the knights at camp, but you left but days later. Here you will have to make Alienor believe—Sire Eustace—so many people who have known François all his life. It will not work, even if I agreed, which I do not!"

"I understand your abhorrence of the notion—I too felt the same. But you are forgetting one important point."

"I am forgetting nothing, Davide! I *knew* you in just moments, did I not?"

"'Tis exactly the point I am trying to make, my darling!"

"I do not understand." Nicolette studied him hard.

"You knew me as *Davide*. No one else knows of Davide's existence, but for Matthew. Davide never *lived* in their world, so how could they suspect I was Davide and not François?"

Nicolette thought silently. Her heart demanded immediate escape from the lies and schemes. She wished never to see St. Aliquis again. But her mind repeated his words and slowly the complicated details gave way to Davide's clear logic. "Poor Matthew . . . I gazed upon him with such hate for I was so certain he had betrayed us!"

"Matthew expected such. He is as devoted to you as he is to me." Pierre smiled. "I believe that were he not my dearest friend I should find him a rival for your heart, my dear wife."

Nicolette blushed. "Davide. Even if your plan works, which I still doubt, for *somehow* someone shall become wise—not even François could have told you all the information you might suddenly need to know —but ignoring such for a moment, we are husband

and wife in the truest sense. But how are we to marry in the church if we are already wed as François and Nicolette?"

"I expected that question." He tenderly kissed her hands. "For me, the Lord sanctioned our union that afternoon in the woods. I do not need a priest, nor the pope himself to act as God's spokesman. But you are so reverent. I do not doubt that deep inside you feel we have sinned. Though your heart tells your soul otherwise, I am afraid that your soul will vex you. Should you wish, after the babe is born we can have another wedding. A glorious celebration. No one could doubt that due to the hurry of the last wedding you were not accorded the pomp a baroness deserves—"

"That would not heal my soul, Davide. For once again I should be pronounced the wife of François Perdant and the Baroness of St. Aliquis. I should be happy to never again set my eyes upon that castle! I have not told you the horrors I suffered—more than you could guess I am sure—"

"Tell me! I am now able to avenge anything that might have been done—" he demanded with a deep resentment for his months of powerlessness.

"Later. I promise. What was done is past. We have so much to decide that will affect the rest of our lives . . . and the life of our babe."

Pierre kissed the mound of her belly. "'Tis more for the babe than for us that you must agree to our plan."

"Perchance . . ." she said, unwilling to yet concede. "Davide, you have held something from me! You told me when we first met that you could not utter your real name nor tell me anything of from whence you came. Surely you can do so now?"

Pierre shook his head and watched her face turn to frustrated confusion. He understood her feelings but 'twas not yet the time. Should anything go awry—for secretly he agreed with her doubts as strongly as he agreed with Matthew's cold logic—the less she knew the safer she would remain. At least until he had the opportunity of visiting his father. For without his father's agreement, he could not break his vow of silence. What *could* he tell her that would appease her, however slightly? It came to him. "Nicolette. I told you from the first that for you to know my true story would place you in grave danger. I have also made a vow to my father that I cannot break without his blessings. Can you understand that?"

Nicolette's face softened. She shrugged. "I do not like it but, aye, I understand your honor. 'Tis one of the reasons I so deeply love you. 'Twas knowing that your word was as good as your life that carried me through some of the darkest moments of our separation . . . " Tears filled her eyes. "Though I am ashamed to tell you, but there were times, before I received your letter, that I doubted every word you had said. I tried not to but I was so afraid"—her voice broke—"that I had been a foolish maiden tricked by a handsome, charming knight." She began to cry. "I am sorry I could have doubted you for even *one* moment, my beloved." She fell into his arms.

Davide held her close, caressing her hair, soothing her like a child as she wept. "To have remained doubtless would have made you a foolish maiden.

SONG OF THE ROSE

Would I, or anyone else, have thought differently, my love? You said yourself that you so feared I would believe your letter that scorned me. Despite the fact that you had so cleverly composed it that the truth rang through it loudly. 'Tis that not so?"

"Aye," she whispered against his chest. "The strength of our love saved us, did it not?"

"And it always will." He gently pulled her away so that he could gaze upon her face. "Finally we are joined. Look in my eyes, Nicolette. My given name is Pierre Delise."

"Pierre . . . Pierre Delise," she said, trying to fit this name to her Davide. "'Tis a nice name," she said. "'Tis so hard for me to know you as anyone but Davide! . . . Pierre . . ." she tried again.

"You may not utter it again. Not until we are at my father's castle."

"Your father, Sire Delise. What is his Christian name? Where is his castle?"

"His name I cannot say. Only that it is not Delise. Nor can I reveal where he rules."

"Mystery upon mystery! Deception upon deception!" she accused as her frustration rose, despite his explanations.

"Nicolette. Do you trust me? Your Davide. The man who lovingly gazes into your eyes?"

"Of course I trust you but—"

"You have proven your love and faith all these months. But I must demand that you prove it once again. I remember that you said, in jest, but still expressing your true wonderfully free spirit, that you wished to honor but not obey me. For you were sick of masters. Once this episode in our lives is over I *swear* to you that you and I shall be husband and wife. I shall never demand, but request. I know 'tis not the way of the world, for husbands own their wives and correct them with words or a blow to their face. My father, he is a man you will truly love. Much like your own, methinks. He taught me otherwise. He is wealthy. Forgive me. I cannot say more as much as I would love to talk to you about him through the night."

Nicolette saw the frustration in Davide's face that more than mirrored her own. How deeply Davide loved and respected his father. Though she thought it impossible, she loved him more than ever for it. "What did your father teach you?" she asked, bringing him back to his thought to help abate his frustration.

Pierre smiled, aware of her sensitivity. "He taught me that the world had much to learn. That one cannot love a woman if he rules her with fear. Men, from kings to barons, think nothing of trusting their wives to run their castles when they are off to war. Yet in their presence they demand greater supplication than they do from their villeins and serfs. He taught me that *true* husbands and wives love and respect one another. They talk through their differences—" He smiled wryly. "As we do presently. A man's strong card is his logic. A woman's is feeling. Combined, my father says, only the Lord's wisdom can be greater."

Nicolette smiled as she reflected upon his father's sage words. She had reflected upon this very subject, for her father had not only showered his love upon her, but he had shown his respect by giving serious consideration to her thoughts and ideas—correcting her without condescension when he disagreed, commending her as he would a fellow knight, when he agreed.

Yet how often Henri had scorned their dear father as a weak man lacking wit and ambition. "He thinks with his heart, like a woman!" Henri had scoffed at him as long as she could remember. And now Davide spoke with deep respect for his father, a man she guessed to be powerful, who sounded so much like her dear father who rested in Heaven. "I long to meet your father, Davide. I love him already."

Pierre was choked with emotion, remembering word had gone to his father saying he was dead. He must return home at the first moment he could. When Nicolette would be safe during his absence of a fortnight. How proud Father would be when he met Nicolette!

"He will love you dearly, too," Pierre said, his voice choked. "I only ask you to agree to the masquerade until our babe is born and you both can travel. I have hopes that Matthew, who so desires the chance to win Alienor's love, might do so. For if she is wed, lawfully St. Aliquis will remain hers. The count could not object as long as he is assured that her husband will prove a loyal vassal and protect the count's interest, come to his aid, serve at his court of 'high justice,' and all the rest you well know."

"Alienor has been the victim of such tragedies. She loved Guy so . . . but perchance Matthew, so fine a man and so handsome, might help to mend her heart. Alienor knows that with her father dead she is at François' mercy—" Nicolette's mouth dropped in sudden realization. "If you be François, she will not be at the mercy of her heartless brother. 'Tis all so confusing that it addles my brain! But I do see you have the chance to do so much good! Oh, Davide, I am no longer certain what I think!"

Her excitement at the possibilities grew. "You, as the baron, can grant permission for Bruge's betrothal. I have told you how deeply she and Gervais love, and he is such a fine young man. Then Henri can no longer hurt me, no longer make me his victim by threatening to wed Bruge to Baron Harcourt, which François would have heartily approved to guarantee no further wars! But you will be François and I shall never have to wake in the middle of the night with the terror of Henri's hands upon my—" She stopped in horror. She had not meant to tell Davide of the hideous things to which Henri had subjected her. Not so soon, for she feared what he would do if he knew. 'Twas too late! Never had she seen Davide's gentle face twisted in such fury.

"You cannot stop what poured from you. Your eyes shone with relief as great as any man's after he escaped what seemed certain death." Pierre kept his voice even. He must know the depth of Henri's vileness she'd accidentally begun to reveal. He had suffered with her the certainty that in order to save herself from being raped by François she would have to subject herself to his amorous advances until the sleeping potion took effect. Nicolette had already told him that the potion had worked just as they planned. She had offered no details and he had not asked, for he knew that such a recounting would rekindle her pain and humiliation. But never had it occurred to him that Henri could be such a barbarian as to attempt to use his own sister. "You must tell me."

"I can not! I fear what you will do if I—"

"Nicolette!" He took her trembling hands into his own to steady her. "I shall do nothing other than what you decide I should do. I have slain more men in the hideous battles than I care to remember. I do not need to prove myself valiant by rash, foolish acts," he said, remembering the countless times he'd seen drunken knights kill one another over foolish words and false pride.

Nicolette folded herself into him. "I can only find the courage to tell you if you hold me tightly," she said in little more than a whisper as she pressed her face against his chest. "Nor can I look at your face as I speak. The pain and rage I would see in your eyes will only make my own the more powerful."

"Tell me . . ." he responded softly as he stroked her hair. "Tell me as if you are recounting a horrifying night dream. For no matter what happened, neither Henri, nor anyone else, will ever harm you again, as long as I live. I swear on my dear mother's grave!"

He had mentioned no mother before. She was dead, Nicolette now knew, and she heard in his voice that he mourned her deeply. Another mystery. But she understood, now, that in time he should tell her all until there were no secrets remaining between them. Now she must do her part in revealing that which was so difficult to speak. "I told you already that Henri somehow saw and heard all that transpired in the momentary meeting between Matthew and myself," she began.

* * *

"What do you wish me to do about him?" Pierre asked quietly after she finished the enraging tale.

Nicolette brought her eyes to his face. He was as pale as death, the wound more scarlet than before in contrast. The muscle at his jawline pulsated. She felt the fury he suppressed for her sake. "I do not know . . . Lord forgive me but I would not shed a tear to see him hanged though he be my stepbrother. But Henri was François' accomplice. Should you behave with the honor and decency that is your character, you would arouse Henri's suspicions. He is quick and clever. There is no limit to his cunning . . . But I am no longer his captive. He can no longer terrorize me or hurt Bruge."

"I have additional knowledge," Pierre began, reluctantly. "François promised Alienor's hand in marriage to Henri if he succeeded in saving St. Aliquis from Harcourt's siege. François sent a letter stating such the day before he was murdered. Henri surely has the promise in writing now."

"Oh, no! I knew he had hoped, but I believed François was too fond of his sister to— How could he agree? I suppose that if François had lived they would have wed Bruge to that scurrilous drunkard Harcourt as part of a settlement of their warring! I thank the Lord François is dead! I hope he burns in hell!"

Nicolette's blazing eyes reflected his own enmity. He wished Henri burned in hell as well. But Nicolette, before her raging, had been correct. He must handle Henri most carefully. It would take time to decide upon the specific course and they had much other ground to cover. Their hours had passed as quickly as moments. Yet the slant of the late autumn sun told him that it would soon be time to dress for supper. "Our fury runs hotly with just reason," he said, calming himself. "We must talk again about the course I should take with Henri after our rage cools into reason. It grows late and we must agree upon matters of urgency now. As you said, 'tis likely that Alienor has already arrived with her party—that stupid maiden Simone amongst them," he spat.

"I truly believe she meant me no harm. Methinks Henri never informed her of her true role. For certainly even a lovesick maiden like Simone would not stand for the man she believed adored her using her to force me to—"

Nicolette did not finish her sentence. He kissed her gently upon her succulent mouth. "I understand," he said. "No more need be said about her. Methinks that if Alienor takes me to be her brother, for the time, we must allow her to believe so. There is no need to burden Bruge. We needn't worry about Henri presently, for I will not see him for at least a few days. Do you gainsay?"

"No. I agree," she said and smiled. "I admit that it seems less complicated by the moment, though we must remain vigilant."

"Aye. I must ask two difficult things of you . . ." he began, knowing the displeasure she would feel at his demands. "They are imperative and never again will I order you, as I swore."

She steeled herself. "Aye. Speak them and I shall comply, Davide." His face took on a cast of stern discomfort.

"Davide is the first. Until we are ensconced safely

within the walls of my father's castle, you may *never* call me Davide again. Not even in the privacy of our bed. You must banish that name from your lips. Burn it from your mind. You must! From this moment on call me François, publicly and privately. You must *think* of me as François."

"But—" she uttered, then let him continue.

"I know how difficult it will be, but you must promise me you will do so. For if you cling to your Davide in the privacy of your thoughts 'tis possible that in the pain of childbirth you will cry out for Davide and not François."

He was correct. The thought had not occurred to her. She could not deny that which he shrewdly foresaw. The man she adored sat before her, alive and loving. What matter was it what name she called him? Why then did her tears fall again? "Aye . . . François," she said. Her tears flowed freely now. She smiled through them and kissed his lips. I kiss your lips, François," she said. "'Tis terribly difficult, for it was I who named you like a newborn, Da—" She stopped herself. "François. Can we not name our son Davide? I pray you! Can we not, François?" She said his name with greater resolve.

"Aye, we can!" Pierre laughed. "But pray tell what will you choose if he is a she?"

"Doreen," she said immediately. "After my mother."

"Doreen . . . 'tis pretty. I feared you would say Davida," he teased. "If he is a boy child he shall be named Davide. Or she will be called Doreen. Which sex be it, Mother?" he teased.

"I carry Davide. Our next child shall be Doreen . . . François."

How her face shone, Pierre thought. "I love you more than you will ever know, Nicolette." He held her close to him again. "I, too, from this moment on will think of myself not as Pierre Delise, or even Davide . . . a name that has meant more to me than you might guess . . . I shall be in my own mind François Perdant. It should be harder for me than for you," he teased lightly, "for I have known myself far longer."

Nicolette burst into laughter and Davide kicked inside her making her laugh the harder. She pulled his hand to her belly so he could feel his son's strength. "Davide laughs too at his amusing father!"

"I knew Davide would be a child of wit!"

Nicolette placed her hands over his. "The second command, François?" she asked, growing serious again. "You said there were two."

"Aye," he replied, sad to end the moment of carefree joy. "Your forced marriage to Fran"—he grinned—"to *me* fooled no one at St. Aliquis. At least not from the talk of the knights. Should you suddenly be seen looking at me with the love I now see in your eyes . . ." He cupped her chin and kissed her lustfully and she sighed with pleasure. He pulled back abruptly. "Or should you respond with even a small measure of the passion that still fills your face, it will be our undoing. Do you understand?"

Most clearly, too clearly, she did. "I must not merely call you François, but you must be François to me," she said and shuddered with the memory.

SONG OF THE ROSE

"Exactly. I will be coarse and loud and overbearing much of the time. I will be François, most simply put. You will reform me *very* slowly. I warned you it would be a difficult command."

Nicolette sighed deeply. "By the time we are free of the charade I hope I will remember something of the man I love," she said. "Why do you grin so?" she asked with irritation, for she saw no humor in this situation.

"Do you swear to do this?"

"Aye, but only if you stop smirking!"

He pulled her down upon the bed. "I never claimed you would have *no* relief," he said. He brought his mouth to her breast.

She struggled but he pinned her arms behind her. "Stop it!" she demanded, in no mood now for his amorous play. Ignoring her, he teased her other nipple, arousing her despite her resistance. "Stop it, I pray you!"

"You pray who, my lady?" he said and worked his mouth and tongue at her neck and ear, causing goosebumps to rise. "Stop it, François!"

"Oh, my lady, your body cries out different words," he said as he slipped into François' pitch and intonation. "I never had the chance, on our wedding night, to show you what a fine lover I am," he said as he mounted her.

No! She could not go through with this after all. She tried to free herself but his mouth caught hers and his tongue played so wickedly, sending chills up her spine. Soon she clung to him, unable to help herself as his fingers slid between her thighs and taunted her with desire. "I want you," she moaned.

"You want who?" he asked. "Tell me how much you want your husband, François, my lusty wench," he said.

Terror clutched her heart as she remembered that moment once before but her tears turned to unbridled passion as he relentlessly tortured her with pleasure. "I want you, François," she cried out.

"'Tis me you want? Tell me, wench?"

"Yes, my lord," she said, and the painful memory of being forced to speak in this same manner lessened in the excitement of the moment. "Yes, François," she whispered.

"Do not lower your eyes," "François" commanded. "I want to see the raw passion in them, my wife."

"Yes, my lord . . ."

"Tell me how much you wish to feel me, hard and hot inside of you," he commanded, his eyes burning, his voice thickened.

She repeated his words, her eyes never leaving his as he sheathed himself inside her. Nicolette cried out as she felt him enter her. Then he withdrew.

"Beg me for it, wench," he ordered, as he taunted her breasts.

"I beg you, François . . ."

"Beg harder, for I am not yet convinced," he demanded.

"I beg you to enter me, François, my lord and husband," she cried out, beside herself as his hands and mouth played at her. His thrust thrilled her and he drove her to a frenzied pitch, then turned her onto her back. He mounted her, the tip of his manhood hot against the delta of her passion.

"Do you love me, Nicolette?" François asked.

"I love you with all my heart," she cried out as he plunged into her. "I love you, François . . . I need you so desperately . . ." He brought her to a wildness she had not thought possible and soon she mindlessly called out, "François, I love you!" again and again until she shook uncontrollably from fingertips to toes and could neither think nor see anything but the blue of François' eyes peering deeply into her. "Oh, François . . ." she moaned as she floated away in a sea of ecstasy.

He watched her with open, gentle devotion, as she slept in his arms as peacefully as a babe. Lightly, he traced the delicate curve of her cheek. "Davide . . ." she muttered in her sleep and smiled, nestling her face against his chest. Though his heart pounded with alarm, he carefully slid away so as not to awaken her.

He rose and stared down upon her. It wouldn't work! Though he knew she meant her promise, calling him François had been a game that her heart and soul rejected. He loved her more than life itself. He had to find a way to force Nicolette to see François when she looked at him. Quickly he dressed for he needed Matthew's counsel. It tore his heart but he knew he had to make Nicolette's Davide dead to her. Cause her to despise him as much as she had François. Until their babe was born and he could take her safely to his father's castle. Until then he had to make her look upon him with the same veiled contempt she felt for François. For now. He prayed that in doing so he would not lose her forever!

Chapter Fourteen

"DAVIDE . . ." NICOLETTE MURMURED AS SHE REACHED out for him, her eyes closed in luxuriant half sleep. Her hand touched the pillow, seeking his face. He was gone, she realized, and turned until she felt the warmth that lingered from his body. She pulled the coverlets more tightly around her and fell back into a calm, sweet slumber.

"Nicolette?" Davide sat beside her, dressed in a fine blue bliaut that reflected his eyes, she saw, as she gazed up at him and smiled sleepily. The room glowed in soft candlelight. She closed her eyes as he stroked her face. She had dreamed that she held her newborn son in her arms, standing before Father Gregoire at the altar of the chapel as he performed the baptismal rites. François stood proudly beside her . . . François smiled at her. Nicolette opened her eyes in sudden alarm. "Davide!" she cried out.

He pulled her upright and cupped her face. "Look at me, Nicolette," he demanded urgently. "Who am I? I am François Perdant, Nicolette. Say my name!" he insisted.

She tried to turn her head away, awash in drowsy confusion, but he held her fast.

"I am François," he continued, hardening himself to the fear that darkened her eyes and paled her cheeks. "Who made you quake with lust? Whose name did you cry out again and again? Say my name, Nicolette."

'Twas François' voice that commanded her. 'Twas François' heartless eyes and hard grasp that held her. I can't! her heart cried out. He kissed her lips and she tried to fight him but she couldn't. His mouth grew more insistent and she answered his kisses with her own. His hands cupped her breasts, his fingers dancing at her nipples.

"Say my name, my wife," he whispered.

"François," she cried out. "François, my husband!" She ran her fingers through his thick blond curly locks. My Davide, she thought. "François . . ." she said as his lips and tongue played at her neck and she clung to him tightly in response.

"You are a lusty wench, my succulent, ripe wife," he whispered. He remembered how François bragged that he'd broken her in as skillfully as he had his destrier. He forced himself to continue. He had to make her hunger, not for Davide, but for François. It frightened him when he felt himself become François, gaze upon her through François' coarse eyes. He would utter words that demeaned her and subjugated her to his lust as he aroused her beyond thought. He felt François' arrogant lust throb within him once again as his manhood hardened beneath his chemise. By the time they were free, would she have grown to despise him? He could not think such now or it would be their undoing. "Rise, my lady," he demanded, as he carefully but quickly pulled her from the bed. He sat as she stood before him, splendid in her nakedness, her taut, protruding belly heightening his ardor.

Nicolette felt as if she were in a trance. She felt the color rise and her face heat as he stared lewdly at her. 'Twas François who leered at her, his mouth curled churlishly in bold desire that narrowed his eyes. Yet instead of repulsion she felt herself mesmerized, her own desire growing as strong as her discomfort.

"Turn slowly," he demanded, "for your blush is most becoming and I wish to see if all of you blushes." He laughed as his words further heightened her cheeks.

'Twas as if he knew he had asked once before.

"Now, my lady!"

The harshness of his command startled her. Her head spun, her thoughts so disordered that she could only obey. Slowly she turned. She faced the blazing fireplace, her back to him, and started to complete her circle.

"Do not move," he whispered in a voice she dared not disobey. She heard the creak of the bed and his approaching footsteps. He breathed heavily against her neck as his arms folded over her shoulders and cupped her breasts so hard that she winced. He lightened his grasp as his fingers taunted her nipples until they hardened and she quivered, forced to lean against him as her knees weakened. She realized then that he had removed his clothing when her back was turned, for she felt his manhood pressed hard against her as his hands roamed her body.

"Do not turn," he demanded and walked her slowly backward until he sat himself upon the bed again and brought her between his spread thighs. She moaned as his fingers fondled the seat of her womanhood. "For all your pretense of reverence and modesty, you are a whore like all beautiful women, Nicolette," he said salaciously. He brought his other hand to her belly. "Madonna and whore." He chuckled. He felt her try to suppress her moan and worked his fingers more deeply inside her, forcing her to sigh with pleasure. "See how you moan and sigh with lust," he taunted. "You do not love me. 'Twas only because of your clever brother's blackmail that you consented to wed me. Yet I thrill you to the core, do I not, my lady?" His fingers taunting her nipple now made her cry out despite herself. "Answer me, wench," he demanded. "For my hand is moist with your desire."

François' nip at the sensitive spot beneath her arm made her cry out, not in pain but in pleasure. Arrogantly he thrilled her body as if she were his plaything—as if she were a whore. But she couldn't help herself, for every physical taunt, every lascivious word drove her harder and she had no will to fight him or the sparks that flamed from her core.

"Tell me how much you want me. Beg me,

François, your lord and master, to take you, my baroness!" He pressed his manhood hard against her.

"Please, my lord, I want you," she cried out. "Pray, François," she said, hearing her voice choked with desire.

"You despise me, though, do you not!"

"I despise you as much as I want you! I despise myself!"

"Address me properly," he said, as he leaned back and raised her upon him, his manhood plunging into her moist warmth.

"Take me hard, my lord. My husband, François!"

He lifted her off his lap and sat her upon the center of the bed. She trembled with unspent desire. "I told my knights stories of your unbridled passion. I told them how I had broken you in, my proud, plucky maiden, as I had broken in my proud destrier who answers my every command. I fear 'twas then an empty boast, though it brought them much pleasure unavailable otherwise in the hot desert sands. I described so well that they could picture every move as vividly as I imagined it." He laughed cruelly. "Now I shall make it a reality," he said, all the time stroking her body.

He turned her onto her hands and knees. "You detest me, Nicolette, do you not? Answer!"

He pinched her and she cried out in pain. "I detest you, François! I always have!" His hand soothed the hurt and slid between her thighs.

"Spread them wider," he ordered. "Just as I told the knights you had."

Trembling with anger, she complied and he laughed as he plunged into her from behind, filling her more deeply than she thought possible as he thrust hard into her.

"Do I ride you well, wench?"

Only her body answered as she responded to his thrusts.

"I want to hear the words from your glorious mouth. Shall I ride you harder? My destrier loves to be ridden hard. Do you wish me to ride you harder?"

"Aye . . . Aye!" She hated herself for the pleasure she could not force away.

"Though you despise me?" he mocked.

"Aye," she said, her passion deeper than her shame. For she loved how François took her as much as she hated him. "Aye, François!"

He thrust slowly, teasing her. "I shall entertain my weary party of knights tonight with each detail. How Matthew will lust with envy. They shall all look at you with veiled lust and it thrills me to know *you* shall know why! I shall tell you how I will describe you beneath me now," he began lecherously.

He was the vilest creature. "Oh God," she cried out as François rode her heartlessly. She hated herself more with each jolt of ecstasy but she could not stop her writhing beneath him, as he humiliated her with strings of coarse expressions and demands, some she had never heard before. "His whore" he called her again and again.

He felt himself at the brink. Tears she could not see ran down his cheeks until François' lust overcame him and he, François, took her, his tears ceasing as he lost himself inside her.

* * *

SONG OF THE ROSE

She lay beside him and he knew that no longer were they the same. *Please, Lord, tell me that I haven't lost her forever . . .*

Nicolette glanced at him. He had taken her twice with humiliating skill. She studied his handsome, sculptured face made even more so by the jagged wound, searching for Davide as he lay in quiet sleep. But all she could see was François. The heat of the passion he brought her lingered in her body. She remembered the sweet knight who had loved her so gently in the woods. *Mother Mary, please bring him back to me,* she prayed, for he was now more an ancient dream than a reality. François, not Davide, lay beside her. She closed her eyes tightly in prayer.

He rose and rested his head upon his arm as he studied her delicate face. "Nicolette?" he whispered. "Do you sleep?"

"I am awake, François," she answered. She smiled as he brought his mouth to hers. A rueful smile, but a smile all the same. In his mind's eye he watched François smile back at her with bold pleasure of victory.

"Shall I dress for supper, François?" she asked. She felt hunger gnaw, despite her despair. François lived. He had made her his wife, his whore, and *worse,* a helpless prisoner shackled to her own lust, God forgive her.

He chuckled. "'Tis after six," he said. "While you slept, I had the maid bring us a tray of food and wine. She giggled and blushed when I said that her lady was too exhausted to dress. Are you hungry?"

"Aye," she answered, trying to ignore his coarseness. "I am." She needed to nourish her babe—he was all she had left of her Davide.

"Good," he said with genuine pleasure as he rose and brought the tray to the foot of her bed. "For I was advised that you had not been eating properly. My son needs his nourishment, may I remind you, my lady." He busied himself preparing the contents of the overflowing silver tray. "Tonight I will feed you, and you must eat every morsel. There is fine soup, cheese, bread, a leg of lamb, and even a most scrumptious-appearing tart for dessert." He pointed to the table where the tray had lain. "And more than enough wine to quench our thirst." He laid a smaller tray onto her lap and fed her a spoonful of the still-hot soup. He then fed himself and smiled with satisfaction. "The heat of the fireplace kept it warm as I had hoped. Another spoonful for you, my wife. No, this one is for my son," he said. He smiled as she laughed in response. "You see, I can be a gentle, caring husband when you behave to my satisfaction."

She nodded and swallowed the tasty ox soup. Had the ghost of Davide reappeared? No, 'twas still François in a moment of kindness she would pay for, she had no doubt.

"I cannot eat another bite," she protested and pushed the tart away. "I have eaten more tonight than I have in days."

"As you should . . . I do not intend to let you rest, without receiving a proper show of your gratitude, as soon as my stomach lightens," he said as he brought the goblet of wine to her lips. He placed the tray of remaining food on the floor. "There is much I want to teach you. After months in the hot desert I have little desire to forestall instruction." He grinned and ran his fingers across her mouth.

"But I am very tired." Nicolette feigned, for her heart beat with trepidation. Each moment she lost herself. She searched for Davide but 'twas François she saw, heard, and hopelessly obeyed.

He brought the goblet to her lips. "Drink," he commanded. "The wine shall refresh you." He watched as she slowly finished half the gobletful of wine. "I shall tell you a story now, while you rest." His smirk told her it would not be the kind of story ladies were usually told by gentlemen. She tensed, but the wine took effect and she leaned back against the pillows.

"One evening, I was riding from Paris and stopped at an inn. I was drinking with Michel when two whores approached us, one more beautiful than the other. One indeed looked *much* like you, though she could not match your beauty, my wife. Michel and I sighed, for we were weary and drunk beyond desire, despite their beguiling loveliness. I forget their names —whores are whores. They followed us to our chamber. Michel told them they wasted their charms, for nothing they could do would rouse our sleeping manhood. The whore who looked like you bet us a tidy sum that they could prove us wrong."

Nicolette flinched, guessing what came next.

"Come now, my lady! I say nothing that should shock you! Do you pretend lingering maidenly innocence?" She flushed in response and he continued. Nicolette did not yet know that a distraught Alienor had arrived hours before. He had to make certain that by the time Alienor told her the heartrending story she had told him in the privacy of her chamber—and surely she would disclose even more details of Henri's vile advances to Nicolette—that Nicolette would not break her promise in order to spare Alienor further copious tears. He would protect Alienor, but only by making her believe he did so for his own advantage. He, François, her brother. Already, with the wine's aid, Nicolette's eyes saw only François. Moment by moment he willfully made Davide a ghost.

"Listen carefully now . . ." he mocked. "For you shall be tested on what you learn." He hid the pain that knifed him as her contempt blazed in her eyes.

Nicolette steeled herself. For she knew that what shamed her most was the certainty that he would have her crying out with pleasure before his humiliating game was over. How could anyone so handsome be so vile? She drank down the remainder of her wine though her head already spun.

"'Tis no use," he whined. "I should have taken the other whore," he complained. "Look at how she pleasures my squire!" he said resentfully, remembering each detail of the story François had told them, with Michel's bawdy interjections, that night around the bonfire in Acre. He lifted Nicolette from her knees on the straw-matted floor onto the bed. "That was when she took on the voice and demeanor of a young innocent virgin. Do you remember that part?" he demanded, forcing himself to ignore her look of horror. "Do you?"

"Aye." 'Twas like a terrible dream. Davide was

dead. François lived; his crudity, his unbridled lust filled the chamber. Took her with no mercy.

"Good. First we shall drink more wine to refresh us." She wiped her mouth and drank with no protest. He handed her her chemise. "Put it on now," he commanded. "I hope 'tis not one of your finest, for it shall be ripped to shreds before our game is through!" She was sufficiently drunk, still her eyes widened with the certain knowledge of what would transpire. "Good," he said and chuckled. "I see you are readying yourself for the part. Even with your belly you look far more like a frightened maiden than the whore did. I shall enjoy this immensely. I only wish Michel were alive to share the pleasure." He was intoxicated enough to laugh at the irony of his own joke.

Nicolette pulled away from his touch as she lay exhausted beside him. "You disgust me," she said. She lifted herself upright as he laughed. Her head throbbed but her shame pained her more greatly. She had not only played the role he demanded but in the heat of passion she had begged for more.

He no longer had to steel himself against her hatred. Already he had slowly grown accustomed to that look in her eyes. He finished his wine and smiled. "'Twas not what you claimed before, my dear wife. You enjoyed the game as well as I. You were surprisingly good at it! I shall have to think of more to amuse us during the long, cold winter nights. Games that will not endanger my son, of course. I shall enjoy watching you grow fatter each day. By the by, I forgot to tell you that my sister arrived late this afternoon while you slept. She asked to speak with you tonight. I suppose it slipped my mind, so full of ardor upon our reunion. Shall I dress and send for her now? I should be happy to take a stroll about the castle and leave you two to private conversation."

He had waited purposely to tell her when she was beside herself with drunken weariness and despair! Nicolette realized. She could barely think. How could she let sweet Alienor see her, after so long, in this terrible condition? "I am too tired . . . I shall see her on the morrow." Nicolette turned and closed her eyes, eager for the relief of sleep.

"My wife, how selfish you can be! Did I neglect to mention how distraught she was? How she pleaded? She is as slender as a twig from despair."

Nicolette rose with alarm. "François, how could you!" Her head spun but she forced herself to alertness. "What has happened?"

"Oh, I am certain she will tell you. She is behaving most thoughtlessly, as you women do. Most unbecomingly. She actually brought herself to her knees before me *begging* me to put an end to her promised betrothal to your brother. I am quite fond of my sister, but surely she has been kissed and fondled before, by Guy, may he rest in peace. Methinks she makes a fuss over Henri's show of his devotion, don't—"

"Send for her at once!" Nicolette ordered him with contempt she did not try to hide. Unsteadily she rose and walked to her washbasin.

"Your wish is my command, my lady," he mocked. He hid his surprise as she walked back and stood unsteadily, but with determination blazing in her eyes.

"If you wish to ever touch me again, François," she

said, "you will immediately put an end to this planned betrothal of your sister to my vile brother!"

"If it upsets you so, I shall think about it. I only promise that." He smiled amiably and took her hand, stroking it gently. "Should you continue to pleasure me as completely as you have tonight, perchance I should come to agree with you and Alienor more quickly." He patted her rump. "I shall dress and have Alienor summoned. May I assist you in bathing and dressing?" he asked with boldly feigned innocence.

"I shall manage quite well, myself, François." She turned and found her way to the washbasin. Davide was dead . . . Her head pounded and her tears spilled as she washed. It had been only a dream, she thought with confusion, or a trick François had played on her most cruelly, pretending to be her Davide . . . "Davide," she murmured.

"What did you say, Nicolette?" he asked, hiding his alarm.

She looked at him with surprise, as if she had forgotten that he stood dressing just feet away. "I said nothing," she replied, so coldly defiant that it broke his heart.

"How I wish Guy were alive," Alienor said as she sat beside Nicolette, tears still streaming from her swollen eyes. Even François' description had not prepared her for how wan and distraught Alienor appeared. She was like a ghost of herself. "Or that your Davide had returned."

"Davide is dead," Nicolette said numbly. "He died in Acre." As she said the words she knew them true.

"I cannot believe—" Alienor sighed deeply. "I do

not know what I can believe any longer . . . Look at you. You should be glowing with the joy of carrying your babe, yet but for your belly you are terribly thin. Too thin. It can not be good for the babe. You are woozy such as I have never seen you. I dare not ask what humiliations my brother has wrought upon you already. I *knew* that he had not relayed my pleas to see you out of his own selfishness! Yet 'tis only François' mercy that can save me, so I dared not anger him by coming to the door of your chamber."

"I feared you would have thought I had ignored your call." Nicolette wiped away her tears. "I think that I have persuaded François to end your betrothal. I pray so!"

For the first time Nicolette saw hope flicker in Alienor's eyes. "Truly? Oh, Nicolette, I can not thank thee enough!" Alienor hugged her tightly. "How did you persuade him?"

"'Tis not yet done," Nicolette cautioned. "Do not ask how, for I can not bear to speak of my—I will try to make him consent quickly. He holds back only to taunt me, methinks."

Alienor paled at her words. "He does not hurt you? Endanger the babe?" she said in a fearful whisper. "For if he does, I care not that he is my brother. He has no right—I shall demand—"

"He does not harm me in body, I promise you. He is quite tender about the babe," she said slowly. She was too ashamed to speak of how he mortified her. Worse, how he made her a participant, made her despise herself for her abasement—for each moan of pleasure, for each unwilling yet freely cried plea for more. She shuddered when she thought of the very words she uttered as he commanded, heightening his lust that in turn brought her to a tortured ecstasy that left her exhaustedly clinging to him. A lust that possessed her, forcing her to endure his mocking smirk of victory, then punished her further as he aroused her again, his mouth, his fingers, weapons of the Devil, surely! She too sinful to fight the pleasure he wove. He had taken her body in almost every way possible, forced her to beg for him as he called her a whore and worse. He had stripped her of her reverence, for she had sinned and pleasured in her lust. He shredded her self-respect as quickly as he ripped her chemise to pieces. Worst of all, he murdered her Davide, and she helped him as surely as if she had stabbed her dagger through Davide's heart.

"Nicolette!" Alienor shook her. How long had she shaken her, Nicolette wondered, with no particular feeling. Strangely she felt little more than a floating sensation from the wine. "Nicolette! Answer me or I shall call for the physician at once!" Alienor's words came to her from a distance, or was it she who was off somewhere? The babe began to kick wildly. Nicolette brought her hands to her belly.

"The babe is awake, Alienor," she said, coming back to her senses. "Here, give me your hands." She placed Alienor's hands upon the spot. Alienor smiled with awe.

"Oh, how strongly he kicks!" Alienor exclaimed. "Nicolette, do you hear me now?"

"Aye . . ." she answered and smiled.

"I do not know how, but everything will turn about. You must endure what is obviously too painful for you to speak, for the moment. I shall be here to help you!

I shall not leave you! Once the babe is born I shall help you to escape my brother, should you choose to. Pray trust my love and devotion," Alienor said and opened her arms. Nicolette fell into them and wept.

"I cannot go on with this charade, Matthew!" Pierre exploded and heaved the empty bottle of wine into the fireplace. He overturned the silver tray and goblets, flinging them as well, then pounded his fists against the wall.

Matthew watched quietly as Pierre expended his fury. Pierre turned to him finally, his face streaked with anguished tears. Finally, he sank upon a bench and with his face hidden in his hands sobbed like a frightened child. Matthew waited until his sobs lessened, then sat beside him, clasping his shoulder tightly.

"I cry like a woman," Pierre finally uttered brokenly, with shame.

"Should it be womanly to weep in torment, then we are all women at one time or another," Matthew answered honestly.

A memory came to him and he looked up at his dear friend. "My father used to say that only the Devil never wept," Pierre said and smiled through his blurred eyes.

"My mother said that tears were Christ's gift to us . . . the same sentiment in different words, methinks." Matthew chuckled. "Certainly the *trouvères* and *jongleurs* sing songs of knights who weep at the mere sight of their ladies' pinky."

Pierre laughed heartily and Matthew poured them fresh goblets of wine. Pierre quenched his thirst quickly. He grew somber again as the memories of the evening tortured him. "When I left Nicolette, she glared at me with utter contempt. She ordered me to end Alienor's intended betrothal to Henri or I would never touch her again. I believe that she could as easily have thrust a dagger through my heart as the most bellicose of knights. She despises me! 'Twas no inkling of love for her Davide in her eyes. I *have* become François to her and 'tis to the phantom of Davide she prays to save her from me!" He wiped his fresh, harsh tears away.

"But 'tis exactly what you had to do, my friend! To save her and your babe, not to mention her sister and Alienor. As much pain as you brought her you inflicted upon yourself. Someday—not far off—you two shall lie comfortably in bed in your father's castle and laugh about it."

"We shall never laugh about it, Matthew. I wish I could tell you now about my father's castle that will one day be mine," he said earnestly. "Do I try your patience by holding this secret from you?"

Matthew laughed. "You try my curiosity. But I understand. You will reveal that part of your life to me when you can. Is Alienor now with Nicolette?"

"Aye. I hope they bring one another a measure of comfort. I have brought nothing but cruel tears to each tonight."

"No worse than your own agony," Matthew gently reminded.

"Matthew, I do not know how to speak of this. I do not wish to further humiliate Nicolette more than need be. But, I—"

"Humiliate?" Matthew scorned. "No woman could

be loved more dearly than she by you, Pierre. You see, I call you Pierre tonight, only because I cannot bear to add to your torment. Speak to me, if you trust me fully enough to believe my heart is in anguish for all of you."

"How could you even question such," Pierre answered. "I hold back because of my own shame. But I must open it before, like a wound, it festers and kills me."

"Another round, first," Matthew declared as he filled their goblets.

"You see, Matthew. Not only did Nicolette come to see me only as François, but may God forgive me, I *became* François. Remember that bawdy story he and Michel told us about the two whores they spent a drunken night with in a tavern outside of Paris?"

"Who could forget," Matthew said dryly. "If François had told it alone I would have thought it a tale from his imagination. But Michel's adding missing pieces convinced me 'twas true and hardly exaggerated at that."

"Forgive me, but during the course of the evening I not only took my precious Nicolette in much the manner François boasted, when he regaled us with his 'night' with her . . . I know of course that most of what he said was lies, but I remembered and made them a cursed reality. Likewise with the story about the whores—"

"Pierre. I understand how it cut against your nature to—"

"Wait," Pierre cried out, at last unburdening his soul, "'tis what sickens me most. For I *became*

François! His lust was mine. My arousal, my ardor was his! I hated each moment, each word, yet they *thrilled* me to the core, God forgive me!"

His eyes filled again. "And I debased my beloved Nicolette in the same way. I fired her with such desire that I forced her to beg for further pleasure, seducing her into deeper humiliation. I spoke to her with the coarseness I would never speak to any woman, not even a whore. And I forced her to speak thus to me, not by physical coercion, which would have been *less* cruel, but through tormenting her with desire, again and again—" He could not go on. "'Twas François she gave herself to, over and over!" he blurted with horror. "And it was I who was François and took her with the most base rapture! Never will we be the same! Neither Nicolette nor I! This is why Davide is dead and she so despises me and herself. For I could go into her chamber and we would both do it again— I, François, taking her at will, she complying as his wife and whore!"

"I understand how you see it that way but 'tis not so!"

"How can you gainsay!"

"Because 'tis not so. Listen to me, I pray you! 'Tis not the way you think."

"Then prove to me how it could be *anything* but what I have said. Do not tell me 'twas only the wine that went to Nicolette's head or my need to protect her from danger—"

"I will not"—Matthew sighed—"for that is too simple and untrue, as you rightly say. 'Tis far more complicated, back to Adam and Eve and the Original

Sin. The priests tell us much nonsense, methinks, but at the bottom they warn of the ultimate truth."

Pierre quieted, eager to hear Matthew's thoughts, for his own self-loathing befuddled his mind. "Which truth? That we are all sinners?"

"Aye. But what *that* means, methinks, is that the Lord has given us, all of us, the animal emotions, the physical sensations to become as debased as François was, as Henri is, and how many others have we seen? Men with men, men with animals, women with women, father with daughter, brother with sister, the whores and men who buy their favors. I could go on endlessly, it seems. The senseless murders, rapes, and carnage after a village or castle is taken continues. Long after the barbarians have disappeared. I believe 'tis little the poor human creature is not capable of. Is that not why we pray daily for our Lord's *mercy*? Do we not *choose* each day between good and evil?"

"Aye. But the pleasure—there should have been *no* pleasure!" Slowly Pierre's mind cleared. "But if there were no pleasure there would be no temptation . . . 'Tis only through resisting temptation that we honor the Lord, truly. For if it comes easily, then we are but superficially reverent, do you agree, Matthew?"

"You have said it in a way I couldn't express. 'Tis what I do believe. I also believe, although you curse yourself as does Nicolette, that 'twas perhaps perverse, but nevertheless *still* an expression of love between Nicolette and Davide. Between Nicolette and *you*."

"No—"

"Pray calm yourself and listen. Do you really

believe that if it had *truly* been François in Nicolette's bed that she would have done more than simply endure? 'Twas it that simple, then François *would* have been the father of your child that hateful night, sleeping droplets or not. And Henri would have had his stepsister and Alienor as well. Do you not see?"

"Perchance," Pierre agreed reluctantly. "But still."

"Pierre. It embarrasses me to speak of matters of religion, far more than of wenching and the like. But I tell you from the depth of my heart that I cannot help but believe that if the Virgin Mother had looked down upon you this evening, she would have understood and blessed you both, though you curse yourself!"

The force of Matthew's sentiments caused them to rest in quiet meditation.

"Even if I take refuge in what you say," Pierre finally continued, "how will I ever regain Nicolette's love and respect?"

"'Tis not dead, but *safely* buried. Now you can act quickly as you said you wanted to. You can put an end to Henri's reign of lust on the morrow. Tell both Nicolette and Alienor tonight. Even if it means awakening them. You, *François,* can arrange for Bruge's betrothal on the morrow as well. How do you intend to rid them of Henri, by the by?"

Pierre couldn't help but laugh. He had yet to see this despicable Henri, but he could imagine the reprobate's reaction when he ordered him to marry Baron Harcourt's daughter. He had learned from François that the poor old maid, nearing twenty-three, was pathetically unattractive with no gifts of song or charm to compensate. He doubted that even such a swine as Henri would bother the poor maiden much. "Wed him to Sabine, Harcourt's daughter."

Pierre roared with laughter, having heard the story. He imagined Henri's sharp, hawklike face, which he had glimpsed but once yet still recalled, red with fury. He laughed the harder. "After what he attempted to do to Nicolette and Alienor, I'd rather see him hang. But I suppose this would be a worse fate for him and yet ensure the peace between Harcourt and the barony of St. Aliquis. I only pity the poor maids at Harcourt," he said and laughed harder.

Pierre rose and walked to the blazing fire. "So I *must be* François until my babe is born," he said with resignation. "But I can do the good François never would." He brightened. "Perchance Nicolette's heart will soften when she sees the results. I can slowly allow her to reform me—however slightly?"

"*Very* slightly, for no one would believe more from François." Pierre smiled at the truth of Matthew's statement. "'Tis one other thing you can do," Matthew said, smiling boldly now.

"Pray tell?"

"Allow me to become Nicolette's protector. Her confidant if she'll trust me. For not only your sakes, but my own."

"'Tis true. I had been too distraught to think about it, but if she hates you too, she will turn Alienor against you. I believe she still thinks you her ally. On the morrow, after I have left for St. Aliquis, do have a private audience with her. Say anything you desire. 'Tis rocky ground we traverse, is it not?" Pierre sighed.

"'Tis that, Pierre. But it *will* end well. I am certain. Do you still plan to ride from St. Aliquis to see your father?"

"Aye. For it pains me much to know that he believes me dead. Also, I shall be able to seek his agreement to my plans to ensure our future safety. Then it will be merely a matter of months. *Merely—* how easily said." He laughed darkly. "In a fortnight you may have to force me to remember who I am again."

"In a fortnight I hope you will have told me!" Matthew raised his hands in mock confusion. "You have more names then anyone I have ever known!"

"That I do," Pierre answered with a cryptic smile. "I will go to Nicolette's chamber. I suspect that neither she nor Alienor sleeps. Perhaps I can at least bring Alienor relief. I do hope you can win her heart, my friend. For you have won mine." Playfully Pierre gave him a mock kiss upon his lips.

Matthew pretended to shove him away. "I do adore blue eyes and fair hair, but only on a woman, François. Is there *no* limit to your lewdness, Messire Perdant?"

"You are not of whom I dream either, Sire Matthew!" Pierre's teasing smile faded. "I pray you, Matthew, bring me quickly a quill and parchment. I shall write a letter to Baron Grieves requesting the betrothal of Bruge Duprey to his son and heir, Gervais Grieves. I shall present it to Nicolette and allow her own chosen messenger to deliver it as further assurance of my sincere intentions. I am certain that Henri retains the letter François sent, granting his permission for Henri to wed Alienor if he saved St. Aliquis in François' absence. I shall nullify that letter in writing, as well as in person, on the morrow. I hope that my present of this letter to Alienor shall allow her to rest more easily."

"I cannot imagine otherwise. And will you now rest more easily, François?" He watched as Pierre easily wrote in François' hand.

"At most I can give fey assurance. I will leave Nicolette to the peace of her bed tonight. She should sleep, if only from exhaustion. As soon as I have completed these letters"—he paused from his writing—"and made their delivery, I shall return to this chamber for the night, so you may have the servants prepare my bed as well." He returned his attention to his scripting.

He watched as his sister and his wife each read the letters he had handed them. Alienor's face lighted with joyous relief as she read. Nicolette's expression remained inscrutable. Dropping her letter upon the table, Alienor ran to him as he sat in the large, carved chair.

"Thank you, my brother!" she said as she kneeled before him, her eyes still reddened and filled with tears. But they were tears of salvation.

He fought back any show of being moved. "Rise, my sister. 'Tis done and I have seen enough weeping for one day, I pray you! You may hold this letter in your safekeeping, for I intend to ride to St. Aliquis on the morrow and inform Henri of my decision. I shall have him betrothed to Sabine Harcourt by evening, in order to solidify the peace between the baron and myself." From the corner of his eye he saw a flicker of something in Nicolette's face, but he was afraid to take it as a sign of hope.

"My dear wife," he said. It had become easy for him to adopt the pitch and cadence of François' voice, though the mean-spirited tone, oh so mocking, pained him. "I will leave the task of picking a messenger to take your letter to Baron Grieves in your capable hands. Does that please you, my sweet?"

"It pleases me, François," she said, but her eyes remained wary. *And what degradation will you charge me for protecting Bruge, François?* she wondered.

He felt an unwarranted anger at her rise within him. Could she not give them both the briefest respite that a genuine smile would provide? He could not leave her on this note. Suddenly he changed his mind as to the sleeping arrangements. For Alienor said Bruge already slumbered in her chamber. "Sister," he said to Alienor. "I wish to be alone with my wife, on this the first eve of our reunion. It would please me if you would stop at my chamber and inform Matthew that I will share my wife's bed tonight, after all." He turned to Nicolette, daring her silently to reject him. "If it pleases you, of course, my lovely Nicolette?"

She was not taken by surprise. "If you wish, my husband. I am very weary and would like to retire." She hugged and kissed Alienor but her smile faded as she turned to him. She walked Alienor to the chamber door.

"Sleep well, François," Alienor said.

"And you, sister," he answered softly.

Nicolette walked to him. "What do you wish from me, François?" she asked with no show of emotion.

"I wish you to undress . . ." Her eyes registered quiet contempt but she stood as quietly frozen as a statue. "And sleep long and well," he said.

Something in his eyes held her. 'Twas her Davide she saw again, and her mind clouded in confusion. Tentatively, she reached for his hand.

"Unless you are feeling amorous again and wish to sport?" He grinned lewdly, demanding her revulsion. "For of all the women I have had—Lord knows how many—you are not only the most beautiful but the lustiest by nature. Methinks there is nothing amorous known to man that you wouldn't perform, despite your pretense of goodliness. My succulent wife, you are at heart a whore. And how it pleases me! A match made in Heaven!" He roared mercilessly as she turned on her heels and unsteadily marched away. He laughed to hide his tears. For he had seen her "see" Davide rather than François and in his joy had almost thrown himself to his knees and begged her forgiveness.

Thank the Lord that he was taking his leave in the morn and would be gone for at least a week. Neither of them could survive otherwise.

Nicolette slipped into her bed and drew the coverlets over her without as much as a glance at François. Yet his lewd grin and mocking laugh stayed in her mind's eye as his vile words replayed in her head. At least Bruge would finally be safe . . . Her eyes were so heavy. She closed them and François' face faded. She saw Davide smiling with loving devotion. He sang

"The Song of the Rose" to her, gently soothing her into slumber as he had every night since the day they met.

"Nicolette," he whispered and caressed her arm gently. She turned to him in her sleep. "Davide?" she whispered. She opened her eyes with a smile upon her face. "François," she said coldly. Her face turned hard as stone. She shifted to her side, away from him. He blew out the candle and lay staring into the night.

Chapter Fifteen

'Twas a bright May morn in Nicolette's dream. Davide stood across the stream, splendid in his mailed suit. She ran to the edge of a jagged, slippery rock, wet from the rush of cool water. Her balance was precarious but she did not notice. "Davide," she cried out, her hands resting on her belly for the babe kicked. "You abandoned me though you promised that you would return for us! Why? Davide, I loved you so!"

"And I you, Nicolette. I did return!" he called over the rushing water.

"'Tis not true. François returned, not thee! 'Tis your babe I carry! 'Tis my love for you I carry!" Suddenly he disappeared. "Davide!" she cried out. "Where are you? I pray you, do not leave me again!"

"I am here, my beloved Nicolette," he said. His voice, close behind her now, startled her, and as she turned she lost her footing and began to helplessly slip.

"Nicolette, you are my love and life," he said as he caught her and lifted her into his arms.

She held fast to him but paled in horror. For 'twas François, dressed in the blue bliaut he had worn today, who held her, his right cheek jaggedly cut. "You are François, not Davide! Put me down! Let me be! Give me back my Davide!"

"You need to sleep, long and well," he said softly. 'I am Davide," he repeated gently. "'Tis the shock of my return and the continuous wine I made you drink that confuses you. I am François and Davide, your beloved husband . . ."

She struggled. "No!" Then she gazed into his eyes and she knew. "Davide, you did come back to me. You didn't die in Acre!" She saw the tears fill his eyes. "Pray forgive me!"

"Pray forgive me!" Nicolette cried out as she bolted up in her bed.

"My lady?" Blanche rushed to her. "My lady," she soothed. "'Tis morn. You had a bad night dream. You are awake now, Nicolette!"

Nicolette glanced around her, her eyes taking in slowly the light of dawn, the sweet sound of chirping blackbirds. "Where is—" She remembered. She remembered everything now. "Where is François, my husband?"

"He awoke me before dawn and asked me to sleep again upon my pallet should you need me. He was about to ride to St. Aliquis. Do you not remember?

Your eyes are swollen and you look most dreadful, my lady."

"My heart pounds," Nicolette admitted. She was now alert, though her head pained heavily. She had never drunk as much as yesterday, she thought, as each detail of the day came back to her.

"Shall I bring you something for the ache in your head, my lady?" Blanche asked. "Daphne has gone with Bruge to chapel."

"Are you certain François has already taken his leave, Blanche?"

"Not certain. Do you wish me to see if I can find him?"

"Aye. I pray thee, ask him to come to me immediately! Hurry, Blanche."

Blanche hesitated, her pretty face a show of uncertainty. "Are you certain you shall be all right? Sire François ordered me not to leave you alone . . ."

"I shall be fine. Hurry off with you or it will be too late!" she snapped. She watched Blanche run out the door. The thud of wood upon wood thundered in her head.

How terribly, cruelly, drunkenly foolish she had been! How could she have lost her senses so? For it all flooded back to her. Davide, nervously standing before her, masking himself as François, though he brushed his locks from his forehead again and again. Davide rushing into her arms with tears of joy after his alarm that she had truly believed him to be François.

How tenderly he held her in his arms. How they joyed in one another. How glorious their lovemaking. Then he had left her to sleep and she had forgotten her promise. She'd called him Davide . . . How clearly she now remembered the alarm in his eyes. And then the rest. Wine and more wine. So cleverly he had forced her to take him for François. He had forced himself to act as François would have. More wine . . . François filling her senses and her body. Yet somewhere, deep within her, she had known 'twas Davide. Her beloved Davide!

She knew now that she had drunk more and more wine to help her play François' wife. His whore. To François she had been one and the same. But he had *always* been her Davide, though she befuddled her mind otherwise. With a shudder she remembered the heavy, cold touch of the true François' hands upon her body the night before she was made to wed him. Her stomach lurched as she forced herself to remember Henri's fingers upon her breast. Yesterday, despite his transformation in voice and look and lustful action, her body had always known 'twas Davide's fingers and mouth—even when her mind had given way to the confusion abetted by the wine. She smiled. 'Twas Davide she'd thrilled to, again and again. A frightening, dangerous, lustful charade—but a charade nonetheless. 'Twas Davide she'd clung to in exhaustion. It had taken her dream to awaken her from her drunken trance.

Oh, poor Davide! She had pained him so. She had become too quick a learner. Yet he had contributed to their pain as well, for he had not trusted her. Despite her one slip, she could love her Davide in private and treat him as François when they were among others. He had done so for her protection but he had been wrong! If only he had known how good she had become at pretense from the day he left her. Had she not convinced François he had taken her that night? Had she not protected Bruge by keeping her blind to their danger? Had she not, for as long as she could, pretended that the very sight of Henri had not engendered fear in her heart? Davide had failed her by underestimating her stamina. Though she had given him little justification to believe otherwise.

They would talk and together destroy the mailed web they had woven, each link cutting their hearts. Despite the pounding in her head, she quickly rose and walked to the washbasin. She would call him François before others. But she was quick enough and strong enough to call him Davide in her heart and whisper his name in his ear, strong enough to even cry it out in tortured, exquisite ecstasy. When the babe came, she knew that she would not betray them just as she would not betray them if she were stretched upon the rack in the watery cell beneath the *donjon*. Now, she had to make Davide believe her strength. She had told him she wanted no more masters—well then, she had to prove to him that she was truly able to be her own mistress! Rummaging through the crowded wardrobe, she picked out a light rose bliaut. One she was certain he would appreciate. She laughed as it came to her!

She would hum the tune of his own song to him, for she had forgotten most of the words after but one hearing. She would hum his song as she opened her arms to him. How happy he would be!

"My lady," Blanche said as she reappeared in the chamber. "Messire Perdant has already taken his leave. He left word that he would be gone a week."

SONG OF THE ROSE

Nicolette did not attempt to hide her disappointment.

"But Bruge waits outside." Blanche continued. "I only asked her to wait to make certain that you were not ill. For I know you always desire that she not become fearful."

Nicolette smiled. "'Tis most sweet of you, Blanche. Send my sister in, please."

Bruge bounded into the room, causing Nicolette to laugh despite her aching head. "Nicolette, you look so lovely!" Bruge exclaimed. "But your face . . . it is happy but different?"

Nicolette hugged and kissed Bruge, dressed in a pretty, red pelisson. "Aye," she said wryly as she led her sister to the chairs set before the windows. "I fear that your sister drank far more wine than she should have. But I was so joyful that my husband, my François, had returned to me."

Bruge's face broke into a smile brighter than the dappled autumn sun. "Oh, I am pleased! For I feared something was wrong."

"Pray tell?" Nicolette asked, masking her concern.

"I encountered François on my way to chapel at dawn. He greeted me most warmly. Called me his pretty little sister," she said with a smile, "and kissed me gently upon my cheek. But he looked as if he forced his cheer. His eyes appeared—I do not know exactly—sad. Aye, very sad."

"I suspect you mistook weariness for sadness. And too much drink as well, Bruge. For we are very happy," she said with a bright smile. For in truth they had been briefly and would be again for the rest of their lives!

"I can see so in your face," Bruge declared. "Nicolette, I almost forgot! François said you had a surprise for me. A wonderful surprise. Pray tell me!"

Nicolette laughed. How she had longed for this moment. Now she would savor it!

"François, my brother!" Henri said effusively. He bowed, then hugged and kissed him on each cheek. "How well you look. Your wound makes you all the more handsome. It shall heal into a delightfully masculine reminder of your valor!"

"Aye. Methinks so, too," Pierre said, falling again into François' easy arrogance. Henri showed no suspicion that 'twas not François he greeted with such obsequiousness. Pierre stared at the slight, rangy, sharp-featured Henri. Surely he resembled his mother, Pierre thought, for there was no more physical similarity between Henri and his stepsisters than there was likeness of character. The man sickened him. Pierre resisted the urge to end the charade and slit Henri's throat. For now that Henri stood beside him, his knowledge of how he had forced himself upon Nicolette, his bony hands touching her delicate, alabaster skin, enraged him. Pierre forced himself to contain his rage.

"Let me take you to my chamber where I have had a fine dinner awaiting. 'Tis after one. You must be hungry and desirous to quench your thirst after your hard ride, François."

Pierre followed him through the great hall, up the stairs, hoping that he seemed as offhandedly familiar with the palais as François would be.

"I am certain it will please you that I took your

former chamber and had your belongings moved into your late father's chamber—may the honorable Simon Perdant rest in peace!"

Pierre gave an inward sigh of relief for Henri's garrulousness. How tricky this charade was, now that he was in François' household that he had never seen before. "I am pleased you gave yourself more commodious quarters," Pierre responded, Henri's smile telling him he had answered correctly.

"As I knew you would be. I shall leave you to wash. I have had a squire lay out fresh raiments for you." Henri looked upon an empty table. "The servants are so slow! I shall discover what holds up our banquet. Oh, Sire Eustace will be by to greet you later. He apologizes but he is in an important meeting with Sire Macaire."

Pierre tried to remember whether Macaire was the provost or the executioner. One was Macaire and the other? He cursed his mind, made sluggish from too much lingering wine.

"For our provost complains that Maitre Dennis is not hanging the criminals quickly enough." Henri chuckled with the air of a baron. "You know how they are always at one another's throats. Worse than the villeins. I still say your father should not have granted those serfs personal freedom except in their obligations to him—to you now, as seigneur of the barony of St. Aliquis. They have become even more boldly demanding and lazy in the past years, just as you always declared, François. I leave you for the moment. Make yourself comfortable, for you know the chamber better than I." Henri closed the door behind him.

SONG OF THE ROSE

Pierre glanced at the chamber, similar to the one at St. Martin's, though less splendid than his chamber in his father's castle. He quickly washed and dressed. For he wanted to foil Henri before his afternoon meal; childish though it might be, it would bring him a measure of satisfaction to ruin the man's appetite as well as his pernicious ambitions.

"To your health and happiness, François!" Henri toasted. "I do hope my dear sister still pleases you!"

You audacious bastard! Pierre thought. He smiled with François' lewdness. Quickly he decided to use such for his own satisfaction, for he intended to see the swine at least squirm before he gave him his final due—far too good for him but unfortunately necessary so as not to arouse suspicion. "Aye. 'Tis why I appear so bleary-eyed today. For your sister is a lusty wench, Henri! Her mouth is as succulent and dewy as a peach picked right from the tree. And her body. Such beauty—it cries out for pleasure! And how she moans and writhes! Insatiable, always begging for more. The lewdest words pour from her sweet, ripe mouth. Now that she is round with child she thrills me more than before. If I did not know her a virgin the night I took her, I would have sworn she had learned the most lascivious tricks from the finest whores in our barony. For how her lips pleasure me! How she loves to watch as my manhood disappears into the hot sweetness of her mouth and—" Pierre roared heartily, for with each lewd description, Henri's face had paled unknowingly. Pierre could almost feel the man's jealous lust. He went on, finding some satisfaction at taunting the bastard so cruelly. "Why, Henri, methinks that your face speaks of your own lust for your sister. Could that be?" he mocked, feigning innocence—for the moment.

Henri reddened and looked flustered. "Oh, no, François, I only—"

"Rise!" Pierre demanded. He watched as Henri thought to refuse. "Rise, Henri!" Pierre stared at Henri's groin—proof positive. Henri stood, mortified so that even his cunning provided him with no words. "Henri . . ." Pierre said and shook his head in derision. He laughed heartily and watched the bulge of Henri's manhood disappear beneath his chausses—for he had worn his suit of armor instead of a bliaut and pelisson, to impress François, Pierre knew. "You give yourself away. You may sit."

Henri sat with the shame of a mischievous child apprehended. "I know not what overcame me! In truth, I am so excited that I shall soon be wed to your sister, the lovely Alienor, that I have abstained from wenching for weeks, out of devotion to my dear Alienor." Henri's color returned as he recuperated.

Henri was even quicker and more cunning than Pierre had suspected. Certainly François was never his match, and he even outshone Michel, despite his somewhat deceptive obsequious chatter.

Pierre refilled their flagons. "A toast to my sister, the sweet, lovely Alienor!" he said as they clinked flagons and Henri drank heartily. "Who shall be wed to Sire Matthew Tregere!" Pierre had to contain his laughter as he watched Henri choke upon his throatful of wine. Henri choked and sputtered, his face deeper red than the wine in the goblet. I should let him choke to death, Pierre thought, but sighed and rose. He slapped Henri's back, harder than need be, until the man breathed properly again.

"You cannot do so, François! You promised me your sister!" All pretense of subservience fled from Henri's face, red still, but now with rage. "I have your letter to prove it!"

"I have changed my mind. Sire Matthew Tregere saved my life. You merely saved St. Aliquis. My sister despises you and seems to look favorably upon Matthew—but that be no matter of consequence. It will benefit us all if you wed the lovely Sabine Harcourt—"

"That ugly old maid!" Henri paled with the new wave of shock. "That dried-out, stupid—"

"Henri! You speak most ungallantly about your future wife," Pierre mocked.

"You have amused yourself enough with me, François!" Henri rose and stood at the table with open fury. "I shall not permit you to toy with me further. For you forget that it was *I* who forced my sister into your bed in the first place. Threatening to give little Bruge to you if Nicolette refused."

"So you say," Pierre replied evenly.

"So the baron knew, as well as Nicolette!"

"My father is dead. I, François Perdant, be messire now." He grinned. "And I do not believe you will have my wife as a willing collaborator. Last night I presented my dearest Nicolette with a letter that she has most assuredly already messengered to Baron Grieves. It requests the immediate agreement of betrothal of Bruge Duprey to his son Gervais. Their marriage to take place upon his knighting, which should be sooner than later, for Gervais has already proven his gallantry beyond that of any squire. For he not only saved my wife and her sister from Harcourt's capture, but with the aid he enlisted from the gallant, worthy Herbert de Leon, he saved them from your clutches."

"What lies have you been fed, François!" Henri sputtered. "I had not wanted to tell you my sister's *true* nature, for when I discovered so—to my horror, —I realized you would find the wench unworthy of you! Do not stay bewitched by her sweet words! For it pains me to say such about my own flesh and blood— though only on our father's side," he hastened to add. "But my sister is a whore and a liar!"

"Go on," Pierre said quietly, and he watched as Henri's face took on the cast of certain victory.

"The babe in her belly. 'Tis not yours. She had a lover. Some knight. The bastard is his. 'Tis your new vassal, your loyal Matthew Tregere, who carried his passionate love letter to her, for her lover fought with you in Acre—perhaps at your side, for all we know. Matthew intended to carry back Nicolette's equally impassioned reply—one in which she plainly stated the child was his. I am only sorry now that I burned it in haste, I see. The knight's name is—"

"Davide . . . " Pierre said loudly, stunning Henri into silence as sharply as if he had stabbed his sword through his heart. "I know it all. Matthew worked for me all along. 'Twas Matthew who sliced Davide's throat one night soon after, as the foolish knight lay in peaceful slumber." Pierre laughed cruelly. "'Tis nothing I do not know. Would you like to hear?

Surely you would. Drink some wine, Henri, as I tell you about the night when only my father's death and the imminent attack of Harcourt's forces saved Nicolette from the final indignities you intended to impose upon her. Shame, Henri. Wenching is wenching, but Nicolette is your sister! I believe the punishment for such is hanging, is it not?"

Henri stumbled from his chair and kneeled before him. His face blanched, his eyes filled with cowardly tears. "I beseech you for forgiveness. I shall wed Sabine Harcourt as you command and become a repentant husband, serving your interests at all times."

"And what of your liberties upon my fair sister Alienor?" Pierre intended to toy with him a while longer, in part for the crumb of satisfaction he derived from seeing the swine crawl, in part to ensure that Henri remained frightened enough to keep his word.

"I admit to you that I perhaps behaved with bold amorous advances, but I do love your sister! I adore Alienor and always have! She is the only woman who has ever been more than a whore to me!"

Despite himself, Pierre felt a surge of pity for this cowering devil with a soul filled with such bile. He saw that for the first time, Henri indeed spoke the pathetic truth. You are François, he reminded himself, pushing back the wave of sympathy that would be alien to François. "Stop your mewling and rise, Henri. Sit yourself again at the table and pour yourself another flagon of wine. For now that I see you have come to realize your position I shall grant you the mercy you seek. I am touched by your declarations of love for my sister, for I believe them, though you are a clever scoundrel. As for your stepsister, my wife, the truth be it as you say, she is a whore."

He grinned lasciviously. "But such a beautiful one, and she pleases me—for since I confronted her with the fact that her lover is dead and that I will graciously accept the child she carries as my own, there is nothing she will not do to please me. Nothing." He laughed heartily as he raised his goblet to Henri's for a toast. "The truth be it that your attempt to indulge in the pleasures of Nicolette's flesh is not what angers me. 'Tis the fact that you would seek to take what was *mine!* Do you understand?"

Henri smiled apologetically, Pierre saw. For in assuming François' logic, he had hit upon their strange, foul code of honor. "I do and I deeply, sincerely, apologize."

"I accept. Prepare to ride to Baron Harcourt's, where we will complete this matter and be done with it. For I have much business to attend to," Pierre said, feigning diminished interest. "I shall seek out Sire Eustace while you dress and prepare your little speech for Sire Harcourt. Make it a sweet one, Henri." He chuckled and strode to the door.

"I will." Henri smiled, seemingly resigned to his fate.

"Oh, Henri, one last thing," Pierre called. "Should I ever learn that you allow yourself to be found in a private moment with either of your sisters or mine, you shall hang in the wind after all," Pierre said lightly. Henri's dropped mouth assured him that he had successfully communicated his message.

Pierre strode down the hall. A squire approached. "François," the youth said with a smile. "Welcome home! May I be of service to you?"

"Aye. Take me to Sire Eustace." Pierre knew that François' rudeness in not calling the squire by name was taken as a matter of course. He only hoped he would successfully pass his interview with the purportedly stern and wise Sire Eustace.

Henri finished dressing quickly. I do not yet know how, he thought as he poured himself a fresh wine, but I shall have my revenge upon you for this, François Perdant. I will play your game for now, but one day the humiliation you have heaped upon me shall cost you dearly!

Pierre rode through the outer bailey of his father's castle right to the bustling inner bailey and dismounted at the entrance of the great hall. Although he had ridden hard for two days and nights and it had rained most of this morn, he felt a surge of energy course through his weary, wet body. How it thrilled his heart to hear the horn on the turret blow as he entered the outer gates of the castle and the gong at the bailey gate reverberate, announcing a visitor of noble rank. Surely his father knew not yet that it was his son, "risen from the dead." Were not his father of such strong constitution, Pierre would not have dreamed of surprising him with his appearance.

Pierre stood with his back to the palais, surveying the familiar inner courtyard with fresh eyes. He started to call out to the kitchen woman, Giselle, who carried two pails of fresh milk, but stopped himself. She merely glanced at him, for to her he was just another knight in full armor, he knew, and he would find her later. He wanted to see his father before any other.

"Sire Duprey?" his father's deep, rich voice inquired. For 'twas Nicolette's surname he had given at the gate to ensure his return remain a surprise. Pierre swallowed hard and turned slowly. His father stood tall before him, but in the almost half year since he had seen him, he had aged so that it shocked Pierre. 'Twas the news of his death that had probably done it. Pierre's hands shook as he removed his helmet and approached closer. Tears filled his eyes. "Father," he said and fell to his knee as he kissed his father's hand.

His father's strong arms raised him. "My son!" his father said as he embraced him tightly. "The Lord has heard my prayers! I could not believe you were dead!" his father cried, as tears filled his large, piercing blue eyes. Pierre smiled with all the love he had always known in his father's presence.

"Are you well, Father?" Pierre asked, as they sat in his father's chamber in private and dined with easy pleasure. Already, Pierre saw that joy had miraculously seemed to fill some of the crags and crevices on his father's ruddy face.

"I am now. You know me, son, as strong as a horse!" he teased, his eyes sparkling beneath his small golden caplet. "The wound on your cheek? Does it pain you greatly?"

SONG OF THE ROSE

"Less each day, Father. What pains me is my heart. I am deeply in love with the most wonderful lady in the world! She carries my child. But we have not yet wed because of terrible circumstances."

"As they say, the apple does not fall far from the tree, my son." His father shook his head knowingly. "But perhaps this time we can manage a happy ending?"

"'Tis what I prayed you would say. I love you dearly, Father."

"I know. 'Tis all that has made my life worth living, despite my riches and power. Tell me your lady's name, son."

"Your week with me has flown so quickly, I feel as if you arrived but moments ago," his father stated sadly.

"I know, Father. But as soon as the babe is born and baptized, we shall return. And then you shall have more of us with you than you will know what to do with." Pierre laughed. "Nicolette, the babe, me, Bruge, Gervais, and perhaps we can persuade Alienor and Matthew to at least visit for a time before they are wed."

"Please, when the time is right, son, extend my offer to Alienor to have her wedding here. It will be the most glorious France has ever seen! It pleases me most to speak of the people you love with some familiarity and I can hardly wait until I have the honor of knowing them." Tears filled his shining eyes. "And seeing my grandchild—"

"Grandson, Father," Pierre teased.

"Be not so certain. Could be either—or both," he

said and laughed. "Should Alienor be reluctant to wed here I will understand—"

"Methinks you should retire to your countinghouse after I leave. For this grand wedding will no doubt empty your coffers," Pierre teased.

"Should you and Nicolette change your minds and decide to have a grand wedding of your own, rather than the quiet ceremony you asked for, I shall be all the more happy to empty my coffers."

"A double wedding? I had not thought of such." Pierre laughed. "We are far ahead of ourselves, I fear. For we can only hope Alienor shall fall in love with Matthew and that even after I follow your sage advice Davide can win back his beloved Nicolette."

"Son, do not doubt the powers of love and prayer. For they brought me your return, did they not? I understand how difficult it will be, but you must speak to Nicolette as soon as you return to St. Martin. I cannot believe 'tis too late to rectify your mistakes. Trust your old father, who has made enough of his own to know!" His face saddened. "'Tis dangerous for you to try to send word to me until the babe is born. I will wait and pray daily for you and your friends, son. The time will pass and perchance I shall finally perfect my backgammon game sufficiently to thoroughly trounce you next time!"

Pierre hugged and kissed his father. "May the Lord go with you and keep you safe and happy until we are reunited!" his father said.

Pierre fought back his tears and mounted his horse. "My advice to you, Father, is to start practicing your backgammon game at once!"

His father laughed. "Aye? But how you shall

become a finer hunter by spring I cannot guess," he countered. "Perchance prayer will help. For if you be as poor as ever, I shall be ashamed to ride with you!"

"You shall eat those words, Father!" Pierre responded with the banter that made their parting less painful.

"With wild boar I pray!" His father followed as Pierre slowly trotted away, his head shaking with laughter.

Chapter Sixteen

Though 'twas a blistery cold, rainy November evening, the musicians who entertained after supper in St. Martin's great hall filled the large, candlelit room with strains of gay song. Nicolette tapped her fingers in time as the viol, guitar, gigue, harp, horn, dulcimer, and even a little portable organ were played dazzlingly well by the troupe that had performed in Paris for the court of King Philip Augustus himself. Nicolette, who sat upon the dais beside Marguerite, glanced across the long table and saw Baron Brouilleaux, seated in his throne chair beside his baroness, break into wild applause as a slim, dark-haired maiden, a member of the group of *jongleurs,* danced out from behind the back curtains of the huge hall to the center of the room. The lesser nobles, the court servitors, groups of skilled villeins who had been invited for supper from the baron's village, all seated at various long planked tables filling the hall, pounded the tables with their drinking vessels. They cheered and hooted as the damsel, scantily dressed as a Palestinian princess, wove through their midst to the clearing before the dais. Nicolette laughed as an overly admiring petty noble had to be pulled back upon his bench seat.

As the dancer performed Herodia's daughter's dance so magnificently, Nicolette could well understand how the legendary Palestinian princess had taken in the gullible king with her acrobatic feats. Why, she could even dance on her head and kick in the air! Nicolette saw that both Gervais and Matthew especially delighted in her feats, though Bruge appeared less moved. Nicolette laughed to herself; she knew just what Bruge was thinking. The *jongleur* who had entertained last week with his tamed bear who could dance and do all sorts of tricks had won Bruge's heart. For three days hence she had chattered about the darling bear.

Nicolette saw Alienor whisper something to Matthew who laughed in response. During the past week and a half, Alienor had taken to spending more and more of her time with Matthew. 'Twas no doubt that the flame of love's light had begun to shine in Alienor's eyes. How pleased Davide would be to learn so when he returned, Nicolette thought. She glanced to her other side again and caught a sweet kiss between Bruge and Gervais. Though winter approached more coldly each day, love bloomed all around her in the palais. Both Daphne and Blanche were infatuated with two of the baron's squires and giggled and whispered happily as they went about their tasks. Nicolette was happy for them but she could not deny her loneliness.

It had been a week and a half since Davide had ridden to St. Aliquis. Matthew had told her he had other business to attend to but offered no more than that. Nor did she press. Nicolette expected that Davide would finally return on the morrow. She could hardly contain her excitement. Since his departure she had practiced calling him François to others while thinking him Davide. With each utterance of the name François, it became easier and was almost second nature now.

Simone gently tapped her upon her shoulder. Nicolette smiled at the heartbroken, stout maiden. For the news of Henri's betrothal to Sabine, Harcourt's daughter, had spread through the castle earlier in the week. While Simone now waited upon Alienor, being her third maiden-in-waiting at that, Nicolette could not help pity the sadly used maiden.

"My lady," Simone whispered. "Messire Perdant has returned. He saw me in the corridor and asked if I would relay that he requests your attendance in your chamber. But he does not wish to interrupt your pleasure at the entertainment unless it pleases you."

Nicolette rose quickly, suddenly as nervous as she was thrilled. During Davide's absence she had arranged for the changes in chambers. Bruge now shared a chamber with Alienor, leaving Nicolette her chamber to be shared in privacy with her husband. She had missed Bruge's presence terribly these past lonely nights, but thought it best to decline her sister's offer to sleep with her until François' return. Nicolette realized that Bruge was truly becoming a young woman and that now that they were safe from Henri's evil schemes, she had to allow a natural separation between them to take place slowly. For Bruge was happily betrothed and she herself was not only Davide's wife but would be a mother in but a few months. "Simone, you need not leave the entertainment," Nicolette offered. "Go back to your table with the other maidens. And thank you." Nicolette quietly slipped out of the great hall.

The strains of bright music and echoes of uproarious laughter followed her as she quickly climbed the steps that led to the chambers above. Nicolette had rehearsed her apology and reasoned appeal to Davide since the morning she'd awoken from her telling dream. But as she climbed the stairs, slowing because of the weight of the babe as she neared the top, her thoughts became jumbled and her heart beat anxiously.

Pierre paced their chamber floor. Simone had informed him that Nicolette had moved his possessions from the chamber he'd shared with Matthew to hers during his absence. Was that a fortuitous sign or merely more of her helpless acquiescence? He thought of his father's warning that she should not be told of his true identity until after the babe was born, but before the baptism. Father had ruefully agreed that 'twas necessary for Matthew to know everything immediately, in the event that something should happen to Pierre. For Father had agreed that Henri's future actions could not be predicted. A man such as

Henri did not take humiliation lightly and Pierre did not doubt that he schemed to seek revenge one day. Pierre poured himself a goblet of wine. He had already hidden away the baptismal dress his father had movingly presented him the eve before he took leave. With Nicolette's consent, their son should be baptized in the dress Pierre himself had worn. How dearly he missed his father, their brief visit merely increasing his loss now.

"François?" Nicolette said. He had not heard her enter. He looked at her. She smiled lovingly. Was it François at whom she smiled? He clasped his goblet more tightly to steady his hands. She was a vision that filled his heart as he took her in. She had grown even more lovely. Her belly extended further but what brought him joy was that her face glowed, her cheeks were plumper, her eyes were bright and brilliant blue, accented by the blush of her cheeks. She appeared healthy, rested, and only her fingers, which played nervously, gave away her otherwise peaceful demeanor.

"My lady," he said softly, forcing himself to take François' voice, and bowed. "You look very well . . ." He was at a loss for words.

Nicolette sat upon the edge of the bed. "And you, my husband, look exhausted and filled with apprehension," she answered honestly. "Pray come sit beside me." She waited until he was seated.

Pierre searched for the words, but the speech he had practiced flew from his head. "Nicolette," he began. "I beg your forgiveness—"

"'Tis I who beg yours, my husband," she said. Tears filled her eyes. "Pray let me speak before my tears stop me." She took his hands in her own. "The morn you rode off, I sent Blanche to find you, but alas 'twas too late. I have waited since that moment to speak my heart and mind to thee. You are François Perdant"—she saw his eyes darken with sadness he could not hide, though he seemed to try—"to everyone else. Until our babe is born and we may travel away. To everyone but *me!*"

He could not believe his ears. He had not lost her! He allowed her to continue for he was too moved to speak.

"But to me, despite the night I was tipsy—" She giggled. "Tipsy be too mild a word. Drunken with confusion and wine, shock at your return—" The words were not coming as clearly as she'd intended but she continued. "Davide . . ." she whispered, seeing the blend of pleasure and alarm mix in his eyes. "You are *my* Davide. I knew you from the first moments and even that night"—she felt the heat rise to her cheeks—"that night, deep within me, 'twas Davide I gave myself to, though we both seemed frighteningly lost in your transformation into François. I understood the next morning that 'twas when I called out to you as Davide that you were so frightened for us—for me—that you had to kill Davide." She fought back her tears. "I believed you had done so . . . But 'tis impossible, I am afraid to say—I am thrilled to say! Oh!" She began to laugh and cry as his eyes showed how he tried to follow her. "I so practiced, but my words will not order themselves! Let us forget the words for now," she said as she brought his face to hers and kissed him.

SONG OF THE ROSE

"Davide, please don't leave me again," she whispered as he took her in his arms, his own tears melding with hers as he tenderly kissed her eyes and cheeks and nose and then his mouth sought her own and did not let go as he lay her gently down upon the bed.

"Some more wine, Nicolette?" he asked, still using François' voice.

Nicolette laughed. "Methinks not. For I desire never to wake with such a throbbing head again as I did that morning, Davide. All that drink cannot be good for the babe. I swear to you that your son slept most of the day, and when he finally kicked again"—she laughed heartily—"he did so most unsteadily!"

Pierre stroked her belly and caressed her breasts, laughing all the while. "Does it upset you to hear François' voice from my mouth?" he asked, growing serious again.

"Only a bit. Just at first. For 'twas not François' voice that was fearful. 'Twas his character, his soul. In truth, your voice be quite similar—his a slightly higher pitch and the cadence different reflecting the different regions you come from—Davide?" She caught herself. "I know," she sighed. "You will tell me all after the babe is born. I shan't even try to guess."

"Nicolette, my visit was most wonderful with my father, as I told you. He is terribly anxious to meet you. Already he loves you," he said softly. He had told her as much as he was able to about his visit. "So you are certain that I can be both François and

Davide to you as I am both myself and François to me?"

"Aye." Nicolette's smile turned to a laugh. "Do not think I did not notice that you do *not* refer to yourself as Pierre Delise. You have *more* names than anyone I have ever known!" she teased.

"Aye." Davide laughed. "Matthew said exactly the same!"

"I do not know how I will become used to your true name—suppose I hate it?"

"Suppose I told you my Christian name was, indeed, Davide?" He grinned mischievously.

"Is it?" she asked with excitement.

"No." He laughed despite himself, for he knew he was further frustrating her.

"Davide!" she exclaimed and threw a pillow at him. He ducked and pinned her arms behind her in play. "Ouch," he cried as her knee jabbed into his groin. He let her go as he fought the pain. Nicolette giggled, though he could see she was sorry to have hurt him. "Will you never learn to behave like a lady!" he teased as his breath returned.

"Oh, I am sorry, my love," she said. She kissed his lips. Her eyes twinkled as she coyly smiled. "Can I somehow make it better?" she asked.

"Can you think of a way?" he teased.

"Let me think upon it," she said with a grin. "Aye . . ." she whispered and kissed his lips, then lowered her head very slowly. "You are certain my touch will not increase your pain?" she taunted.

"I am willing to discover so . . ." he said with a sigh as her sweet, loving lips began to soothe him. How she pleasured him! "I do not mind you being master at all, my love . . ." He sighed. "Do with me what you will!"

She raised her head. "Only if you do the same," she said with a gloriously lustful smile.

"Michel, 'tis you! I'd been told you were dead!" Henri exclaimed. "Quickly, come to my chamber where we may speak in privacy."

"Certainly," Michel answered ruefully. "But I do not think anyone should recognize me, Henri," he said as he followed Henri down the hall.

Henri forced himself to look upon the deformed, burned face that had once been Squire Michel's glory. "You are right, I am sorry to say. Still, we must speak in private. I have no doubt that François has well-placed spies in the castle. Oh, how he has turned upon me!" Henri did not understand why the horrifyingly distorted face of Michel broke into hard, loud laughter.

"Michel, bless you!" Henri declared as he filled another flagon for him. He watched as Michel lifted it awkwardly with his left hand, for his right arm hung at his side, burned beyond use in the fire. "I must say that this Pierre Delise took me in so cleverly! Everyone believes him to be François. I know you said they had appeared like brothers, but still 'tis uncanny. My sister, who has been forced to know him *most* intimately, is reported to believe he is François as well. Wait!" He jumped up from the table and threw his flagon against the fireplace in rage. "It all comes to me now! All the pieces fit! Matthew, his *loyal* vassal and intended husband to Alienor!" Henri spat. He walked back to the table.

"Tell me, Henri," Michel asked.

"I have not much time, for I must ride to Harcourt's for Christmas dinner with my future wife." The words curdled in his mouth. "You of course shall remain here. I shall see to that. We shall give you another name—we'll decide what later. What I now clearly see is that Pierre Delise and the mysterious Davide I told you of, they are one and the same! We shall prove it. On the morrow we will begin to prepare our case. You are our key witness, for surely you seek vengeance?"

"I seek retribution! And a proper estate to see me through my days, whatever their number shall be. I wish to do no more than wench and drink myself into oblivion. But with my demonlike visage, wenching is costly." He laughed darkly. "I no longer find young maidens eager for my embrace." He laughed harder, causing Henri to feel the chill of malevolence creep up his spine.

Henri forced himself to smile amiably. "I understand and sympathize. We must build our evidence carefully, for I fear they could cleverly say that you had become mad from your injuries. We have much time, for my sister's bastard child will not be born for at least another month. I have *graciously* been invited to the baptismal celebration—otherwise I am banned from St. Martin's. But I shall not be attending alone. We will arrive with the duke, for 'tis he who is our suzerain and should rule in such a matter of 'high justice.' Their celebration will turn into a trial before the bastard child can be baptized," Henri said with glee. My revenge will come sooner than I could have hoped, he thought. "Tell me more. Everything you remember about this Pierre Delise while I dress," Henri demanded.

Chapter Seventeen

THE SUN REFLECTED BRIGHTLY UPON THE SNOW ON THIS first morn of February. Yet it paled in comparison to the glow on Nicolette's face. Had Pierre not been the wiser, he never would have guessed that she suffered through twelve hours of pain before the babes were born. Now the boy child and girl child, warmly swaddled, rested at her side, sleeping peacefully.

"Twins," Nicolette uttered as she held them close. Wonder filled her eyes. "I had not imagined . . . to my knowledge there have been no twins in my family."

Pierre tried to maintain his neutral expression. Nicolette suddenly rolled her eyes. "Methinks you have *far* more to tell me than I could have imagined, my dear husband. I have waited long enough! Begin at once." She broke into a smile. "But kiss me first?"

Playfully he gave her a brotherly kiss upon her lips and pulled away.

"Davide!" she whispered. "The nurse and maids wait outside. Finally we are alone again. Kiss me, I pray thee."

"My lady Nicolette. Mother of my children. I am not certain 'tis proper to kiss a *mother* in the manner you suggest!" he teased. "I certainly have never done so before!"

"I should hope not, my husband!" She laughed. "Bring your lips to mine and I shall show you how passionately even a mother can kiss!" Her laughter fled as she reveled in the touch of his mouth upon hers.

"I love you so, Nicolette," he whispered and kissed her again. He bent and tenderly kissed the foreheads of each of his babes. "How do I begin, Nicolette?" he asked with a laugh.

"I haven't the slightest idea. Perchance with your name, Lord help us—wait! Before I hear *another* name, are we agreed that our babes shall be called Davide and Doreen?

"Aye . . ." He smiled.

"Good. Now, if you will kindly tell me what their family name will be?" She grinned.

"Perhaps I should begin at the beginning . . ." he said nervously

"'Tis amazing . . ." Nicolette whispered when he finished his story and answered all the questions that had come to her mind. She nursed the babe, Davide, at her breast, for he had awakened hungrily though Doreen still slept quietly in her father's arms. He had been terrified, but with Nicolette's encouragement he now tenderly held his sleeping daughter. "So you wish me to speak first with Alienor?" she asked.

"Aye. As I explained, Matthew has known since I returned from my father's castle. Do you still wish to have our babes baptized on the morrow or would you rather wait?"

"No. I do not think we should wait. The babes are as healthy as they are beautiful," she said tenderly. "On the morrow we shall be able to speak their true names and yours, finally. Though, as I said, I have decided that from me you shall be shackled forever with Davide."

"Shackled happily." He laughed. "Actually, I do believe Davide suits me best. 'Tis the most handsome of all my names and since I am so very beautiful—"

"Such vanity, you peacock."

"I say so only now because I am safe from your kick at my delicate manhood!" he bantered.

"But not for as long as you think, my cowardly husband."

"Not so long—'tis music to my ears! For I have allowed you to trample over me these past months, my lusty wife. But soon you will receive your due."

"I can hardly wait!" she said.

"Nicolette! Thank the Lord our babes cannot see their mother grinning so lasciviously." he teased, as his heart swelled so fully he thought no man had ever been graced with more love and happiness. Doreen suddenly woke with a wail, frightening him. "What should I do?" he asked helplessly, as he rocked her.

"Since you can't feed her, I suggest you hand Doreen to me and take Davide," she answered with a laugh.

"I tell you, Nicolette," he said as he carefully switched babes, "being a knight is far easier than being a father."

Alienor sat beside Nicolette, staring at her, her eyes wide as she tried to absorb all Nicolette had delicately explained to her. "Alienor? Do you hate us?" Nicolette asked with mounting apprehension. From the beginning of her recounting, Alienor had not uttered a word, though tears had fallen from her eyes. "I pray thee, say something. Anything."

Alienor sighed and wiped her tears away. "I shall forgive that you did not take me into your confidence —both of you—under one condition," she said sternly.

"Speak it," Nicolette said. She could not tell what Alienor thought or felt.

"That I shall be Doreen's godmother and Matthew Davide's godfather." Nicolette cried with joy and relief as Alienor hugged her tightly. "'Tis all so hard to absorb!"

"I know! Nicolette whispered. "Shall I have the nurse bring the babes in now?" she asked.

"First I would like to speak with Davide. Does he wait outside?"

"I would suspect he has worn through the floor planks in the past hour." Nicolette laughed. She watched as Alienor rose and opened the chamber door. "Daphne," she said. "Would you ask Sire François to join us?"

Alienor had just reseated herself upon a chair by Nicolette's bedside when Davide entered the chamber. His face was filled with apprehension.

"Well, my brother," she mocked gently. "I believe we have much to discuss. The most important being that Matthew and I shall be the godparents to your babes. Before I forget in all this confusion"—Alienor looked from Nicolette back to him "—Matthew has asked for my hand in marriage, and I have accepted! I hope you are both as pleased as we are!" Her shining smile dimmed for a moment. "Methinks that Guy would be happy for me as well . . ." She swallowed hard and smiled again. "How does a double wedding at your father's castle strike you?" she asked him.

He could not speak. He walked to Alienor, kneeled, and kissed her hand

Since it was too cold to risk taking the newborn babes outside the warmth of the heated castle, it had been arranged for Father Gregoire, who had arrived yesterday afternoon, to baptize the babes in Baron Brouilleaux's chambers. Just the immediate families would be in attendance. Tonight, a festive banquet would be held to celebrate the occasion. Baroness Brouilleaux had presented Nicolette with Guy's baptismal dress, which touched them all deeply. Especially Alienor, for last night she had informed the Brouilleauxs of her betrothal to Matthew. Not only had they given her their blessings, but offered her their palais for the wedding and celebration. Later, when "François" had spoken with them, they grew to understand Alienor's hesitancy. 'Twas agreed that since Alienor's parents were dead that the Brouilleauxs would be at her side when she was wed to Matthew. 'Twas only the babes who slept well that night, for Nicolette had recounted the stories to Bruge and then again to Bruge and Gervais.

Now Nicolette and Alienor, with Bruge's eager help, dressed the babes while their father recounted his story once more to Father Gregoire and Sire Eustace in the privacy of the baron's chamber. Marguerite and the baroness supervised the preparations for tonight's celebration. The baron busily received the guests who had been arriving since early morning.

Denise bounded into Nicolette's chamber. "How curious!" she declared. "Emissaries of the Count of Reims have arrived. I thought that—" She looked at Alienor who smiled with equanimity. "One is the archbishop himself! I suppose that they were invited by the baron?"

"Look, Davide smiles!" Bruge exclaimed.

"Oh, let me see!" Denise demanded. "And you, Doreen, will you not give me a smile?" she cooed. "Look, she smiles at me. She smiles at me!" Denise said with great excitement.

"Methinks 'tis just wind," Bruge declared jealously, causing gales of laughter to fill the room. "Laugh all you wish. I am certain!" Bruge stubbornly maintained, as the babes were dressed and ready to be baptized.

"I see that Henri has had the good taste not to show his face," Nicolette whispered to Davide as they stood before Father Gregoire and the archbishop, she holding Doreen, he holding Davide.

The chamber door swung open and there stood Henri. An entire party behind him filled the hall. She had spoken too quickly, Nicolette thought.

"Stop this baptism immediately!" he bellowed. "The babes are bastards! 'Tis not François Perdant who stands before you. François is dead. Pierre Delise, an imposter, and the father of the bastard babes, shall be hanged!" Henri pushed a horribly disfigured man before him that Nicolette had not seen. "Here is my witness, Michel Chantois! François' squire who watched François' throat cut and saw him burn in the fire that almost killed Michel himself!"

Nicolette gasped in horror. Not at Henri's vengeful fury, nor at his foul words spat at her babes. Poor Michel, disfigured beyond recognition! She had hated him, but now her heart went out to any man who should have to live with such a fate. Her gasp echoed through the room.

"Enter the chamber, Henri, and pray calm yourself," Sire Eustace declared, shaking his head with pity. "You too, Michel."

"Have you not heard a word I've said!" Henri sputtered.

"We have heard it all. 'Tis now your turn to listen."

Cautiously, Henri entered, followed by Michel. Nicolette saw from the way his right arm hung at his side that he was crippled as well as disfigured. The poor soul, she thought, as she watched them sit upon a bench. Nicolette shook her head in wonder as she saw not only the provost, Sire Macaire, enter, but the

Count of Champagne himself. Henri must have planned to have Davide found guilty and hanged on the spot, she thought, and shuddered, fully expecting to see Maitre Dennis, the executioner, enter next.

"Do you deny you are not François Perdant but are in fact Pierre Delise!" Henri began again.

Davide handed the babe to Alienor and ushered the ladies to their seats. Father Gregoire and the archbishop sat as well. Davide and Sire Eustace, who hovered above Henri, were the only two who remained standing in the hushed room.

"I do not deny so. Nor would anyone else in this room," Davide said simply.

Henri's mouth opened in astonishment but no sound came forth but for a slight gasp.

"I am almost sorry to disappoint you, Henri. For you are a clever scoundrel, I will grant you that." Davide laughed darkly. "My given name is Christophe Garnier. I am the son and heir of Christophe Garnier, the Count of Reims. My mother was Lady Adela Perdant, may she rest in Heaven."

Henri paled further but remained silent in obvious shock. "I have repeated this story more times in the past twenty-four hours than I'd ever thought I would in my entire life. So forgive me, Henri, if I give you a less detailed recounting." He smiled banefully at Nicolette and Alienor. "My father's emissaries, who rest in a guest chamber in the palais, have with them the documents that I am certain you will wish to see to confirm my story. The Archbishop of Reims"— Davide gestured to the august member of the clergy who sat beside Father Gregoire, dressed in his full regalia—"can also corroborate my story, for 'twas he who baptized me and my brother, François. My twin brother—though not identical, as you may have already surmised."

"François, your brother?" Henri whispered.

"You see, my mother and father were deeply in love. But she was forced to wed Baron Perdant—I shall not privilege you with the details that do not concern you. The story went that she had been kidnapped and held in captivity during a war between the baron and my father. But the truth was that she had fled to the man she loved. My father. For 'twas his babe she carried. Or I should say, babes."

"I do not believe—" Henri began.

"Such a *striking* parallel between my mother's story and Nicolette's plight, would you not agree, Henri? François and I were born at my father's castle. The Duke of Burgundy, who had for a time ruled Champagne, largely due to Baron Perdant's aid, came to his side and threatened to turn his many forces—for he controlled many fiefs and had the reluctant fealty of hundreds of knights—against Reims. My father held fast, but my mother could not stand to see Reims destroyed. Moreover, she feared that she and my father might be killed and her babes left to be raised by the less than scrupulous Baron Perdant." His face darkened. "Forgive me, my sister," he said to Alienor.

Alienor smiled at him through the tears in her eyes. "'Tis nothing to forgive when the truth be spoken, my loving brother."

"So she decided to return with one babe, presented

as Baron Perdant's son. François was picked for no particular reason. Mother arranged that I should be secretly carried to the village in Perdant's barony and raised by the cobbler and his wife—the Delises. A warm, loving, childless couple, whose passing I shall always mourn. For the first three years I lived happily in the village. I even remember Papa Delise, as I called him until the day he died ten years ago, taking me on trips to the forest. 'Twas this fond memory that caused my detour to the forest, on the way to join the forces of the Count of Champagne last May."

Nicolette's eyes filled with tears, for Davide smiled at her with such tenderness.

"'Twas there that providence brought me to Nicolette. And introduced me to my brother, who had become a reprobate at best. I am sorry for Alienor that our mother died but glad that she did not live to see how François had—but I jump ahead. I lived here in the barony of St. Aliquis until it came to the baron's attention that there was a child in the village who looked almost like the young sire's twin. My mother so feared for me that she decided to send me to Reims with the Delises, where I should be raised safely and with love of at least one natural parent. Although the Delises were very loving, as I said. I have only vague memories of a beautiful lady who sometimes came to visit and brought me a toy, but I am told that my mother visited me all she could until the baron became suspicious."

He smiled lovingly at Nicolette again. "So, with the aid of a gallant knight—your father, Henri—whom my mother had taken into her confidence from the time he helped 'rescue' her from my father, my stepparents and I were spirited off in the night to my father's castle.

"My stepmother caught the fever two years later and died. My stepfather lived on until I was thirteen. Upon his death my father, the count, whom I'd thought of as a kindly, powerful lord who had offered to 'nourish' me so that I could become his knight and vassal, told me this story. For he could not bear for me to believe I was an orphan, though my mother had died when Alienor, my half-sister, was born."

"If this is all so, " Henri said weakly, "why would you baptize your babies in the name of Perdant? And seek to take over St. Aliquis."

"I do neither, Henri. Your mind is clever but apparently incapable of thinking with *any* sense of honor. Our babes are being baptized Davide and Doreen Garnier." He turned to the father and archbishop. "Tell him if you would, Father Gregoire."

"They *will be* if you ever allow us to proceed, Henri," the priest said with less than saintly patience, causing titters among the others.

"St. Aliquis belongs rightfully to my sister Alienor and Matthew. They will be married with Nicolette and myself in Reims as soon as the babes are old enough to travel." Davide sighed. "However, Henri, you are as trustworthy as you are scrupulous. Methinks that to prevent any further perfidy from you or others that might threaten St. Aliquis—for I have no doubt that you will run off to Harcourt with any number of schemes—I suggest that with Father Gregoire's consent, Alienor and Matthew wed immediately after the baptism, making Matthew official Messire of St. Aliquis!"

Nicolette looked from Alienor to Matthew. No dissent would come from them, she thought, as they smiled and boldly kissed, causing the maidens to giggle and applaud.

"Nicolette and I will live most happily at my father's castle, where Bruge and Gervais shall join us. Methinks that answers all your questions, Henri," Davide said with less pleasure at Henri's defeat than he'd expected. "Do you wish to add anything, Nicolette?"

Nicolette handed Doreen to Baroness Brouilleaux. "Aye," she said and walked to stand beside Davide. "Each day I grieve our father's passing, Henri. But I am glad he never lived to learn what you have become. I cannot bear the thought of inflicting you upon even Baron Harcourt's daughter. We will provide you with enough funds to find your way out of France. Shall you ever be seen or heard from again I will personally see to it that you are hanged. I need say no more than that for you to understand, I believe. No one doubts your cleverness, Henri. I will not disparage the word by calling you 'brother.' I do not wish your bedeviled eyes to as much as *glance* at my babes. Leave St. Martin's at once!"

"You cannot order me such!" he exploded, his hatred of her spilling from his eyes.

"I can and do," Baron Brouilleaux said. "I will have my men escort you if you do not leave willingly!"

Alienor passed the babe Davide to Bruge and rose. "I, in turn, order that you do not return to St. Aliquis.

Sire Eustace will have your belongings packed and sent to you, will you not, Sire?"

"It will give me the greatest pleasure to do so, my lady," Sire Eustace said, his deep voice resounding through the room.

"As for you, Michel," Nicolette said softly. "My heart goes out to you, though you do not deserve it. But still, we will help you, should you find it in your heart to repent."

Michel looked at her through his tortured face. "I shall speak honestly to you, Nicolette. I have no heart to repent with. Nor do I wish to see any more destruction. I should like to take leave and live out my days in Paris. I wish you neither good nor evil. I wish you nothing." He turned toward Matthew. "You, Matthew Grieves, I thank for attempting to save my life. I give my word of honor, whatever that be worth to you, that I shall never haunt any of you." Michel rose and walked from the chamber. He turned at the door. "Henri. Have you not made enough of an ass of yourself for one day? Are you leaving or do they have to throw you out?" Michel laughed darkly and disappeared down the hall. Henri followed.

Doreen began to squall and awakened her brother, who cried even the more loudly. Nicolette rushed to her babes, as she and Alienor tried to soothe them. "They are hungry," she said above their cries.

"As am I," Sire Eustace said with pretended gruffness. "May we get on with this baptism before the babes are old enough to be wed?"

"'Twas a long day, was it not?" Nicolette said as she lay in Davide's arms.

"Aye . . ." he sighed.

"But it went well and finally we live in peace." She smiled and cuddled closer to him.

"Hmm . . ."

Was he asleep? "Davide, I think we should take a walk in the garden for it is a beautiful summer eve . . ."

"Aye . . ."

She laughed to herself. She brought her lips upon his and began to tease him awake. "Davide?" She ran her hand across his chest, tracing her fingertips over his nipples in a manner she knew aroused him. "Davide . . ."

"I am awake, my lady," he said in a voice thick with sleep.

"I do not believe you," she said as she caressed his neck, but then he pulled her into his arms and kissed her long and deeply.

"You shall be the death of me yet, wench," he teased and she kissed him in her bewitching manner. "Oh, Nicolette," he said as he caressed her body. The wail of one of the babes pierced the room. Davide began to laugh. "Which one cries, can you tell?"

"*Your* son," she said, only half in play, as she rose from the bed to comfort her babe.

"Thank you, my son!" he called with pretended relief. "*You* shall see to it that your father lives to be an old man after all!"

"'Tis not funny!" Nicolette declared hotly.

"'Tis so!" he countered, laughing heartily. Suddenly he heard both babes crying.

"Come get your daughter!" Nicolette ordered.

He rocked Doreen but he could not still her.

Davide cried as well. "How long does this last?" he asked with awe.

"Two or three years!" Nicolette replied. She saw his face pale with horror as he sat and rocked Doreen by the candlelight.

"Do not look so stricken, Davide," she finally said. "'Tis only in jest!"

"'Tis not humorous!" he declared.

"'Tis so!" The laugh was hers this time. After she quieted her son and placed him back in his crib, she took her whimpering Doreen from Davide's arms . . . Soon Doreen too slept.

"Oh!" Nicolette whispered as Davide caught her by surprise, sweeping her up into his arms.

"Quiet, or you'll awaken them," he whispered. "How long do you think they shall sleep?" he asked, as he lowered her upon their bed, resting her against the pillows.

"A few hours. Then they will be hungry . . . Davide!" she cried as he pinned her arms over her head, showering her with kisses.

"I know we cannot yet do *that*," he whispered, reading her mind. "But I intend to have you all to myself until the little devils wake again," he said as he ran his fingers across her lips and brought his mouth to her breast ever so gently.

"I thought you desired sleep?" she whispered and sighed with pleasure.

"I did, but I have a strong constitution. Methinks I can wait on sleep for two or three years—ouch!" he cried as she kicked him with precise aim. "You did it *again*! This cannot be the manner in which a lady should treat her husband!"

"We are not married yet, you might remember," she teased, as his hands and mouth thrilled her.

"Must you bother me with such *trifles* in a moment like such?" he bantered. "You women! Always worrying about this or—" She caught his laughing words with her mouth and wrapped her arms tightly around his neck.

"She is the rose . . . the lily too . . . the sweetest violet . . ." Davide sang softly. "Do you remember, my love?" he whispered.

" 'The Song of the Rose.' Each night you were gone I heard you sing it to me in my mind as I tried to sleep. Sing it fully, Christophe Garnier, my beloved Davide . . ." She closed her eyes as his lilting baritone softly echoed through the chamber.

Davide finished singing as he held Nicolette. "Nicolette?" he whispered. "Nicolette?" He smiled as his beloved slept secure in his arms.

Tapestry

HISTORICAL ROMANCES

___ LOVING DEFIANCE
Joan Johnson
54426/$2.95

___ FIELDS OF PROMISE
Janet Joyce
49394/$2.95

___ LADY RAINE
Carol Jerina
50836/$2.95

___ LAND OF GOLD
Mary Ann Hammond
50872/$2.95

___ CHARITY'S PRIDE
Patricia Pellicane
52372/$2.95

___ MASQUARADE
Catherine Lyndell
50048/$2.95

___ BANNER O'BRIEN
Linda Lael Miller
52356/$2.95

___ PIRATE'S PROMISE
Ann Cockcroft
53018/$2.95

___ GALLAGHER'S LADY
Carol Jerina
52359/$2.95

___ TANGLED VOWS
Anne Moore
52626/$2.95

___ CAPTIVE HEARTS
Catherine Lyndell
54396/$2.95

___ SECRETS OF THE HEART
Janet Joyce
52677/$2.95

___ GLORIOUS DESTINY
Janet Joyce
52628/$2.95

___ FRENCH ROSE
Jacqueline Marten
52345/$2.95

___ PROMISE OF PARADISE
Cynthia Sinclair
53016/$2.95

___ SILVERSEA
Jan McGowan
54282/$2.95

___ PRIDE AND PROMISES
Adrienne Scott
52354/$2.95

___ WILLOW
Linda Lael Miller
52357/$2.95

___ GLORIOUS TREASURE
Louisa Gillette
52343/$2.95

___ GILDED HEARTS
Johanna Hill
52484/$2.95

___ NEVADA NIGHTS
Ruth Ryan Langan
54427/$2.95

___ CORBINS FANCY
Linda Lael Miller
52358/$2.95

POCKET BOOKS

- GOLDEN DESTINY
  Jean Saunders
  61744/$3.50

- SWEET REVENGE
  Patricia Pellicane
  61761/$3.50

- HEARTS ECHO
  Jan Mc Kee
  61740/$3.50

- AN UNFORGOTTEN LOVE
  Jacqueline Marten
  52346/$2.95

- SILVER MOON
  Monica Barrie
  52843/$2.95

- BELOVED ENEMY
  Cynthia Sinclair
  53017/$2.95

- WHISPERS IN THE WIND
  Patricia Pellicane
  53015/$2.95

- MIDWINTER'S NIGHT
  Jean Canavan
  54686/$2.95

- VOWS OF DESIRE
  Catherine Lyndell
  54397/$2.95

- FOX HUNT
  Carol Jerina
  54640/$2.95

- TENDER LONGING
  Rebecca George
  61449/$2.95

- BRIGHT DESIRE
  Erica Mitchell
  54395/$2.95

- SONG OF THE ROSE
  Johanna Hill
  62903/$3.50

- ENCHANTED DESIRE
  Marylye Rogers
  54430/$2.95

- JOURNEY TO LOVE
  Cynthia Sinclair
  54605/$2.95

- GENTLE WARRIOR
  Julie Garwood
  54746/$2.95

- THE GOLDEN LILY
  Jan McGowan
  54388/$2.95

- RIVER TO RAPTURE
  Louisa Gillette
  52364/$2.95

- A LOVING ENCHANTMENT
  Cynthia Sinclair
  60356/$2.95

- SEPTEMBER'S DREAM
  Ruth Ryan Langan
  60453/$2.95

- LOVING LONGEST
  Jacqueline Marten
  54608/$2.95

- A MINSTREL'S SONG
  Marylyle Rogers
  54604/$2.95

- HIGHLAND TRYST
  Jean Canavan
  61742/$3.50

Tapestry

Pocket Books, Department TAP
1230 Avenue of the Americas, New York, New York 10020

Please send me the books I have checked above. I am enclosing $_____ (please add 75¢ to cover postage and handling. NYS and NYC residents please add appropriate sales tax. Send check or money order—no cash, stamps, or CODs please. Allow six weeks for delivery). For purchases over $10.00, you may use VISA: card number, expiration date and customer signature must be included.

Name_____

Address_____

City_____

State/Zip_____

TAPESTRY ROMANCES

___ **DEFIANT LOVE**
Maura Seger • 45963/$2.50

___ **MARIELLE**
Ena Halliday • 45962/$2.50

___ **BLACK EARL**
Sharon Stephens • 46194/$2.50

___ **FLAMES OF PASSION**
Sheryl Flournoy • 46195/$2.50

___ **HIGH COUNTRY PRIDE**
Lynn Erickson • 46137/$2.50

___ **KINDRED SPIRITS**
DeAnn Patrick • 46186/$2.50

___ **CLOAK OF FATE**
Eleanor Howard • 46163/$2.50

___ **FORTUNES BRIDE**
Joy Gardner • 46053/$2.50

___ **IRON LACE**
Lorena Dureau • 46052/$2.50

___ **LYSETTE**
Ena Halliday • 46165/$2.50

___ **LIBERTINE LADY**
Janet Joyce • 46292/$2.50

___ **LOVE CHASE**
Theresa Conway • 46054/$2.50

___ **EMBRACE THE STORM**
Lynda Trent • 46957/$2.50

___ **REBELLIOUS LOVE**
Maura Seger • 46379/$2.50

___ **EMERALD AND SAPPHIRE**
Laura Parker • 46415/$2.50

___ **EMBRACE THE WIND**
Lynda Trent • 49305/$2.50

___ **DELPHINE**
Ena Halliday • 46166/$2.75

___ **SNOW PRINCESS**
Victoria Foote • 49333/$2.75

___ **FLETCHER'S WOMAN**
Linda Lael Miller • 47936/$2.75

___ **TAME THE WILD HEART**
Serita Stevens • 49398/$2.95

___ **ENGLISH ROSE**
Jacqueline Marten • 49655/$2.95

___ **WILLOW WIND**
Lynda Trent • 47574/$2.95

___ **WINTER BLOSSOM**
Cynthia Sinclair • 49513/$2.95

___ **ARDENT VOWS**
Helen Tucker • 49780/$2.95

___ **DESIRE AND DESTINY**
Linda Lael Miller • 49866/$2.95

___ **ALLIANCE OF LOVE**
Catherine Lyndell • 49514/$2.95

___ **JADE MOON**
Erica Mitchell • 49894/$2.95

___ **DESTINY'S EMBRACE**
Sheryl Flournoy • 49665/$2.95

POCKET BOOKS, Department TAP
1230 Avenue of the Americas, New York, N.Y. 10020

Please send me the books I have checked above. I am enclosing $_____ (please add 75¢ to cover postage and handling for each order. N.Y.S. and N.Y.C. residents please add appropriate sales tax). Send check or money order—no cash or C.O.D.'s please. Allow up to six weeks for delivery. For purchases over $10.00, you may use VISA: card number, expiration date and customer signature must be included.

NAME _____

ADDRESS _____

CITY _____ STATE ZIP _____